GHOST STORIES
AND MYSTERIES

Borgo Press Books by ERNEST FAVENC

Ghost Stories and Mysteries (edited by James Doig)

GHOST STORIES AND MYSTERIES

ERNEST FAVENC

Edited and with an Introduction by James Doig

THE BORGO PRESS

MMXII

CLASSICS OF
FANTASTIC LITERATURE
NUMBER FOUR

GHOST STORIES AND MYSTERIES

FIRST EDITION

Published by Wildside Press LLC

www.wildsidebooks.com

DEDICATION

For Ewa, Cass, and Nick

CONTENTS

INTRODUCTION

BY JAMES DOIG

Ernest Favenc (1845-1908) is arguably the most important Australian colonial writer of Gothic and supernatural fiction. The thirty one stories assembled here were first published in some of the most popular and important periodicals of the day and were read and enjoyed by a large audience. In his day Favenc was a prolific author of short stories and he wrote under several pseudonyms, most frequently Dramingo and Delcomyn.

Favenc is often described as a 'romantic,' in contrast to the literary realism of his better known Australian contemporaries such as Henry Lawson, Barbara Baynton and Edward Dyson. While it is true that he wrote many tales of mystery and the supernatural and his two adventure novels were certainly influenced by the popular romances of H. Rider Haggard, the strength of his work is drawn from his own experiences as a station hand and explorer in remote regions of Australia.

In his best stories, which were published in the first half of the 1890s, Favenc celebrates the mystery of the Australian outback. His characters—drovers and fossickers and explorers—range across an ancient landscape in which the supernatural can erupt at any time. These stories are written in a spare and uncomplicated style and Favenc attains an imaginative power that is unusual in the popular fiction of the time.

His tales are based on personal experience, of places he has seen and stories he has heard, enhanced by his interest in Australian history and legend. Thus, in "A Haunt of the

Jinkarras" he adapts Aboriginal myth to his literary purpose, while "Spirit-Led" is based on the notion that seventeenth century Dutch sailors may have explored northern Australia. In this sense Favenc has something in common with the English tradition of the antiquarian ghost story exemplified by M. R. James and the American regional supernaturalists like Sarah Orne Jewett. Favenc weaves his tales from the stuff of Australian history and tradition in much the same way that M. R. James drew from his knowledge of British antiquity, or Jewett from the landscapes and traditions of New England.

This fictive naturalism sets Favenc apart from other colonial writers who dabbled in Gothic forms. Most Australian writers of the supernatural followed the model of the English ghost story, which had reached a standard form by the middle decades of the nineteenth century: a ghost interacts with the living in order to exorcise or ameliorate past sins or unrealised promises. A consequence of this limited dynamic is that the vast majority of ghost stories are conventional and unremarkable, and Australian colonial ghost stories are no exception—most are commercial offerings of little literary merit. Favenc, however, was able to extend the form mainly because he was conscious of the Gothic possibilities inherent in the Australian landscape and heritage. His interest in and knowledge of Australian history and legend coupled with his first hand experience of the remote outback gave him unique insights into the colonial experience. In stories like "Spirit-Led," "A Haunt of the Jinkarras," "The Boundary Rider's Story," and "Doomed" he modernised the Australian supernatural tale.

Part of this modernising is Favenc's awareness of the interaction between the supernatural and the psychological. In several stories, madness, physical extremity and guilt are just as likely explanations for the events that transpire as the supernatural. In stories like "Jerry Boake's Confession" and "In the Night" we are never quite sure whether we have passed that tenebrous boundary into the realm of the supernatural. This marks a maturity of conception, where the boundaries between realism and romanticism are not clear cut.

Perhaps Favenc's greatest strength as a writer is his ability to create a feeling for the unknown. In his best stories there are no plot twists or convoluted explanations of events; the purpose of these stories is to tell us that strange things are out there and the lasting impression is that the outback has infinite possibilities and forms. This sense of the unknown is grounded in Favenc's feel for the Australian landscape.

Favenc was a versatile writer who dabbled in a number of different genres: adventure, romance, humour, crime and the supernatural. His aim was to entertain and thrill, and he was attune to sensational plot devices and Gothic props that would entertain his readers: animated corpses, decaying bodies, madness, cannibalism, starvation, and so on.

He appears to have had a genuine interest in the occult, and some of his stories draw on occult themes and ideas, most notably "My Story," "The Dead Hand," "The Unholy Experiment of Martin Shenwick, and What Came of It," and "Spirit-Led." His adventure novels also reveal an interest in contemporary views about the lost continent of Lemuria and its association with theosophy.

A number of Favenc's stories can be described as proto-science fiction. "What the Rats brought" is set fifteen years in the future when Australia is decimated by a plague and overrun by monstrous vampire bats from Asia. In "The Land of the Unseen" the invention of a machine allows people to see the invisible monsters lurking around them, while "A Haunt of the Jinkarras" involves the discovery of a race of primordial creatures.

Favenc was also adept at the humorous tall story, and his comic yarns still hold up well today; "The Ghost's Triumph" is a good example. His early tale, "The Lady Ermetta; or, The Sleeping Secret," is an amusing, if somewhat exhausting, parody of the type of convoluted tale that appeared in the Christmas number of the popular Penny Dreadfuls of the day.

Although he is an important writer who should be better known, Favenc was a professional who was paid by the word and some of his stories show the weaknesses that plague much popular writing. Many of his longer stories have overcomplicated and convoluted plots, clearly designed to fill a quota of words, and lack the precision of his most accomplished stories. Sometimes his plots are derivative and hackneyed; stories like "The Island of Shadows" and "The Haunted Steamer" conform to the standard mechanics of the contemporary ghost story.

Another negative aspect of his writing is the casual racism that permeates his work. This was a common enough attitude for the time, and in some respects Favenc was uncommonly sensitive to the plight of indigenous Australians; however, Aboriginal violence, especially in stories like "In the Night" is an ever-present reality for colonial Europeans and Aborigines and other perceived subordinate races like the Chinese are often disparaged.

Regardless of his shortcomings it is hoped that this collection will demonstrate that Favenc deserves to be regarded as a pioneer of Australian speculative fiction.

Favenc's Life and Work

Ernest Favenc was born on 21 October 1845 at 5 Saville Row, Walworth, Surrey, the son of Abraham George Favenc, and his wife, Emma, née Jones. His father was a merchant by trade and his occupation appears to have sent him to different locations as Favenc was educated at Temple College, Cowley, in Oxfordshire, and in Berlin.

With his two sisters, Edith and Ella, and his bother, Jack, Favenc came to Australia while still a teenager in 1863. After a few months working in Sydney, Favenc moved to a cattle station owned by his uncle in north Queensland where he worked as a drover. He spent the next sixteen years in north and central Queensland working on stations, usually as a superintendent. His experiences as a drover in the outback provided the backdrop for a number of the stories in this volume, including "An Unquiet Spirit," "The Boundary-Rider's Story," "The Ghostly Bullock-Bell," and "The Red Lagoon."

By 1871 he was writing fiction and poetry for the *Queenslander*, and in 1878, Gresley Lukin, the proprietor and literary editor of the *Queenslander* placed Favenc in charge of an expedition to survey a route for a railway line from Brisbane to Port Darwin. After travelling from Brisbane to Blackall in central-western Queensland, the small party set off northwest into the Northern Territory, discovering and naming natural features like creeks, lagoons and lakes as they went. Near disaster occurred in November 1878 when they were stranded on Creswell Creek due to water shortage, and they were forced to wait until rain replenished the water supplies. Their supplies almost exhausted, they reached the Overland Telegraph Line north of Powell's Creek station in mid-January 1879.

Although the proposed railway line was never built, the expedition had a profound influence on Favenc's prose and verse. Of his tales of mystery and the supernatural death from thirst occurs in stories like "Blood for Blood," and "A Haunt of the Jinkarras", and the threat of it is present in many other tales, while the country he explored during the expedition was used in stories like "Spirit-Led." He also wrote several accounts of the expedition that appeared in newspapers and periodicals.

Favenc's journalism and his successful land speculations in the Northern Territory in the early 1880s allowed him to marry and settle down in Sydney. On 15 November 1880, Ernest Favenc married Bessie Mathews, whom he had first met in Brisbane in the mid-1870s, at St John's Baptist Church, Ashfield, Sydney. Bessie was born in Whimple, Devon, on 22 November 1860 and had come to Queensland in 1871-72 with her parents and eight siblings; her father, Benjamin, worked as a teacher for the Education Department. Ernest and Bessie had a daughter, Amy Eleanor, born on 24 September 1881, while another child was stillborn in late 1882 or early 1883.

At this time he was working as a journalist in Sydney, contributing substantial serial essays to the *Sydney Mail* on topics like "The Queensland Transcontinental Railway," "White Versus Black," "The Far Far North," and "The Thirsty Land." "The Far Far North," which appeared in August and September 1882, described an expedition Favenc took from Normanton in far north Queensland to Powell's Creek station in order to establish cattle stations. "The Thirsty Land," serialised in November and December 1883, describes a journey to the same region made during March to May 1883. On this occasion Favenc was accompanied by Harry Creaghe, a business associate of Favenc's, and his wife, Caroline, who left a detailed diary of the expedition. Leaving the Creaghes at Powell's Creek station, Favenc continued north-east with two companions, exploring the headwaters of the Macarthur River, which they followed to the coast. They then travelled west, arriving at Daly Waters on 15 July. Soon afterwards, Favenc led a survey ship, the Palmerston, commissioned by the South Australian government to chart the mouth of the Macarthur and the Sir Edward Pellew group of islands in the south-west corner of the Gulf of Carpentaria.

The years following this flurry of activity were relatively barren, in terms of both writing and exploration. Favenc appears to have returned to Sydney where he experienced ill health, which according to Favenc's biographer, Cheryl Taylor, could be a euphemism for the drinking problem that affected him intermittently for the rest of his life. It was not until the end of the decade that he began to write regularly again. The monograph *Western Australia, Its Past History, Its Present Trade and Resources, Its Future Position* was published in 1887, and resulted in a commission to explore the Gascoyne region northeast of Geraldton, which he undertook between March and June 1888. In the same year he published the magisterial *The History of Australian Exploration*, which has remained a classic of its kind and is still regarded as a useful source. Dedicated to the Premier of New South Wales, Sir Henry Parkes, the book reveals Favenc's passion for exploration and adventure; he wrote in the preface that a complete history of the exploration of Australia can never be written as "[t]he story of the settlement of our continent is necessarily so intermixed with the results of private travels and adventures." To some extent Favenc filled out his history in his fictional accounts of explorations into the outback.

The 1890s were Favenc's most productive period as a writer, and his best tales of mystery and the supernatural were published between 1890 and 1895. By this time he had abandoned the discursive, over-complicated plots of his early short fiction in *The Queenslander* in favour of tightly controlled shorter pieces like "Doomed," "A Strange Occurrence on Huckey's Creek," and "The Red Lagoon."

The 1890s also saw the separate publication of two novels and a novella. *The Secret of the Australian Desert* was serialised in the Queenslander in 1890 before being published by the London publisher, Blackie & Son, in 1895. Like the best of Favenc's fiction, the novel weaves fact, fiction and speculation. *The Secret of the Australian Desert* traces the fortunes of an expedition that sets out northward from Central Australia in search of fate of Ludwig Leichhardt's famous expedition, which disappeared without trace. The novel crosses over into fantasy in its portrayal of a lost tribe of aborigines "wholly unlike any tribes known ever to have existed," which draws heavily on contemporary interest in the lost land of Lemuria.

Similarly, *Marooned on Australia* (1897) is based on fact. As indicated by its subtitle, *Being the Narrative of Diedrich Buys of His Discoveries and Exploits "In Terra Australia Incognita" About the Year 1630*, the story speculates about the consequences of the wreck of the Dutch ship *Batavia* and the depredations committed by the mutineers. The first person narrator, Diedrich Buys, is one of the two mutineers who escaped execution and were instead marooned in North West Australia. As he battles to survive in a hostile land he comes across the Quadrucos, a race distinct from the Aborigines because its technology is too advanced and culture too sophisticated.

A novella, *The Moccasins of Silence,* was published by the Australian publisher, George Robertson, in 1896, and featured strange native shoes that were worn to attack enemies by stealth at night. The same shoes appear again in the late story, "The Kaditcha: A Tale of the Northern Territory" (1907).

During the 1890s Favenc worked mainly for *The Bulletin*, which was edited by J. F. Archibald whose preference for the unadorned bush yarn may have influenced Favenc's style. Known as 'the bushman's bible,' *The Bulletin* was an important newspaper that helped shape Australia's national literature and published important work by Henry Lawson, 'Banjo' Patterson, Barbara Baynton, Miles Franklin and the cartoonist Phil May, in whose *Summer* and *Winter Annuals* Favenc would contribute.

A selection of seventeen stories published in The Bulletin between 1890 and 1890 was published in *The Last of Six: Tales of the Austral Tropics* (1863), the third volume of *The Bulletin's* short story and verse anthologies. In 1894 the London publisher, Osgood, McIlvaine published *Tales of the Austral Tropics*, which dropped six stories from the earlier collection and added two others. A third collection of stories from *The Bulletin*, *My Only Murder and Other Stories*, was published by the Melbourne publisher George Robertson in 1899; this collected twenty four stories published between 1890 and 1895. Of the thirty one stories gathered here, six were published in *The Last of Six: Tales of the Australia Tropics*, and seven appeared in *My Only Murder and Other Stories*. A collection of verse, *Voices of the Desert*, was published in 1905.

Favenc was a part of the acclaimed group of *Bulletin* writers living in Sydney during the 1890s, and was a good friend of Louis Becke who was also a master of the short form, compared in his day with Robert Louis Stevenson. In 1898 Favenc joined the Dawn and Dusk Club, a group of Bohemian writers and artists and it was around this time that his alcoholism began to take a toll on his health again. Certainly, by the end of the 1890s he was less productive and there was a marked decline in the quality of his work, although between 1899 and 1903 he did write six stories for Phil May's *Summer* and *Winter Annuals* with Gothic and supernatural elements. At that time, the annuals were edited by Harry Thompson, who preferred tales of horror and the supernatural.

By May 1905 Favenc was seriously ill in Royal Prince Albert Hospital, and later in year a bad fall that broke his thigh confined him to St Vincent's Hospital. He died on 14 November 1908 in Lister Hospital in western Sydney.

Further Reading

Cheryl Frost, *The Last Explorer, the Life and Work of Ernest Favenc* (Townsville: Foundation for Australian Literary Studies, James Cook University of North Queensland, 1983).

Ernest Favenc, *Tales of the Austral Tropics*, edited by Cheryl Taylor (née Frost) (Sydney: University of New South Wales Press, Colonial Texts Series,1997). This book collects the stories in *The Last of Six* and *Tales of the Austral Tropics* with a full scholarly introduction and critical apparatus.

Index of Stories in Ernest Favenc's Short Story Collections

The Last of Six: Tales of the Austral Tropics (Sydney: Bulletin Newspaper, 1893)

The Last of Six
A Cup of Cold Water
A Haunt of the Jinkarras
The Rumford Plains Tragedy
Spirit-Led
Trantor's Shot
The Spell of the Mas-Hantoo
The Track of the Dead
The Mystery of Baines' Dog
Pompey
Malchook's Doom: A Nicholson River Story
The Cook and the Cattle Stealer
The Parson's Blackboy

A Lucky Meeting
The Story of a Big Pearl
The Missing Super
That Other Fellow

Tales of the Austral Tropics (London: Osgood, McIlvaine, 1894)

A Cup of Cold Water
The Rumford Plains Tragedy
A Haunt of the Jinkarras
Trantor's Shot
Spirit-Led
The Mystery of Baines' Dog
The Hut-Keeper and the Cattle-Stealer
The Parson's Blackboy
A Lucky Meeting
That Other Fellow
Stolen Colours
Bunthorpe's Decease
The Story of a Big Pearl

My Only Murder and Other Tales (Melbourne: George Robertson & Co, 1899)

My Only Murder
A Tale of Vanderlin Island
Blood for Blood
The Other Mrs Brewer
The Burial of Owen
The Red Lagoon
Tommy's Ghost
The New Super of Oakley Downs
An Unquiet Spirit
George Catinnun
Bill Somers

A **Note on the Texts**

The texts of the stories in this collection are taken from their book appearance, for which they were often substantially revised, apart from those that saw their first and only publication in periodicals. The stories are arranged in order of their first publication.

MY STORY

(1875)

I have tried to relate the following adventure as plainly and truthfully as possible. That it appears simply wild and impossible, I well know; but I have herein related nothing but the facts.

It was in the year 1871 that three of us left the Cloncurry diggings, intending to push through to Port Darwin, prospecting as we went. We reached to within one hundred miles of the Roper River, when the strange event occurred which altered all our plans.

My two companions were named, respectively, Owen Davy and Charles Morton Hawthorne; my name is James Drummond. Davy was an old friend; Hawthorne a comparative stranger, a well made, handsome fellow, middle aged, with dark eyes of peculiar force and brilliancy. He had a habit of looking intently into your eyes when speaking, with a weird stern look that would, without doubt, confuse any man of nervous temperament. His face was marked with a scar extending in a diagonal direction across his upper lip; his mustache partly covered it, but you could trace the course of the seam by the unequal growth of the hair.

Davy and I had made his acquaintance by accident, about a fortnight before leaving the Cloncurry. He had expressed a great wish to join us when our proposed expedition was spoken of, and it ended in his accompanying us.

For the first few weeks we agreed together capitally; our new mate made himself an agreeable companion, and proved to be a good bush man. After a time, however, the novelty wore away, and he showed decided symptoms of laziness, besides assuming an authoritative, dictatorial tone, when any of our movements were under discussion. At last, beyond saddling his own horse in the morning, and perhaps making a languid attempt to light a fire, he fairly shirked all his share of the necessary work of the camp. Davy, a hot-tempered little Welshman, had had several quarrels with him; and one evening but for my interference they would have come to blows. The conviction was forced upon me that night that Hawthorne, in spite of his lordly airs and stern looking, black eyes, was at bottom but a coward. I could see the look of relief come upon his face when I stepped between and insisted upon the dispute ending; and many times afterwards I saw gleams of hatred in his eyes that showed the tiger cruelty he harbored within him. An older man than Davy, I had my temper more under control, and though I knew that Hawthorne disliked me, we managed to continue our intercourse with one another upon the terms of ordinary civility. In the days of good friendship, Hawthorne had contributed greatly to relieve the monotony of our journey by his brilliant and to a certain extent fascinating conversation; he evidently knew a good deal of the world, and of fast if not good society. He had often spoken mysteriously of being in possession of a wonderful secret, but his hints were always so vague, that Davy and I thought but little about the matter until after the strange event occurred that I am going to relate.

Davy and Hawthorne had ceased to speak to each other; the day's journey was generally performed in a moody, discontented manner; and I was thinking of proposing to abandon all prospecting and make straight for Port Darwin, when the whole aspect of affairs was suddenly changed. We had been out between four and five weeks, our horses were still in capital condition, and our supply of rations good. Since leaving Bourketown we had not seen the face of a white man, we had met with but slight difficulties with the blacks, and were now we thought within about one hundred miles of the Roper River, without having found the slightest indication of payable gold. This was the state of affairs on the 31st of November, 1871, when we unsaddled for our midday camp on the bank of a small creek.

The country through which we had been travelling for the last three days had been of a poor, sandy description, covered with forest tea-trees and stunted ironbark. The ridges were badly grassed, but here and there, on small flats on the banks of the creeks, we got good picking for the horses; and it was on such a small flat, situated in the bend of a sandy creek, that we turned out on this particular day. After unpacking, Davy took the billies and went down to the creek to get water; he was some time away; when he came back he put the billies down, and said:

"I saw fresh horse tracks in the bed of the creek."

Hawthorne, who was kneeling down lighting a fire, looked up eagerly, but did not speak.

"Many?" I asked.

"Seems only two," he replied; "one of them has been rolling in the sand."

"Who on earth can it be?" I conjectured. "People prospecting or looking for country, I suppose. But if so, there must be more tracks about, for they would have more than two horses."

"They may have left or lost them higher up the creek; they seem to have come down, and cannot be far off, for the tracks were only made this morning."

Hawthorne had not before spoken; he now remarked, in a strangely conciliatory tone, that "Davis was doubtless right— the horses must have come up the creek, and that if we followed the creek up, we should find the camp of their owners."

Davy, who at any other time would have opposed any proposition emanating from Hawthorne, on principle, now seemed struck by the altered tone of Hawthorne, and agreed with him that it might be as well to spend the rest of the day as proposed; I gave my consent to the proposed vote, and in an evil hour we started on our fatal errand.

Davy and Hawthorne went to gather the horses together when our meal was over; they found two strange horses had joined in with them—a bay and a chestnut, —both poor and saddle-marked. As we expected to overtake the owners of them, we drove them on with our spare horses.

We proceeded about five miles up the creek, the country getting more broken and barren. Small white sandy hills, covered with low wattle scrub, and here and there huge piles of granite boulders, were on either side of the creek. The creek itself had grown considerably deeper and narrower during the last two miles, the bed of it being full of holes of white, milky looking water. The tracks of the two horses were plainly to be seen the whole way, crossing and recrossing the creek.

Hawthorne was riding ahead, Davy and I were driving the horses after him; presently we saw him pull up, beckon to us, and then point ahead. We looked, and saw in the distance a rough humpy. We drove the horses up to within a few hundred yards, and then left them, to feed about; the three of us rode on to the camp. No fire was burning; a few crows rose up as we approached, and flew away, cawing loudly. Davy rode his horse up close to the gunyah and peered through the boughs.

"There's someone asleep inside," he said, and dismounted; Hawthorne and I did the same. Davy entered the rude place unceremoniously.

"Asleep, mate!" he called out.

No answer. "Hi!" he cried; then stooped and looked into the sleeper's face.

"By God, he's dead!"

Hawthorne and I crowded in, and saw a man lying upon a blanket spread over some dried grass, his head pillowed upon some articles of clothing folded neatly up. He was lying upon his back, his eyes half open, no trace of decomposition visible; life seemed to have but lately fled. Lifting my eyes from the dead man, I happened to notice Hawthorne and was startled by the look of combined joy and recognition visible in his face. Again I looked upon the corpse, and the dread fancy seized me that the dead and senseless body was aware of the evil glance directed upon it, and that a fearful, haunted, terrified look was now visible in the glazed eyeballs. I could stay no longer; calling to Davy, I hurried outside, Hawthorne, with a half concealed smile, following.

What were we to do? was our next question. Examine the camp, and see if we could find any clue as to his name, was the unanimous opinion. We did so. Outside the humpy were a riding saddle and a pack saddle, also a bridle and halter; inside were some ration bags, containing a little flour, tea, and sugar, an empty phial labelled "Laudanum," a quart pot with some tea leaves in it, and a pint pot smelling strongly of laudanum. That the man had poisoned himself was self evident; his body was well nourished, and free from any marks of violence. We next removed the articles of clothing from underneath his head, and in the pockets found about thirteen pounds in notes and silver, and two horse receipts in favor of George Seamore; underneath the pillow, as though pushed underneath, was a Letts' Diary, scribbled all over with writing in pencil; there were also such slight articles as tobacco, pipe, and matches. We then carefully examined the body, and made perfectly certain of the absence of life. He had been a tall man, with a fine determined face, fair chestnut beard, and gray eyes; the eyelids would not remain closed, and the eyes still seemed to me to wear a startled, shrinking look.

We now unpacked our horses, arranged our own camp, and proceeded to dig a grave, this of course being easy with our prospecting tools. That task finished, it was growing dark, and we carried the body to the grave. I had a prayer book in my swag, and read a part of the burial service over the body; the sandy soil had proved easy digging, and the grave was about four feet deep. The body was laid at the bottom, rolled in the blanket on which we found it lying. We filled in the grave just as it fell dark; I can see the whole scene before me as I write, the desolate looking hills, an unnaturally large red moon rising from behind them, and making the fantastic looking piles of boulders show black and grim against its light, my two companions and myself standing silent beside the mound of earth, ere we turned away.

Now, during the time that we had been digging the grave, Hawthorne left us and went down to the camp where the body was then lying; soon afterwards I called to him to ask him to bring some water when he came back. Receiving no answer, I went down myself, being thirsty from digging; on passing through the camp I saw Hawthorne inside the bough humpy bending over the body, making what looked like mesmeric passes. I called out sharply to know what he was doing; he started, and stammered out that he was only making sure that there were no indications of breathing. I said crossly that there seemed to be no occasion for that, and he went back to the grave.

After our supper was finished I tried to decipher the writing in the diary, but it was too illegible to read without a great deal of trouble, so I put it away under my head when I turned in. From the little that I had been able to make out, it seemed to be an account of the life of the man whom we had just buried, written by himself during his last hours. We talked for some time of the strange affair, dropping off to sleep one by one; we were sleeping round the fire, having been too busy to pitch our tent.

About the middle of the night, the moon then shining very brightly overhead, I was awakened by feeling something moving beneath my head; on lifting my head I saw Hawthorne feeling with his hand underneath my pillow. Angrily, I asked him what he was doing. He made no reply at first, but glared savagely at me, looking straight into my eyes, and seeming as though he would awe me by the very fierceness of his gaze; but my nerves were strong, and I looked back boldly and defiantly, and saw his eyes drop baffled; but his strange superhuman look had affected me more than I was then aware of.

"I was feeling for your matches, mine are all used; I am sorry that I disturbed you," he said.

I handed him my match-box without a word, and he went back to his blankets and lit his pipe. After a short time I again fell asleep, first feeling for the dead man's diary, as I felt certain that that was the object of Hawthorne's search; it was there where I had placed it. Once more was I disturbed; Davy shook me by the shoulder, and called me by name. I raised myself and looked around. The cold breath of the coming dawn was making itself felt; the moon sinking low in the west gave but a dim half light, and threw long shadows of the I stunted trees upon the white sandy soil around us; a few tall gum trees on the bank of the creek standing out white and spectral like. Davy was standing beside my bed, evidently greatly excited. "What do you think," he said in a frightened whisper; "Hawthorne has gone away with the dead man!"

I stared at him in astonishment. "I saw him, saw him go, and as I live, the dead man rode with him."

My courage has been put to the test in many lands, and I do not think I have been found wanting; but I must confess that when this weird communication was whispered into my ear in the ghastly failing moonlight, in the desert far from our fellow men, I felt a thrill of abject fear run through me. I laid my hand upon my companion's shoulder, and at the human contact the cowardly superstitious feeling that I had weakly given way to left me.

"What can you mean? How could he take a *dead* man with him?" I asked.

"I tell you that I saw them go. Listen! Can you hear anything?" We both listened, holding our breath, but the dead silence was unbroken; not even the scream of a curlew or the howl of a native dog could be heard.

"No," said Davy, "they are out of hearing now. A short time ago I awoke and thought that I heard the horses galloping about in their hobbles away down the creek. I put on my boots, and taking my revolver, went down to see what was up, as I thought the blacks might be knocking about. When I got near where the horses were I heard a strange noise, and was on the point of turning back to call you, but changed my mind, and went a little closer, sneaking along under cover as much as possible. I saw two men amongst the horses, catching and saddling some of them, saw them mount and come straight towards where I was hidden. I had my revolver ready to fire, when I saw that it was Hawthorne and—" He pointed towards the grave.

"The man could not have been dead."

"What time is it?" said Davy, in reply. I looked round; the dawn in the east was growing bright and clear.

"Half-past four or so," I said, and stooped for my watch.

"And what time was it when we buried the man?" my companion went on.

"About six o'clock."

"Say then that he was in a trance when we buried him, would not the weight of earth have killed him? Would he not have been suffocated in less than an hour?

I could only answer, "Yes." "But," I was going on to say, "could not Hawthorne have dug him up directly we went to sleep;" and then I remembered that I had seen Hawthorne in the camp in the middle of the night.

I looked for the book, and found it still under my pillow. I told Davy of the occurrence; he was on his knees, busy making up the fire; the bright cherry blaze seemed partly to scare away the dismal horrors that lingered round the haunted camp.

All Hawthorne's things were gone; he and his unearthly companion must have carried them down to the horses. We both shuddered at the thought of the living corpse moving about the silent tamp, and stepping perhaps over our sleeping bodies. Our horses were all there, Hawthorne's four and the two strangers being away.

"Shall we track them up?" I asked, when we were ready to start.

"No, no!" said Davy. "Let us get away from here. I don't feel myself; I feel quite nervous and cowed."

So we started, first inspecting the grave, which we found empty. We pushed on during the ensuing few days; and in my spare hours I managed to make out the blurred manuscript. The history revealed by it coincided so strangely with the scene that we had witnessed, that we could doubt the evidence of our senses no longer. It was so unheard of and incredible, and it brought back all the horrors of that night so forcibly and vividly, that our only wish was to reach a settlement of fellow beings, in hope that our minds would cease to dwell and brood upon what we had seen.

In a little more than a fortnight we reached the overland telegraph line, and following it along, we came to a working party; and then Davy fell sick and could not travel. He rapidly grew worse; everybody was most kind, but we could do but little. I could see the end not very far off.

I was watching by his side one evening, when he turned and spoke to me.

"I have told you all that I want you to do for me, excepting one thing, old fellow, and that is that when I die that you will watch over my grave for at least a week; promise that you will save me from that horrible fiend; make sure of it before you leave me."

I pressed his hand, and told him, "Yes."

"Good-bye, old friend; it's hard to die like this, but I feel easier since your promise."

That night he died, and I was left alone, the sole possessor of the horrible secret. I dared not tell the others, for they would only have laughed at me; but I determined not to break my word to the dead.

We buried him the next morning near the line; all hands knocked off work, and attended; and then my watch commenced.

They thought me mad thus to carry out a whim of my dead comrade's; and had they known against what I sought to guard his body, they would have been sure of my insanity; but I did not tell then. With snatches of broken rest during the day time, I kept my promise for more than a week, until all semblance of life must have departed from the body underground; and then, when my time expired and I could relinquish my armed watch (for man or ghoul, living being or ghost, I had determined that he should not make an attempt unscathed), I left poor Davy in his lonely grave, with the silent messages that had travelled so many thousand miles flashing past his resting place, and hastened to port. I went to Melbourne to recruit, and for a while forgot to a certain extent my hideous experience; until, after three years, I found myself here in Brisbane, and the other day it was all brought home to me again.

My resolution is taken—I will keep the story secret no longer. In a few days, if I live, I shall leave the colony, and if the body of that poor wretch found no peace in the wilderness, perhaps the depths of the sea will be more kind to me, when my time comes.

GEORGE SEAMORE'S MANUSCRIPT

I stayed about a week longer in London; and then, at the repeated request of my parents, hastened down to spend Christmas with them in Devonshire. I left fully persuaded that Fanny Berrimore was beginning to love me, as well as I loved her; and my visits had been as frequent as I could consistently make them. Christmas seemed to me but a weary time; and my absent manner was a great source of wonderment to my friends, to whom of course I had not confided any of my late adventures.

I told Fanny that I could not possibly return under a month; but after about a three week's stay at home I was troubled with a strange dream, in which Hawthorne bore a prominent part. My mind, only too ready to receive an idea that would send me back to Miss Berrimore, accepted this as a sign that my presence was wanted in London; and without in any way excusing my sudden change of purpose, I started next morning for town. Arrived at my rooms, I only stayed long enough to change my clothes, and then I bent my steps towards Grace-street. The servant, knowing me as an old visitor there, admitted me without hesitation; and I hastened upstairs to her sitting-room. Waiting but to give a light knock, to which I received no answer, I opened the door, and saw Hawthorne and Fanny Berrimore standing by the fire-place, she apparently leaning against his shoulder, as he encircled her waist with his right arm, whilst with his left hand he appeared to be caressing her face. My entrance had been unnoticed. For a moment I stood a spectator; and then with a deadly curse, sprang upon Hawthorne. He turned at the noise, and a look of fear paled his face, as he released his embrace of Fanny, who sank into a chair. The next moment we were engaged in a hand to hand struggle. He stood no chance with me, and in a few moments was stretched bleeding at my feet, my last blow having cut his upper lip quite open.

"Shall I kill you, you dog?" I muttered savagely, as I glared down upon him where he lay, afraid to rise; then I turned to look at Fanny; she was sitting with her head bowed down between her hands, in the same attitude almost as when I saw her after telling her of her brother's death; and but for the wrath boiling within me, I might have been touched by the graceful drooping attitude, and the remembrance of her desolate condition. But contempt alone predominated; I felt utter scorn for them both; and spurning my prostrate enemy with my foot, as unworthy of me, I left them both without another word.

I walked home quietly enough—my rage was too deep for any outward demonstration. All ideas of Hawthorne's pretensions to infernal knowledge—for such it really amounted to—were lost sight of in the jealousy I felt in the discovery of Fanny's duplicity. I could not help brooding over it; for like most men of ordinary sluggish temper, when once aroused, my passions were both deep and permanent. My dislike to Hawthorne had been scarcely augmented by the late event. Fanny seemed to be in my eyes the most guilty of the two; perhaps the thrashing I had inflicted upon my apparently successful rival before Miss Berrimore's face had something to do with the almost pitying contempt I now felt for him.

The next morning I was on my way back to Devonshire, and moodily sulked there for about three months. Then, as the spring was dawning upon the earth, I took a fresh resolution, and returned once more to London, determined to drown all saddening reminiscences in a burst of dissipation.

A day or two after my arrival, my wayward steps led me into Grace-street, but I saw nothing of Miss Berrimore; again and again I loitered about there and the old place in Farringdon street, but she never came. Thinking that she must have changed her place of abode, I one day knocked at the door, and enquired for her. The same servant that formerly lived there answered my knock; and in reply to my enquiry for Miss Berrimore, stared at me amazedly.

"Did you not know, sir; I thought that she was a friend of yours."

"Know! Know what?"

"She is dead."

"Dead!" and the sharp pang that I felt told me how well I must have loved her.

"When did she die?"

"Just about a month ago, sir. She caught a cold one day; and after being ill for about a fortnight, she was suddenly taken worse, and died."

"Was there anybody with her—any of her friends?"

"No, sir, I don't think anybody came near her until just before she was taken worse; and then a tall gentleman came here, and used to enquire how she was nearly every day."

"Tall with dark eyes and hair?"

"Yes, sir; and asked me if I had seen you lately—if you had been to call on Miss Berrimore, that's to say."

"Did he see her?"

"Not while she was alive; but after she was dead he went with the doctor, and he seemed very much cut up; and afterwards, in the evening, he came again before she was screwed down in her coffin."

I left the street after getting all the information I could from the woman. Hawthorne, then, had dared to come back, and death had stepped in and robbed him of his prey. But what was the meaning of his visiting the dead body? and a horrible fear struck chill to my heart. I went to Kensal Green Cemetery, where she was buried, and finding but a very plain and simple stone, had a pretty and ornamental tomb erected, for in her grave I had buried all animosity that I had harbored against her.

Three months dragged slowly on. I was an aimless, moody man, praying to meet my enemy, but finding him not; nor could I gain any information of his whereabouts. I one day fancied that I saw him at a distance, but could not come up with him in time to be certain.

About a week afterwards I was leaning moodily over the parapet of London Bridge one night. The hour was late, and the streets almost deserted; the night was dark and cloudy; occasional squalls of drifting rain came up the river. I stood there for some time looking at the lights of the town and the shipping, at the dark water running beneath my feet, listening to the chiming of the clocks, and weakly giving way to melancholy and despondent feelings. I was perfectly sober, and my brain clear. A solitary policeman was watching me a short distance away, as though he thought that I meditated suicide. A female figure hastily approaching from the opposite side brushed close to me, almost touching me; a strange thrill passed through me, an unrestrainable impulse made me spring after her; I overtook her just as she passed underneath a lamp; it was her!—the woman over whose body I had had a tomb erected in Kensal Green Cemetery was by my side! My exclamation of surprise and horror seemed not to affect her in the least; she kept on her way, and I by her side. The policeman looked keenly at us; he little thought that it was a dead woman who passed him. Some merry party came along, chatting and laughing loudly; how their mirth would have been checked had they known that the nice-looking girl—as I heard one loudly remark about her— had stepped forth from among the buried. She never looked at me as I kept up with her, but steadily pursued her way. I dropped a little behind, as the joyous thought came into my brain that by following her I might find Hawthorne. What an account should he render to me!

On we went, the dead and the living, until she turned down a narrow blind lane, reached a door in a wall at the side, opened it with a key she took from her pocket, and passed in; before she could re-close it I had pushed in, too—into a small courtyard, high buildings rising in the gloomy night all round. She seemed scarcely to notice my intrusion, but hurried on into one of the houses, I still keeping close behind her—into a dark passage and up a narrow stairway; from thence I followed her into a lighted room, where three men were sitting. They took no notice of either of us. A hasty glance assured me that Hawthorne was not amongst them. She opened a door leading into an inner room. I saw a man sitting in a lounging chair, his back towards me. She went up and handed a note to him; I followed, for I saw who it was—at last, I had him! He read the letter through, I standing quietly behind his chair, my heart leaping gladly. He tore the note up, laughing lightly.

"Well, Nelly, you have—" He turned as he spoke, and saw me. His exclamation of fear and terrified retreat was, oh, such music to me! The next instant he called loudly for help, for he saw murder in my face. The men from the other room rushed in, but before they could come I had hurled him half strangled on the floor, and was standing over him with a hastily snatched up decanter in my hand. "Order them back!" I cried, as they were rushing at me, "or your life pays the forfeit first! I'll beat your brains out! quick!"

"Back! back!" he cried in an agonised voice. "Don't kill me, Seamore!"

"Send them out of the room."

He did so.

"Now, what have you done to her?" I pointed to Fanny, who was sitting on a sofa in the old attitude I knew, the bowed down head and clasped hands.

"What shall I do? what do you want?"

"Remove your power from over her, if you can; give her back to me."

"I cannot; she will die again if my influence is removed. She knows you no more; her name now is Nelly Hotham."

"I care not whether she lives or dies, so that she is no longer your victim. I will give you but a few moments to make your mind up. Consent or—"

"I consent to anything," he said, cowering and shrinking.

"If I swear not to take your life, nor ever again to seek it, you will relinquish any hold you may have over her mind or spirit, and allow me to take her away wherever I like?"

"I will; never again will I seek to interfere with her."

"Then I spare your life. I do not trust your word, but I do your cowardice. If you dare to break your bond, I will find you, no matter where you hide yourself. I fear no more the punishment that I should incur through murdering you, than I do you yourself."

"She will die, as I told you; but you shall have your wish." He turned to "Nelly," as he called her.

"Nelly, go with this gentleman, and do whatever he tells you. You will never see me again." He made two or three quick passes with his hand—for I had allowed him to rise,—though I kept between him and the door, which I had locked. She looked at me dreamily, and shook her head as though confused; then she advanced and took my hand, and looked long into my face.

"Do you know him?" said Hawthorne.

"I do—that is, I think that I remember him, and will go with him."

I turned to Hawthorne again. "Before I leave you, you must tell me one thing—was Miss Berrimore untrue; or was it some devilish trick of yours that misled me that day?"

"She was always true to you; and on the day that you interrupted us she was under mesmeric influence," he sullenly replied. "But," he went on, "it was your desertion that killed her; she could not recall anything that passed that day, after she awoke, and believed that she had given you no cause to leave her without explanation."

I took Fanny away, and have never seen Hawthorne since, though the last glimpse I caught of him, standing looking at me with deadly hate, is still present to my imagination. His prediction was true—Fanny sank slowly, and died about three weeks after I rescued her from Hawthorne. I visited her constantly in the home that I found for her. She had lost all distinct remembrance of her past life; me she remembered more by some mysterious influence that I appeared to possess over her, than by reason of our being formerly acquainted. Of Hawthorne she never spoke at all; by some means he had bound her over to keep a silence that she dreaded to break.

At last she died, painlessly and quietly, and I buried her in the same cemetery where her body was even then supposed to be resting. I let her sleep under her assumed name of Nelly Hotham, and I watched over her grave for many weeks.

How Hawthorne first obtained possession of her body in order to bring her back to life I never could learn. Now she is safe. Since then I have wandered far and wide, but have never heard of him. Were it not for the want of physical courage, his power would be immeasurable; for I am at last convinced that he claimed no more than he could accomplish. Of my own life I am weary. I have found in this solitude a place where I think my body will meet with no worse fate than to moulder and decay, unnoticed and unburied. This is my birthday, and in a few hours my life will be spent; and hundreds of miles from my fellow men, I will render back my soul, in the hope of at last finding peace.

THE END OF THE MANUSCRIPT

The reason I leave here, the reason that I now make this public, is that the other day I met the man whom we buried, the man called, I believe, George Seamore, face to face in the street, and he turned and followed me.

THE LADY ERMETTA; or,
THE SLEEPING SECRET:
A SENSATIONAL NOVELETTE IN THREE PARTS, WITH AN ORTHODOX CHRISTMAS INTRODUCTION
(1875)

INTRODUCTION

It was Christmas Day, and I, the wearied super of a cattle station far out in the back country, was swinging idly in a hammock, in an iron-roofed verandah, where the thermometer stood at a hundred and ten; and imagining that I was keeping a merry Christmas. Not a sound, save the indistinct hum of insect life, was to be heard; all hands on the station, having succumbed to the influence of colonial rum and pudding, were asleep; and I lay and perspired, and smoked, and thought—of what? That is a question that will be answered directly. With my hands clasped under the back of my head, one foot projecting over the side of the hammock, and occasionally touching the verandah post in order to keep myself swinging, I began gradually to lose full consciousness of surrounding objects. I knew that it seemed to be getting hotter and hotter, that the iron roof overhead appeared to be assuming a molten appearance; that I was getting too lazy to keep myself rocking, that my eyelids were growing heavy, and that I should soon give it up and fall asleep, when I heard a deep, deep sigh close to me. I turned—

Saw throned on a flowery rise,
One sitting on a crimson scarf unrolled.

Well, not exactly.

This was a man, and he was sitting in one of the squatter chairs leaning against the slabs, and a curious looking figure he was to see in such a situation. I knew him at once; he was the Genius of Christmas. There he was, holly wreath, white beard, laughing countenance, and all the attributes complete.

I said, "Good day, old man —how are you?" for I felt astonishingly bold somehow. He was reading in a large book, the print of which seemed possessed with life, and to be constantly moving and changing; but when I made this remark he raised his head, and gazed at me with "a countenance more in sorrow than in anger," but did not speak.

"I know who you are," I went on; "you're the Genius of Christmas."

"I am," he said.

"And you're going to show me all manner of pictures and scenes of human life, and I shall awake by-and-by and find that it has all been a dream; and I shall be very good and charitable all the rest of my life."

"Not you," said the Spirit; "you couldn't be charitable if you tried."

"Spirit," I said, "that's very hard, why could I not be charitable if I tried?"

"When you couldn't show mercy to a poor old ghost who's been harped upon, and written about, and carolled over,—there, I'll say no more; but man's inhumanity to me makes a Christmas Spirit mourn."

"Spirit," I said, "you mistake, surely, I who esteem and venerate the Christmas season."

"You do, do you? Now, answer me truly, were you not trying

to compose a Christmas tale as you lay in that hammock?"

"I confess it, I was."

"And you say you venerate me; pretty veneration I call that, but I'll be revenged. I'll stand it no longer. I'll read Christmas poetry to you for the next three hundred and sixty-five days."

"Spirit, do not judge me unheard; be calm."

"Be calm! Who could be calm under such provocation? Listen! We are seven,—that's Wordsworth isn't it,—never mind, as I said before, we are seven; seven spirits, one for each day in the week. I'm Saturday. When Christmas Day falls on a Saturday, as it does this year, I have to attend to it. Now every leap year one of us has to do double duty, and as next year is a leap year I am told off for the extra day's work; but there is a chance for any of us to get out of this extra work, thus," —he went on as though quoting from some rule or regulation, —"If a Spirit when in the execution of its duty, can find a place upon earth inhabited by Christian, or supposedly Christian people, where no Christmas Literature is to be found upon Christmas Day, he shall be able to claim exemption from extra duty on leap-year, and the Spirit following him shall do his work."

"Spend your Christmas here," I cried, starting from the hammock. "Search the house from garret to basement (it was only a two-roomed hut), and see if you can find a Christmas magazine or paper."

"That Christmas story," the Spirit sternly replied, "That Christmas story, which shall never see the light, by its mere presence in your idiotic skull has spoilt my chance of a holiday, and I wanted to put Sunday into it"—the long faced sanctimonious hypocrite. "But I will be revenged, revenged!"

"Spirit," I cried, casting myself at its feet and clutching its robe, "have mercy; I am not strong-nerved. I could not bear to be transported to regions of ice and snow, and see poor people kind and generous to one another, and pretty girls playing at blindman's-buff, and all the many signs you would show me— have mercy!"

"Can you ask it knowing that during the whole of the past year

I have wandered to and fro seeking for a place wherein to rest on this twenty fifth day of December? I marked this spot, noted the dense stolidity, not to say stupidity, visible in your face, and I said here is a place where I shall be safe; nicely situated in a warm comfortable climate, mails always a month late; here I am secure for my holiday. This morning I took a turn through Europe, Asia, Africa, and America, just to see that everything was going on all right, come here to finish my day quietly and peace fully, in the virtuous frame of mind that a Spirit feels in who has done his duty, and I find, what! That you—a being than whom a generation of apes could not produce a greater fool—have dared to compose a Christmas Story; that you have committed two pages of it to paper, and it is even now lying there in your bedroom. Can you deny it?"

I could only bow my head in guilty assent.

"But vengeance can still be mine—yes, Vengeance! Vengeance!! Vengeance!!!" Here his voice rose to such a shriek that I expected to see the stockman and cook come rushing in to see what was up; but no help came to me, and he raged on.

"I will read to you, commencing with your own wretched two pages, *all the Christmas literature that has been published in the world this season!*" Uttering this awful sentence he leaned back in the chair, and glared furiously at me."

"Mercy, mercy," I said faintly.

"No mercy, I know it not; I reckon it will just comfortably occupy us until the end of next year to get through it all."

"Spirit!" I cried, "I have sinned, but I repent; I will be a new man, Christmas shall be to me a season of mourning and desolation; spare me."

Its only answer was to open its book and commence reading.

As though its first word was a blow, I fell back spell-bound and motionless, and there I lay whilst the Genius began to read my now detested production of two pages. First he read it in an ordinary colloquial tone, then he gabbled it over, next he sung it, then he tried to chant it. Then he read it in a facetious manner, stopping to laugh every now and then; then he read it in a dismal manner, pretending to cry; then he tried to make blank verse of it, and I tried to stop my ears, but all in vain; over and over again he read the horrid sentences I knew so well, until at last he seemed out of breath, and stopped.

"How do you like it," he said, "will you ever do it again?"

"Never, never," I groaned. He chuckled, and turning again to his book, the pages of which produced anything he liked without his having to turn over the leaves, he inflicted the following story upon me:—

THE LADY ERMETTA; OR, THE SLEEPING SECRET— PROLOGUE

Calm in the serene solemnity of their solitude; grand in the outstretched vastness of their extent, and golden in the Pactolean wealth of their beauty, lie the sands of Plimlivon. But what huge, gloomy object is that, the rugged outlines of which mar the tranquil beauty of their level expanse? Like the fossilised form of some gigantic inhabitant of a world long forgotten, or like a Brobdignagian bandbox labelled, "This side up, with care," stands a mighty isolated rock, and casts upon the otherwise unflecked extent of stainless sand around it, a shadow, weird, gloomy, and mysterious. Why does that rock— that grim, portentous sentinel, challenging the gladsome sunlight, with its ominous "*Qui vive*," stand there and throw its gruesome shade over sand-grain and pebble that would else be revelling in the glorious radiance of day? Say, why does the shadow of some awful secret crime fall across the otherwise unblotted course of a fair, fresh life, and turn the rich colors of the flowers of life into the sombre hues and tints of death? I know not, gentle reader, but that rock stands there because I intend to use it in the third and last chapter.

Chapter I. THE SECRET

"My daughter," said the Marquis of Marborough.

"Yes, my father," replied the Lady Ermetta, who was of a most dutiful disposition, and when she did not say "No" said "Yes" with undeviating regularity.

"The hour has now arrived when I feel it incumbent on me to reveal to you *the secret* —the secret upon which hinges your future welfare and happiness, and is also the central point of interest in this story in which we are two of the principal characters. Therefore, arm yourself with fortitude, and prepare to hear it as becomes a heroine."

"Very well, my father," returned the dutiful girl, but will you kindly tell me exactly what to do."

"Clasp your hands convulsively, lean forwards attentively, and with an expression of anxious horror on your beautiful features, exclaim, 'Speak, speak, my father; I can bear the worst'"

The Lady Ermetta followed his directions to the eighth part of an affygraffy.

"You know, my child, that in the third and last chapter you are to be married, as becomes a heroine; and you also know that Baron Gadzooks is the bridegroom elect. But you do not know that a dark secret hangs over his birth, a secret which I am now about to reveal, therefore listen attentively."

"I am all ears," said the lovely girl.

"My dearest, that is a most irrational remark; now, really, how can you be all ears?"

The Lady Ermetta blushed to the tips of the articles in question, and muttered something that sounded like a request for her father to go and put his boots on.

"Silence, Ermetta!" said her father sternly, "such conduct is unbecoming in the heroine of a novel. Now, listen to me— The Baron was changed at birth."

"Then Baron Gadzooks—"

"Is somebody else."

"And somebody else?"

"Is the Baron. You now comprehend the situation."

"Not altogether, my father, you have neglected to inform me

who somebody else is."

"That, my dear child, is a question that even the author could not answer."

"Then supposing that I marry the Baron, I in fact marry 'somebody else,' and as you say that 'somebody else' is the Baron, why of course my husband will be the Baron."

"How the deuce is that?" said the Marquis; "let's see. If you marry the Baron—, but you can't marry the Baron, because he's not the Baron—he was changed at birth,"

"He's somebody else."

"Yes, exactly."

"Then, as he is not the Baron, somebody else is the Baron."

"Well, yes, I suppose so."

"Then, again, if I marry Gadzooks, I marry 'somebody else,' and somebody else, you say, papa, is the Baron," said the Lady Ermetta, triumphantly. "Come now," she added rather maliciously, "I think you are a little irrational now."

"Really Ermetta, you will look at the matter from only one point of view; don't you see that he's not the right somebody else. There are any amount of somebodies else; but let me tell you all about it. This important secret came out in a conversation that was overheard to pass between two servants. One was the nurse of the then infant Gadzooks, the other was a fellow servant. The nurse was heard to make the following remark about her youthful charge:— 'The blessed dear was a layin in my arms as quiet as a lamb, and smiling like a cherrup, when he *changed* all of a sudden, and has been that cross and frakshus ever since that I ain't had a minnit's peace with him.' The person who overheard this startling disclosure was a devoted friend of the family; he acted with decision and promptitude. The servants were first got rid of—one was strangled, the other hung. He then took the secret, hushed it into a sound sleep, wrapped it carefully in tissue paper, and put it into a box."

"Then where is the danger to come from?"

"Here lies the danger. When that devoted friend put the secret into the box he made a fatal mistake—he put it into the wrong box, and the secret might awake and find itself."

"In the wrong box! How truly awful."

"It is indeed; it might awake at the very moment of your marriage, and forbid the ceremony to proceed. There's no knowing to what lengths a secret that's been kept asleep, in the wrong box for many years might proceed when once awakened."

The Lady Ermetta sobbed deeply. "I can never give up Gadzooks," she said, "I have never seen him, for he has not been introduced personally into this story yet, but I feel that he has my poor heart."

"Restrain your feelings, my child; picture to yourself what would be the result if the secret should awake after your marriage, and announce to an astonished world that you had married somebody else; why you might almost be tried for bigamy."

"Have you the secret, my lord?"

"I have; the two boxes are in my study, but calm your agitation, for you know that Squire Hardpuller will soon be here, and should you bring yourself to think of giving up Gadzooks, why, he is rich, and I do not object to the idea of having him for a son-in-law." So saying, the Marquis left Ermetta to her tears and lamentations.

Chapter II. THE SECRET DIES

Now that she was alone, Lady Ermetta gave full vent to her grief. "I can never give him up," she murmured, between her convulsive sobs; "I feel that he is entwined around the very tendrils of my existence. We were to have been married in the third chapter, and now— this is the second, and we are to be separated. And what separates us? A secret! A secret that sleeps. Sleeps, why should it awake, why should it not die:" and uttering these last words in the strange hissing tone used by people who have determined on perpetrating some crime, Ermetta raised her head and stared into vacancy, with a cold hard look stealing over her sweet face.

The tears soon ceased to flow, her hands clenched themselves tightly, and she who might but just now have stood for a statue of the weeping daughter of Tantalus, was transformed into Lady Macbeth, demanding the daggers. Muttering sternly, "It shall be so," she left the apartment with a step befitting a representative of that strong-minded woman.

Let us watch her as she enters her father's study, where the light falls but dimly through the deep-set windows, as though winking at the deed about to be done. Watch her as she kneels before two quaintly carved ebony boxes, and applies her ear to the keyhole of each in turn. Watch her as the look of gratification steals over her face on detecting, in one, a low but perfectly distinct and regular respiration, the ghost of a feeble snore. Watch her as she applies the key to the lock, lifts the lid, and takes out the secret—takes it out gently and carefully, with the tender touch of a woman, so as not to disturb the slumber that has lasted now so long. Watch her, the guilty thing, as she starts at hearing the sound of voices in the hall, and, concealing the secret in her pocket, passes from the room to hasten to receive her expected visitor. As yet the deed is not done. As yet she can gaze out of those clear blue eyes with a soul unstained by actual murder. But how long will her innocence last; even now as she stands by the window in the morning room where she intends to receive her would-be suitor, the weird, wild look that must have been ever on the faces of the Di Medici and Brinvilliers is visible. She has deposited the secret (still asleep) on a chair, and she abides her time.

He comes. The door opens, and Squire Hardpuller is announced. She greets him with a winning smile that makes his heart bound again; poor man, he little thinks that she is bent upon making him accessory to her deed of death. Skillfully she backs him on to the chair of doom. Blandly she bids him be seated. Cordially she welcomes him. Will he look behind him? Will he apologise, and remove the innocent secret slumbering upon the seat of the chair?

No, Ermetta, your eyes have him spell bound. What man

could look away when you smilingly desired him to take a seat? You have—alas! for beauty, for youth, for guileless innocence, and sweet simplicity—you have made a murderer of him. He is a heavy man, and he *sits down on the secret*. It is done, and fiends may chuckle ha! ha! Now to keep him there.

Squire Hardpuller was a sporting character; he had been introduced into a great many novels, and was always looked upon as a great bore by the other characters, on account of his endless stories of horses, dogs, runs, and other sporting anecdotes. In the present case nobody could have answered Ermetta's purpose better; once fairly started upon his favorite and only topics, he prosed on contentedly for over two hours; then, blushing to find that his visit had trespassed on her time to such a length, he rose and made his adieux. She beamed on him to the last with her siren-like smile, and then, when he had gone, the re-action set in, and she who had listened unmoved for two mortal hours to a lot of sporting anecdotes, quailed before a dead secret. But such is human nature. She went to the chair in which he had sat; she lifted up the tissue paper containing the secret; with one white hand she held it to her ear, and with the other held her breath.

Not a sound, not the faintest suspicion of sound was to be heard. For nearly ten minutes did that high-bred resolute girl strain every nerve tighter than wire in a sheep-fence, but all was still. The secret, then, was dead. For a moment the rush of feeling overpowered her, then curiosity came to her aid; she would open the paper and see the secret. She had never seen a secret; she had often heard one. Nay, she had read a book called the "Dead Secret;" now she held one in her hand, she would see it.

She was about to unfold the covering of tissue paper, when a shadow fell across her, and somebody knocked at the window. She looked up startled. The car of a balloon was dangling in front of the glass, and seated in it was her father. She went to the window and opened it

"Come, my child," he said, "the third chapter is at hand, and we must be at the appointed place. Step in." Putting her hand on the sill, Ermetta sprang lightly into the car of the balloon, which immediately commenced to ascend. She at once communicated the important event that had just taken place to her father, and carrying them with it the balloon soon became a mere speck in the blue regions of the infinite.

But a close observer, one of unequalled vision, might have detected a small minute object come fluttering down from the empyreal vastness. Down it descended, gyrating hither and thither, the sport of every wandering zephyr. They tossed it mockingly about, played with it, then let it fall lower and lower, until the broad bosom of the pitying earth received and sheltered it. It was the corpse of the poor murdered secret. And the shadow of the rock, on the sands of Plimlivon, is darker, and deeper than ever.

Chapter III. BARON GADZOOKS

Baron Gadzooks was walking up and down on the sands of Plimlivon. He looked out to sea, and tapped his teeth with the top of his pencil; in his hand he held a note-book. He was composing a poem. Presently he commenced to read it over.

> Exsuffolating memory, get thee hence,
> Nor seek to melodise the scathful past;
> When rampant Ruin, drunk at my expense,
> Rose, and the empty bottle at me cast.

"That's rather good," he said, thoughtfully; "the simile in the last line particularly, the empty bottle, stands for the dregs of life."

> That rounded throat, that wealth of tumbled hair:
> That mouth so rose-like, kissable, and tender,
> She'd glue to mine, as if she didn't care
> If suffocation should ensue and end her.

"Hem! that ought to fetch her," he went on; "quite in the modern style; now for some thing hot and strong."

Must I forget all these; if so, then let me
Be chained within a sea of fire volcanic.

"What will rhyme with 'let me'? Let's see. Wet me, pet me, bet me, get me, net me"; and the Baron cast his eyes upwards, for inspiration, and caught sight of a speck in the canopy of heaven overhead that made him shout "Ball-o-o-n!" Then suddenly remembering that he was one of the principal characters in a novel, and as such bound to act with propriety, he blushed, sat down, and commenced to pick his teeth with one of his gilt spurs. On second thought, however, he started up again, frowned fiercely, and in deep tragedy tones said:— "Ha! ha! they come." Then he picked up a telescope that had been left behind by a party of excursionists, because they knew that it would be wanted for my plot, and, applying it to his eye, gazed at the rapidly increasing speck.

"Ah!" he muttered, "I see her, there—now she winks; now— yes, she's about to blow her nose. Angelic being! But hold! What's this?"

The noise of horses galloping at top speed had struck upon his listening ear. Nearer they came, and two horsemen appeared tearing along the level sand. And hark! the beat of paddles. Over the surface of the hitherto tenantless deep glided a mighty steamer, with crowded decks, the captain standing on the bridge, and shouting, "Full speed ahead! full speed astern!" alternately. A shrill whistle drew the Baron's attention again inland. A traction engine, dragging a long string of carriages, appeared, full of characters out of all sorts of novels, who had got in for the sake of a ride. Amazement held the Baron dumb, so he said nothing. Nearer and nearer everything came, everybody cheering and waving another man's hat. At once the occupants of the balloon stepped upon *terra firma*; the two horsemen, one being Squire Hardpuller, alighted from their panting steeds; the train disgorged its occupants, and the people from the steamer sprang into the sea and waded on shore.

They all approached and surrounded the Baron; they waited for him to speak, but he was silent.

"Read the will," said a tall man who looked like a lawyer.

"I have no will," said the Baron, "or I should not be here."

"Then reveal the secret," said another.

"Unfold the plot," exclaimed a third.

"Open the red box," said a fourth.

"Produce the real heir," said a fifth.

"Bless you, my children," said a sixth.

"Last dying speech and confession," said a seventh.

Then spake the Lady Ermetta: "Baron, papa has consented; the Bishop is ready, and here are the witnesses."

"Hurrah for the witnesses!" shouted everybody.

"Good heavens!" said the astounded Baron, "I know now what you mean. I was only introduced in this chapter; how the deuce am I to know what's been done in the other two chapters?"

"He jibs!" said the Lady Ermetta, "and I have sinned in vain." She would have fainted, but nobody seemed inclined to catch her, so she didn't.

The Marquis then advanced, and in his usual dignified tone said, "Are there any bad characters present?"

Nobody was fool enough to answer yes.

"Then," said the Marquis, turning to the Baron, "I am afraid that you must be the bad character of this story, and if so, Poetical Justice demands that you must be punished."

"This is hard," said the Baron, whose high bred composure did not desert him under these trying circumstances. "I came out here simply because I was informed that I was wanted for the proper completion of the plot, and now I am to be made a scapegoat of."

"There is some show of reason in what you say," said the Marquis; "so one more chance shall be given you."

"Are there any bad characters present?" he again asked in a

louder voice. As before, nobody was fool enough to answer yea.

"If there are any bad characters present," he went on, "let them step forward and be hung instead of this innocent nobleman."

At these awful words three bad characters, who had been hiding behind the big rock, waiting for a chance to commit a murder, or some thing of that sort, tried to sneak away unseen.

Squire Hardpuller, who had been anxiously looking out for an opportunity to cry tally-ho! and thereby identify himself as a sporting character, saw them, and immediately cried, "Stole away! yoicks! yoicks! away!"

With one consent the whole assemblage joined in the cry, and rushed in pursuit, with the exception of the Marquis and his daughter.

The Lady Ermetta had big feet and thick ankles, which she was frightened of showing if she ran, and the Marquis thought it beneath his dignity to go out of a walk.

"Ermetta," said the Marquis gravely; "we are flummoxed."

"Perhaps they'll come back," said Ermetta.

"I'm afraid not," said the Marquis, looking after the fast vanishing multitude.

He was deceived, however. Nerved by despair, the three bad characters ran well, and now doubled back and came once more to the isolated rock on the sands.

Instantly new life seemed to enter into Ermetta; she whispered something to her father, who shook his head, and said, "too late," but suffered his daughter to lead him behind the rock.

Breathing heavily—with their pursuers, headed by Hardpuller and Gadzooks, close upon their heels—the three bad characters approached;— they passed and made for the sea. As Gadzooks, in hot haste, pressed after them, running close by the fatal rock, a foot clad in a French kid boot, and a very substantial white-stockinged ankle, was thrust forth from behind it, right in front of him; he tripped, he fell; and the next moment the Marquis was holding him down.

"Poetical Justice!" he cried. "Poetical Justice!" echoed Ermetta, who limped a little, for the Baron in falling had inadvertently kicked her on the shin, and she didn't like to rub it before so many people.

Everybody halted, glad of a spell, and the bad characters swam out to sea.

"Where's the Bishop?" said the Marquis.

"Here," cried his lordship, coming forward hot and perspiring.

"Look sharp, or the end of the chapter will be here," said the Marquis.

Gadzooks was dragged to his feet, and held firmly, in spite of his struggles and protestations.

"Quick, or we shall be too late," reiterated the Marquis.

"Never mind, papa, we have got him fast, and I can be married in the Epilogue."

"Nonsense, my child, epilogues are only to tell the reader what he knows already."

The Bishop gabbled over the service,—"keep-thee-only-unto-her-as-long-as-ye-both shall-live?"

"I will!" yelled everybody, drowning the voice of the wretched Gadzooks, who said, "*I won't.*"

Away went the Bishop again, etc, etc.

"I will!" said Ermetta; and she meant it

"Thank goodness!" said the Marquis; "she's off my hands!"

* * * * * * *

Years have passed, and the rising tide has washed away the footsteps that were imprinted that morning on the sands of Plimlivon. But that lonely rock still holds its steadfast watch, and the shadow it casts is deeper and darker than ever. But the shadow on the heart of the stricken Gadzooks is deeper and darker still.

EPILOGUE

Now, during the reading of the latter portion of the forego-ing story, a gleam of hope had shot across my brain. As soon, therefore, as the Spirit had finished, I proceeded to put it into practice.

"What do you think of that!" said the Spirit.

"I like it immensely," I replied; "really you can't think what a jolly year I anticipate; it will be all beer and skittles."

The Spirit, I thought, looked slightly crest fallen.

"You've no idea," I went on, "how dull it is up here; and now to have you to read these charming little stories to me—really, old fellow, it will be delightful."

"Don't be so sure of that," he answered. But I fancied that he seemed staggered.

"Now," he said, opening his book again; "for the next, one of the real old sort—"How the King got his own again."

"'Twas Christmas Eve, and a bitter cold one to boot. What of that? It but made the crackling log fire seem the warmer and snugger. 'Be-shrew me!' said mine host of the Holly Bush, as he stood with his back to it, warming his portly calves; 'but if sad-colored garments and cropped heads are to be the fashion of the day, we shall scarce know Merry England.'"

He had got thus far before I could well stop him; then I interrupted him as blandly and politely as I could, "Excuse me; one moment. That promises to be a most interesting tale, but you will be tired and hoarse if you go on reading without pause. Now just to give you a spell I'll sing you a song."

"A what!" he said.

"A song—a carol. *A Christmas carol.*"

"You daren't," he said; but the blow had gone home I could see.

"No trouble at all, my dear fellow, just the reverse, and it's one of my own composing too," I added boldly, for I thought that I could see victory ahead.

I have no more voice than an alligator with a cold in its head, and scarcely know one tune from another, but without more ado I struck up:—

Come, your hands entwine, for this toast is mine,
A health to Christmas bold.
Round his head the leaves of the holly shine,
In his arms he does earth enfold.

"Patience! Grant me patience," muttered the Spirit; but he seemed to clench his teeth firmly, as if with a determination to sit it out. I went on, and hurled the next verse at him like a boomerang:—

When over the ground he spreads around
The snow that he so does love,
The robin comes out, and he looks about—

With one wild yell of anguish that made every sheet of iron in the roof ring like a bullock bell, the Spirit of Christmas started from the chair.

"Man! man! You have conquered. I forego my revenge. That robin is too much for me. Live unharmed by me; but," and here his voice softened into a tone of beseeching pathos, "as you have some charity in your disposition, as you may stand in need of consideration and forbearance yourself some day, do not add to the heavy woes of a tortured Spirit by casting your additional stone. Do not ever again attempt to write a Christmas story."

I was deeply touched, there was such a look of heartfelt anguish on his face.

"You promise?" he asked.

"I do."

"Then, we part friends; but, ah! that robin," and, waving me a parting salute, he stepped out into the glaring sunshine, and passed away.

THE MEDIUM
(1876)

Chapter I

The end of a dry season; the roads foot deep in dust; the grass, what was left of it, as brown as grass could be; the waterholes dwindled down into puddles of liquid mud—in fact, everything looking just as it always does after an Australian drought, as though it only wanted a fire-stick put into it to burn the whole concern up, and forestall the last day.

It was just sundown one day, during this desirable period of the year, when a traveller came cantering along the road leading to the Stratford station. On he went, raising as much dust as a marching regiment would in any other country, until he pulled up at the slip rails, dismounted, let himself and horse in, and wended his way up to the homestead.

The house he was approaching was the usual style of thing in the bush: two or three rooms, and verandah, with smaller huts scattered around. A very tall man was leaning against one of the verandah posts, smoking. He turned as he heard the horse's tread, and welcomed the horseman by the name of Jackson. They shook hands, Jackson unsaddled his horse, and they went inside.

The tall man's name was Starr, and he was the owner of the place.

Jackson handed him a couple of letters, remarking as he did so that he heard he was mustering, and had come down to look after his cattle if it was the case. "No," said Starr, as he broke the envelopes, "I was only getting some fat cattle for Blatherskyte; I start to-morrow with them."

"The beggers told me you were mustering down here, so I've had my ride for nothing. Luckily I am not very busy, for one can't do much till we get some rain."

"Well, I'm glad to see you down here. Tea will be in directly."

"I will just rinse some of the dust off," said Jackson, stepping into one of the bedrooms.

A trampling was just then heard outside. Starr went out, and was immediately greeted by name by one of the new comers—a young and good-looking man. The other was dark-eyed, with a black moustache, and rather a theatrical looking personage.

"Why, Starr, you are looking jollier than ever. I think you have grown even taller since I last saw you."

"Glad to see you back again, Harris," returned Starr as they shook hands.

"Mr. Haughton," said Harris, indicating his companion. Starr bowed, and Jackson made his appearance, giving his face a finishing rub with a towel. Harris and he were old friends, so his greeting done, and Mr. Haughton having been presented for the second time, they went inside.

"What is the news from Blatherskyte, Harris," said Starr, when they were all seated at tea.

"Any amount of gold being got by some; nothing by others. Mr. Haughton is one of the unlucky ones."

The other two glanced enquiringly at the stranger, who had scarcely spoken as yet. He remarked that he had been up there for the last six months, that he went on to the field with money, and had now scarcely enough left to carry him off; so his luck had not been in.

"Everybody drunk last night," said Harris, taking up the thread. "We were going to have a concert, but the singers got too drunk to sing, and the audience to listen—so that it was a failure as far as the melody of the affair went. You are going up to-morrow, did you not say, Starr?"

"Yes, I start in the morning, with some bullocks, and expect to get in some time during the next day. Any water at the twenty-mile creek?"

"Yes, enough to do you, and that is about all. When will you be back?"

"I intend to come straight back the day after I get in. I am going down to Imberwalla, to take down some gold I want to get rid of."

"You will be worth sticking up."

"Yes, I shall; for old Jawdon, the butcher, owes me for half of the last draft, which I shall get this time. I shall have about seven hundred, mostly in gold."

"Well, that is not such a great sum, but many a man has lost his life for less."

"I hope that is not going to be my case," replied Starr; and after the usual bush talk about horses and cattle they rose from the table.

"Where is your old hutkeeper?" said Jackson, after the things were cleared away.

"I had a row with him this morning; he had been here too long, and was getting cheeky, so he went this morning. This man happened to be passing, and wanted a job, so he got the place."

"I never did like that other fellow, he had an evil look about him," remarked Harris.

"He was a very good cook," returned Starr.

"Let us have a game at whist," he said, rising. "Do you play, Mr. Haughton?"

"I don't mind taking a hand."

They sat down, Harris and Jackson against Starr and Haughton. They played for some time, but after the first game or two all the luck went over to Haughton and his partner. Harris, who was a volatile sort of fellow, after a great deal of restlessness, proposed changing the game to euchre. The game was changed, but not the luck; Haughton and Starr still won. It was about ten o'clock when they left off playing, the winnings then amounted to a couple of pounds or so. Haughton proposed to his partner that they should play off—who took the lot. They did so, and Haughton won. Starr rose, and, going into his room, brought out a couple of pair of blankets.

"You will have to be contented with a shake down to-night, Mr. Haughton; I have no spare bed to offer you."

"Oh, I will do right enough," said the other, smilingly. "I will sleep in the verandah; it is cooler."

He went outside, after bidding the others good night. Jackson was sitting on the table, playing at patience with the cards.

"Well, I intend starting early to-morrow, so shall say good night," said Starr.

"All right, but don't go just yet; it is not so very late. I have any amount of news to tell you, but I cannot get it all out at once," returned Harris.

"Well, let us hear some of it"

"You know Rowdy Jack, who was horse breaking for you?"

"Yes."

"He has got bored and is lodging at the expense of the country for three years."

"It is certainly news that he has got it, but none that he deserved it. Anybody else come to grief?"

"Yes, two or three married."

"You call that coming to grief, do you?" said Jackson, putting the fourth story on a card house.

"In most cases I do," said Harris. Jackson's card house came down with a run.

"What do you know about it," he said.

"I am a married man, and speak from experience."

"You married, Harris! You are only joking."

"No, unfortunately, I am not. You two fellows are old friends, so I will tell you all about it.

"When I came out here ten year ago a regular new chum, I went up to live at Bloomfield's station, on the Wantagong. I had been up there about two years, and being only a raw, foolish boy found it very dull after the first novelty wore away. The place is all cut up into farms now; it was pretty well selected on even when I was there. I got very intimate with one of the selectors, an old fellow named Delaney, who used to live upon his wits I suppose, for it was very little I ever saw growing on his selection. I said that I got intimate with him. I ought to have said with his daughters. They were the attraction. The eldest I thought a regular beauty. Looking back on her now with the utmost detestation, I must admit she had remarkable good looks. She possessed a great deal of tact, too, and concealed her defects of manner and education admirably. I fell over head and ears in love with her; she was two or three years older than I was, and could do anything she liked with me. One day I called just as the priest, one Father Carroll, was leaving. I went in and found Mary crying, sobbing at least. Of course I was up in arms directly, and when we got by ourselves I insisted upon knowing the cause of it. After a great deal of feigned bashfulness and reluctance, she told me that Father Carroll, whom the Lord confound, had been warning her, telling her that my visits were becoming common talk, that I was only trifling with her, meant nothing serious, and all the many hints you can imagine. I am convinced now that this was nothing else but lies from beginning to end. Father Carroll, who was much respected in the neighborhood, knew too much of her to talk in that strain; repentance was the subject he would be most likely to choose for his homily. I confounded him just now, for if his name had not been introduced I do not think I should have been worked upon like I was. How I could have been such a mad infatuated fool is incredible to me now. But I was only a boy, and she and the devil had regularly ensnared me. I had a little money, not much; rumor had greatly magnified it, and they thought they had a prize. Anyhow, to make short work of it I married her that day week. I left the cottage immediately after the priest had married us, and hastened home to prepare a place to take my wife to. When within two miles of home I met a man on horseback. He pulled up at we came together, and I recognised a young fellow who had left the station shortly after I arrived on it.

"I was looking for you," he said. "They told me I should find you down at old Delaney's. I am looking for some horses of mine that are running down this way. Mr. Morgan (the superintendent) told me that you knew where they were running."

I was in a hurry, but the horses were no distance away I knew, so I turned off to show him the place. He commenced asking me about the people in the neighborhood as we went along; he said that he had been in Queensland ever since he left the station, and only came back two or three days ago.

"You have been down seeing the Delaney, girls," he went on to say; "how is Mrs. Morgan?"

"Mrs. Morgan," I said. "I don't know her."

"Why Mary Delaney, of course. Did you not know that she consented to be Mrs. Morgan for six months or more? She might have become Mrs. Morgan in reality, for she was making a regular fool of him, but old Bloomfield in Sydney heard of it, and he saw that he had either to lose her or his billet, so he sent her away. That is not the first trial she has had of married life, and her sisters, I suppose, are running the same track. They say that you are down there pretty often."

"He had scarcely finished speaking when we caught sight of his horses, and he started after them, leaving me to meditate on the pleasant piece of information he had just imparted to me.

"I did not do anything sudden or rash, but rode quietly home. Next morning I left the district, never to return. I wrote to her a letter I do not think she would forget very easily, and have made her an allowance—as much as I could afford—ever since, on condition that she never called herself by my name or attempted to join me. She consented perforce, for I went to New Zealand, and remained there for three years."

"Have you heard of her lately; are you sure your information was correct?" said Starr, after a pause.

"I have; and her conduct since my departure fully comes up to, nay exceeds, the character I heard of her."

There was a pause of some minutes, during which the regular breathing of the sleeper outside could be heard.

Jackson's attention was attracted by it.

"Who is he?" he said, in an undertone to Harris, indicating the object of his remark by a move of the head.

"I don't know; I only met him a day or two ago, and we travelled down together. He says that he has been in the army."

"Looks more like a skittle-sharper," said Starr, rudely.

"Don't be spiteful now, because he won when you played off!"

"Not I, but I saw something that you fellows didn't see. The stakes were not worth making a noise or a scene about, but the cards know him as well as he knows them."

"What! Did he cheat?" said Harris, turning as red as fire.

"Something very like it."

"Confound him forever. To think of my having brought him here. Old Fitzpatrick introduced him to me; he seems to have been educated, and I supposed that he was as good as most of the other men you meet. "

"Of course, Harris, it is impossible to know what a man is from just riding along a road with him. Good night," he went on, shaking hands, "we shall have breakfast at sunrise to-morrow, but you need not get up unless you are going to start early too."

"I am off the first thing," replied Jackson. "And Harris, of course you will come to my place to-morrow?"

"Yes. But I have a good mind to wake Mr. Haughton up, and tell him something that will stop him from proceeding with us to-morrow. I feel almost as though I had been found out doing something dirty myself."

"Oh, nonsense," said Starr, "it is not worth speaking about; only don't play at cards with him any more."

By sunrise next morning breakfast had been despatched, and the horses were ready, saddled. Haughton complained of an attack of fever, and declined any breakfast. Starr and Jackson bade him good morning, and made some ordinary remarks.

Harris stalked by him like a muzzled tiger past a shin of beef.

Haughton took no notice of his changed behaviour, though it was open enough. He said that he would ride slowly and overtake them in an hour or two if he felt better.

The station was soon tenanted by the cook and stockman only. Haughton's horses were in the yard, and about an hour after the others had left, the men saw Haughton catch and saddle them, then ride away along the same road taken by Jackson and Harris.

They had pushed on, and by three o'clock arrived at Jackson's station, Glenmore. Harris was easily persuaded to stop the next day, the station of which he was superintent being only fifteen miles distant

"Mr. Haughton does not seem to be showing up," he said, as he was preparing to start the following morning.

"No, he could not help noticing your behaviour towards him. I will be down your way in a day or two—good bye."

Chapter II

On the second day after Harris' arrival at home, Jackson rode up to the station, a black boy following him. Harris came out to meet him, and was immediately struck by the gray expression of his friend's face.

"Why, Jackson, you look serious enough for half-a-dozen parsons; what is the matter?"

"Starr has been murdered," returned Jackson, shortly.

"Good God! You can't mean it"

But Jackson's face assured him that he did mean it.

"He was found dead at Yorick's Lagoon, shot through the head. Here is his black boy, Dick, who found the body."

Harris turned to the boy.

"Mr. Starr been killed?"

"Yöi; ben shootem here," touching the top of his head.

"Had he been robbed too, Jackson?"

"There were no tracks of any other horse but his own within two miles of the place; no signs of a struggle, and his body appeared to be untouched by anybody after falling."

"And the gold?"

"No gold was found upon him. Some papers, two or three £1-notes, and some loose silver, were all the articles of value on his person. His horse was found with a mob of station horses, but without the valise, which Dick says was on the saddle when he left the Blatherskyte diggings. This is all I can learn from Dick. If you can come we will start back at once. An inquest will be held to-morrow or the day after; Williams has gone up to Blatherskyte."

All that was elucidated at the inquest was, that on Monday, the 24th of January, James Starr had left Blatherskyte diggings alone, leaving a stockman named Williams and the black boy, Dick, to come on slowly. He was not again seen alive by anybody then present. Williams stated: That he was a stockman in the employ of the deceased; assisted him to drive a mob of fat cattle to Blatherskyte; that he left the diggings on the same morning, though some hours later, than the deceased did; a storekeeper of Blatherskyte, named Thompson, and the black boy, Dick, accompanied him; went as far as the creek called the "Twenty-mile," and camped there that night; arrived at Yorick's Lagoon about twelve o'clock; saw the body of a man lying at the edge of the water; the upper portion of his body was on a log; went over to it and found it to be the body of his employer, James Starr; a bullet wound was visible on the top of his head; appeared to have been dead about twelve hours; the body was quite stiff; deceased had some gold in a valise in the front of his saddle when he left the diggings; did not know the amount; found his horse close to the station, with some other station horses; the saddle was on the horse, but no valise.

Thompson's testimony was to exactly the same effect.

Jawdon, a butcher of Blatherskyte, stated that he paid the deceased the sum of one hundred and sixty ounces of gold, and a cheque for £155, before he left the diggings; it was in payment for cattle sold and delivered to him by the deceased; saw the deceased put it into a valise and strap it on in front of his saddle; made some remark at the time about the horse getting away with it on; Starr left his place immediately afterwards; did not see him stop anywhere as long as he was in sight; believed that he went straight away. Williams, recalled, stated that after finding the body the black boy, who was an excellent tracker, went round with him to look for tracks; saw no fresh tracks of wither horse or man, excepting the track of deceased and his horse; knew the track of deceased's horse by his having been newly shod on the diggings, and having a very peculiar shaped hoof; could swear to it; had shod the same horse himself at various times; the track of Starr's horse went straight to the place where the body lay, and from then back to the road, and along it until the horse joined the mob he was found with; the lagoon was a small piece of water, about five miles from the station, close to the road; saw no horse tracks on the other side of the lagoon; it was about thirty to forty yards broad; cattle had been watering on the opposite side of the lagoon during the previous night; saw fresh tracks of a large number; saw the tracks of Starr's horse all the way along the road to Yorick's Lagoon; saw no other fresh tracks; met no one on the road.

The medical testimony showed the cause of death to have been a bullet wound in the top of the head; bullet produced was a small one seemingly, belonging to a very small bored rifle.

Jackson and Harris were examined, but of course their testimony threw no light on the affair. Suspicion first settled on Starr's discharged cook. He was found at a public-house, some fifty miles from the scene of the murder. Had gone there direct from the station, and had been there ever since, "on the spree." Several witnesses could swear to his presence there at all hours of the day and night.

Haughton was then enquired for, and found at Imberwalla. Proved to have stopped at a shepherd's hut, six miles beyond Glenmore station, the night after he left Stratford; he accounted for not calling at the station by mentioning the changed manner of Harris towards him; arrived at Imberwalla three days afterwards; had to camp on the road, on account of sickness; was still suffering from fever; did not possess either a rifle or revolver; had not had one for the last six months.

A verdict of willful murder against some person or persons unknown was returned; but years passed and nothing ever transpired.

Dick went into the service of Harris, and one day passing the scene of the tragedy he persuaded Harris to ride over, and then made an explanation which seemed to have been troubling him.

"You see, Mitter Starr bin get off to drink, lay down, like it there, doss up along a log. Some fellow been come up along a nother side, you see, where cattle track big fellow come up. That fellow bin shoot em Mitter Starr when he bin stoop down drink. Then go away along a cattle track. Cattle come up along at night, look out water, put em out track all together."

Dick's conclusion struck Harris as being correct, but it went no further towards pointing out the murderer.

Chapter III

More than twelve years after the events of the last chapter, Jackson and Harris met in Sydney. They had not seen each other for several years, both having left the district in which they formerly resided.

"Jackson, you must come and stay with me for a while. I want to introduce you to my wife. No! not the one I told you about. She is dead, died from drink I believe. I heard she was dying, and went to see her. If I had not seen it, I could not have believed that a woman could alter so. I am not a hypocrite, Jackson, nor are you, so I can say thank God she is dead without fear of your pretending to be shocked. No! I can show you a wife I am proud of."

Jackson stayed several days with Harris, whose wife certainly merited her husband's praise. One evening the conversation turned upon spirit rapping. Mrs. Harris remarked that some friends of hers, who were devout believers in it, had pressed her strongly to accompany them to a séance the next evening. She did not at first mean to go, but on Harris and Jackson saying that they would accompany her, they made up their minds to see the wonders of spirit-land the next evening.

Mrs. Harris' friends called at about three o'clock in the afternoon, and the party, after proceeding down several rather shabby streets, stopped at a more than rather shabby house.

Jackson whispered that he wondered the spirits did not select a more fashionable, or at least a cleaner, neighborhood to make their communications in. After payment, they were shown into a dimly-lighted room, where several other well dressed persons were present. Some were seated round a table, others standing. The medium and another person, who was not a medium at present, only a disciple, were holding a conversation on spirit-rapping for the good of the company.

The medium was a thin-faced, crafty-looking man, evidently in bad health. Not bad looking, but still not exactly prepossessing. After a time, he seated himself at the table, the disciple left the room, and silence was demanded. The medium having explained the meaning of the knocks, what one knock stood for, etc, put himself into communication with the spirits. Several people asked questions of deceased relatives, some trustingly and confiding, others sneeringly. Sometimes the answers were strangely correct, to judge from the countenances of the enquirers; others, and by far the greater number, were as evidently wrong. Presently a conversation arose, which soon ended in a discussion between believers and unbelievers.

The medium then took a pencil and paper, and stated; "that any of the company might write a question on a piece of paper, fold it, and lay it on the table; that his arm would be guided by the spirits to write the answer, without having seen the question. This was evidently the display of the evening, and the company evinced a good deal of interest in the proceeding.

As before, some few of the answers seemed to be correct, and the majority wrong. The spirits, to judge from the manner in which the medium jerked his arm about, were fighting for possession of the pen.

Harris and Jackson determined to ask a question out of fun. Harris took out a note-book, wrote a question on a leaf, tore it out, and then handed the book to Jackson. He took it, but did not write anything. Harris walked up to the table and placed his folded paper on it; at the same time looking half-laughingly, half enquiringly, into the face of the medium, immediately afterwards though turning his gaze on to his wife.

The medium's sharp black eyes looked for a moment disconcerted, as they met Harris' frank look, but they noted its after direction, and a curious puzzled expression came into them. The spirits at first did not seem inclined to answer the question, but presently the mystic arm moved, and with a doubtful look, which soon changed into a triumphant one, the seer handed the answer to Harris.

It was a small piece of paper, and there were only two words on it, but they were quite enough to make Harris look at the medium with a scared face that was quite ludicrous; he drew back without speaking.

Jackson, who had been intently watching his friend's success, wrote a question rapidly on a sheet of the note-book, tore it out, folded it, strode forward, and laid it on the table.

The medium looked at Jackson, his lips moved, but no sound came. His face grew very pale, and his gaze turned with a fixed look on the folded paper; it deepened into such an expression of intense and absolute horror as to startle the surrounding company. It was evident to the most sceptical that there was no acting now. His hand moved over the paper and formed a few hasty words, he folded it, trembling as he did so, handed it to Jackson, and fell with a deep groan on to the floor.

Jackson, nearly as startled and scared-looking as the prostrate medium, put the paper into his pocket, and stooped over the fallen man. The rest crowded round, the people of the house were called, and they conveyed the pallid conjurer, now slowly recovering from his swoon, out of the room. The séance was broken up, and the company began to disperse. Some expressed great curiosity to see the answer which had produced such a commotion. Jackson, however, did not satisfy them, they looked for his question, but that and the former one had disappeared.

"Taken by the spirits," one devout believer suggested. In reality quietly pocketed by Harris during the confusion occasioned by the medium's collapse.

Harris, his wife, and Jackson, left their friends a short distance from the spirit's residence and went home. Scarcely a word passed between them on the way. Jackson appeared to be lost in deep thought. The only remark he made was—

"Did you ever see that fellow before, Harris?"

"Never that I know of," was the answer.

Jackson was silent the rest of the way.

When Jackson and Harris were alone in the room, Mrs. Harris having gone upstairs to remove her bonnet, etc., Harris drew forth the two questions, his own and Jackson's. He handed his to Jackson. It was—

"If the spirit of my first wife is really present let her sign her name."

"Here is the answer," he said.

"Mary Delaney."

Jackson looked very scared and excited as he almost whispered, "Look at my question, then we will look at the answer."

Harris read—

"Who was the murderer of James Starr?"

Jackson opened the paper, the writing on which no one but the unhappy seer had as yet seen.

On it was written in a good, bold hand, differing entirely from the writing on Harris' paper—

"Rudolph George Rawlings, known to you under the name of Haughton"

"It was him! I knew it!" exclaimed Jackson, in a voice which brought Mrs. Harris into the room in a fright.

"Who? Who?" cried Harris, nearly as excited as his friend.

"Haughton himself; I thought I knew him. No wonder he should faint; he wrote and handed to me his own death warrant."

Harris still held the paper in his hand.

"Look Jackson," he said, "it is Starr's handwriting,"

He went to a bookcase and took down a book, on the fly-leaf

was written, "T. C. Harris, from James Starr." The handwriting was identical!

"Let us go at once and get a warrant, and have him arrested," said Jackson, whose excitement could scarcely be controlled.

"We have no evidence to do so," replied Harris; "we are no nearer towards doing justice on Starr's murderer than we were before. This may carry conviction to you and me, but what magistrate would issue a warrant on such a lame story. We can inform the police that suspicious circumstances connect this medium—who you may be sure is well known to them—with the Haughton who was mixed up with Starr's murder. They may find out some further evidence, but we are powerless. "

A knock at the door. Mrs. Harris, who was listening with a white face, went and opened it. The servant said that a woman wanted most particularly to see Mr. Jackson. Harris looked at him, then told the servant to show her up. She came in, a faded-looking woman, who handed a slip of paper to Jackson.

He read on it— "Come and see me before I die. R. Rawlings." He passed it over to Harris; his wife read it over his shoulder.

"I will come with you," said Jackson to the woman.

"And so will I," said Harris.

She led them back to the house of the séance, to a room with a miserable bed in it, wherein lay the man they had seen acting the part of medium. He gazed wistfully at Jackson and spoke very feebly, and in abrupt sentences.

"I am dying, but I will tell you how it was done."

The woman left the room, and closed the door.

"That night, which you remember as well as I, I went out on the verandah to sleep. I did not go to sleep until long after you all went to bed. I heard every word you said. I heard Harris tell the story of his marriage, which enabled me to make the lucky answer I did today. I knew you both directly you came in. I heard Starr expose me about the cards in a contemptuous sort of way that made me hate him. This led me on to recall your talk about the gold. I determined to rob him, but I was a coward, and assassinated him. I had not the courage even of a common bushranger to stick him up. I knew the exact day he would be back, as you know. I feigned sickness the next morning, and only went as far as the shepherd's hut. The next day I went on a short distance past Harris' place and camped. That night after dark I started back to Yorick's Lagoon.

"I meant to conceal myself behind the bushes growing on the bank, and shoot him as he rode along the road, which, as you know, is close to the lagoon. I reached the neighborhood of the lagoon about daylight. My keeping off the road as much as possible led to my coming in along the cattle track, on the side of the lagoon opposite to the road. I had a short rifle in my pack, the barrel taken off the stock, which was the reason you did not notice it. I tied my horse up some distance off, and went down the dusty cattle track to the water's edge on foot. There I waited the whole of the morning—how long it seemed! It was about three o'clock when I saw Starr coming. I was about aiming at him, when he pulled up, got off and stooped down to drink. He was right opposite to me, his horse drinking alongside of him, his head down on the surface of the water. I was a dead shot, and struck him right on the top of the head. He scarcely seemed to move; his horse gave a slight start and snort, stretched his neck, and snuffed once or twice at the body of its rider; presently, finding itself free, began feeding, and after a few minutes' nibbling at the grass, walked towards home.

"I was in doubt what to do, but determined to follow the horse and obtain the valise. Should the gold not be in it, I would have to return and search the body. During the latter part of my watch, several mobs of cattle had come along the track I was lying on, smelling me when they got close; they had run back again. This gave me the idea of following the track back for a couple of miles, trusting to the cattle to obliterate all marks of my presence. Starr's horse seemed to be making straight home. I determined to chance finding him somewhere along the road. I followed the track out, took a circle round, and came on to the road just as Starr's horse and some more he had picked up with came along. He was quiet and easily caught. The gold was in the valise. The presence of the other horses prevented my track being noticed, and by midnight I was back at my camp. At daylight I looked along the road, and saw by the tracks that no one had passed during my absence.

"I was safe. You know all about the inquest. I am ill of a terrible disease which plagues me with fearful torments. I must die in a day or two, perhaps to-night. Remorse now is useless, but I tell you that I have known little peace since I shot Starr. Leave me now, and don't attempt to preach to me."

Neither of the two friends felt either fitted or able to attempt it, and seeing that their presence there availed nothing, they left. But when they reached the foot of the stairs, Harris called the woman, and, giving her money, told her to call and inform him of the fate of Rawlings.

She came next morning and told them that he died a few hours after they left, never having spoken again.

THE DEAD HAND

(1881)

In the town of Souviers in France there resided an English doctor named Cranstone. Late one night an old woman—a countrywoman of his—came to see him with a short note requesting his immediate attendance.

"How is Monsieur Varillon?" he asked after glancing at the few words the note consisted of.

"Dead, "replied the dame; "died this morning."

"And Madame?"

"Miss Lucy is with me, and she wants you to go with her to-night to see her husband."

"To see her husband! You say that he is dead?"

"He's as bad dead, as he was living; but she'll tell you all about it."

Without more questions the doctor accompanied the old woman; and they presently reached a little cottage, the interior of which presented a strange jumble of French and English furniture.

Sitting by the fire burning in an open fire-place was a fair-faced girl, unmistakably English, who the doctor addressed as Madame Varillon.

It was some time before she mooted her real object for sending for him; then she watched his face narrowly with her big hazel eyes, as if dreading ridicule.

"He made me promise," she said, speaking of her dead husband, "that for the two nights before he would be buried I should come and pray beside his coffin, and watch there from 2 o'clock until daylight."

"What a childish whim," replied the doctor. "You are certainly not strong enough to redeem your promise, so you can make up your mind for a good night's rest to-night."

"But I must go."

"Nonsense, it might be the death of you. Why did you send for me if you won't take my advice?"

"It was not for your advice I asked you to come," she said apologetically, "but to ask a greater favour. I *must* go, but I confess I feel timid. Will you go with me?"

"Of course."

"There's nobody in the house but old Jeanne, and she sleeps below; the *sœur de charité* leaves at nightfall."

"I will go to Miss Lucy," said the old woman.

"No, nurse, I won't let you; you know I shall be safe with Dr Cranstone."

"Such a foolish whim," grumbled the old dame.

"What could he mean by such a whim?" asked the doctor angrily.

"I can scarcely tell you what he said," and her voice dropped, and she glanced fearfully around, "that somebody—somebody not living, you know, would come to his body if I were not there."

"Gracious me! What nonsense," cried the old nurse; "who'd like to go near his ugly body if they could help it, I'd like to know."

"Go to bed at once, and dismiss these childish notions," said the doctor.

"I must go, I feel I must."

"A wilfu' woman maun gang her ain gait," muttered the doctor; "but if we must go I see no reason for leaving this snug room until necessary. I for one object to doing more penance than I can help."

The doctor tried again to dissuade his young friend from her purpose, but in vain; and after one o'clock they were traversing the deserted streets. After some walking they reached a gloomy square, in a quarter that Cranstone was very little acquainted with. On one side of the square rose the dark towers of a church, the remaining three sides consisting of large houses. High up in one of these a dim light shone through a window, and before it they stopped. After pulling at the bell for some time, somebody in the porter's lodge seemingly awoke, for a small door cut in the large one opened, and the doctor and his companion entered. The hall was intensely dark, and the air close and unwholesome as if the place were always shut up. Madam Varillon took the doctor's hand, and led him on a few paces, then giving him a whispered and very necessary caution to mind the stairs, they commenced to ascend. Like the hall, the staircase was unlighted, save by such meagre starlight as struggled in through the uncleaned windows; and as the doctor followed his silent guide, he could scarcely help feeling a slight thrill of superstitious feeling creep over him. They stopped on the third story, and entered the room where burned the light they had seen from the street. In one corner of the room stood a heavy old-fashioned bedstead; on it was an open coffin, and in the coffin the body of a man. A flickering candle burnt on either side of the corpse, and on the breast lay a wreath of immortelles.

The girl looked on the dead with a half-terrified gaze, and then, throwing back her cloak, knelt down beside the bed, and, burying her face in her hands, seemed to pray. Hardly knowing what to do, Cranstone stood beside her, and gazed curiously around at the place in which he now found himself for the first time. It was a large room, and the furniture in it was cold and dilapidated. The uncertain light of the two candles only illumi-nated that portion of the room in the immediate neighbourhood of the bed, and the far corners were shrouded in grim obscurity.

Having finished his unsatisfactory survey, he then exam-ined the corpse. Its face was that of a man above middle age, evidently of a stern, forbidding aspect during life, and now looking doubly so as he lay still in death. The hair and beard were dark, streaked with grey, and contrasted in a ghastly manner with the white face.

The spell was broken by the girl rising from her knees. She gathered her cloak about her, as though cold, and stooping over the corpse, put her left hand on one of the lifeless ones, and resting her right one on the edge of the coffin, bent down as if about to impress a farewell kiss upon the cold lips.

In the very act she started back with a quick cry of pain and terror; a cry that seemed to the astonished doctor to be mockingly re-echoed throughout the building. "My hand! My hand!" she gasped, in horror-stricken accents.

Startled and astonished, Cranstone saw that the dead hand had closed upon the living one the girl had laid upon it. No other change or motion was visible in the body; the set face showed no signs of returning life; but the bony hand had grasped the delicate one that had rested on it, and was crushing it in a fell grasp that made the sufferer wince with pain and terror.

Recovering to a certain extent his presence of mind, Cranstone caught hold of the wrist of the corpse with one hand, and with then other tried to disengage Madame Varillon's hand. But he failed in releasing the hold of the fingers in the slightest. Again he essayed, putting forth all his strength, and using both hands in his endeavours to wrench the hand open, but still in vain. Excited and incensed by the sight of the girl's suffering, Cranstone strained every muscle, throwing his whole will and energy into the endeavour to free the imprisoned hand. This time he seemed to have made some impression on the iron clasp; but it required the exertion of all his strength to retain the slight advantage he had gained. Suddenly the thought of Mesmerism as applied to cases of trance occurred to him; and, concentrating every wish and thought of his mind on the completion of his object, he continued the struggle mentally as well as physically. He felt that a mind of equal power and determination was opposed to his, and the combative faculty on either side was so equally balanced that one supreme effort must give the victory.

The horrible notion that a dread being of another world was in the once-living form and fighting him for possession of the tortured hand, made him almost shudder at the contact of the cold dead flesh; and he at once felt the fingers closing with renewed tenacity. Enraged by his own weakness, he strove to banish from his mind every feeling of terror at supernatural influence, and threw his utmost vigour into his tired and strained muscles. He felt, to his joy, that now he was succeeding, and that the rigid hold was failing beneath his desperate clasp. Animated at this, he essayed his utmost to accomplish his object, when the clock in the neighbourhood church struck three. At the first stroke, and with a suddenness that—coming so unexpectedly—almost caused him to lose his balance, the dead hand opened, and the girl, with a low shuddering moan, dropped fainting on the floor.

Cranstone raised her at once, and looked vainly round the room for some water. Noticing a door other than the one he had entered at, he went and opened it, and looked in. It was evidently a dressing room, and in it he saw the water he sought. A low couch was also there, and thinking that his patient when she recovered would be better out of the presence of the dead body, he carried her in and laid her upon it. After bathing her temples with the cold water, he got one of the candles, and examined her hand.

So ever had been the grasp to which it had been subjected, that the blood was oozing from beneath the finger-nails, two of the bones of the palm of the hand were broken, and the rings she wore were bent, and pressed into the flesh. After dressing the injured member as well as he could, he went to inspect the dead man.

Here he was entirely at a loss; no trace of life could he discover. Every test that his professional knowledge suggested he put into practice—but without result. The man was dead, and had evidently been so for some time.

Just as he finished his inspection of the dead body, the noise of the door through which he had first entered being opened attracted his attention. Holding the remaining candle high above his head, he turned round. The door opened slowly, and a woman came in and advanced to the side of the bed. She was robed in a loose dressing gown, her long hair hanging disordered down her back. Two dark wistful eyes looked out of a pale handsome face—eyes solemn, sad, and holding in their depths some haunting secret horror that gave them the fixed and glassy stare almost of insanity.

She took no notice of Cranstone, who had put down the light and stood silent and fascinated—a creeping sensation of awful overwhelming fear almost overmastering him as this ghostly figure came to the side of the bed. She stood regarding the dead body for some time, her eyes never losing their set stare, her hands clasped loosely in front of her. And Cranstone noticed with a fresh accession of horror, that a hideous gash was across one of her wrists, nearly severing it to the bone. The blood was slowly dripping on the floor, with a perfectly audible splash. The doctor tried to move or speak, but was powerless.

The silent figure then turned and went into the room where lay the still insensible girl. She paused, as before, beside the couch—still visible to Cranstone through the open door. Presently she lifted her wounded arm, and holding it over the prostrate form on the couch, let the blood trickle on to Madame Varillon's face.

Breaking the charm that held him by a mighty effort, the doctor sprang forward, uttering an expression of disgust. He saw the woman look menacingly at him as he advanced, he saw the girl's face with the disfiguring blood-stain upon it; and then to his astonishment the standing figure disappeared, and when he reached the side of the couch, the insensible face on the pillow was as fair and pure as it had been before.

Doubting the evidence of his own faculties, and utterly mystified, the doctor stood bewildered for a few minutes. Then he recalled his coolness, took one of the candles, and minutely examined both rooms, but failed in discovering any mode of egress save the door he had entered at.

He stepped out on to the dark landing, leaving the light behind, and closing the door, listened patiently and motionless for some time, but could not detect the slightest sound in any part of the house. Dense darkness and absolute silence seemed to reign everywhere.

He returned to the room, and tried to reason himself into the belief that it was all an illusion. It was the creation of his own imagination, the premonitory symptom of illness, perhaps; such things had been in his experience. But when he looked at the bruised hand of his patient (who was beginning to recover), he had to confess that something had happened that was beyond him. It was some time before Madame Varillon was sufficiently restored to return to the old nurse's cottage; and as the slightest allusion to the scene through which they had passed seemed to excite her, the doctor forbore to press for any explanation—even if she could have given any.

He deemed it his duty, however, to look up the doctor who had attended Monsieur Varillon during his illness, and see if any symptoms of trance had shown themselves.

Doctor Buvert proved very communicative, and did not seem to trouble himself about his confrere's motives for making the inquiries. Without much diplomacy he was led to talk of Carillon's past life.

"He was married before," he said, "to a woman whose heart and soul were given to another." She was forced by her parents to marry Varillon, a cold, stern, abstracted man; you can fancy how happy she was. Well, the result was inevitable: the lovers met again, and he heard of it. He gave no sign, but bided his time.

Her lover—his name was d'Heristal—ventured into the house to bid her a last farewell. They reckoned on his absence. They were deceived. When about to separate, his step was heard coming slowly and deliberately towards the room.

There was no escape; from the ground to the window was over forty feet at least; there was but one door—that by which the husband would directly enter. Anxious to screen her from disgrace, and not to save himself—for all stories unite in giving him the character of a bold young fellow—d'Heristal got out of the window, and standing upon the precarious footing afforded by the ornamental portion of the façade beneath the old-fashioned window, stooped down low, sustaining himself with one hand on the window-sill.

Varillon came into the room, and his quick eye must at once have seen the hand on the window-sill; for, in her alarm, Madame Varillon never thought of diminishing the light in the room.

He said nothing of what he suspected, but, after a few ordinary remarks to the trembling woman, he caught her by the hand, and tried to lead her to the window.

She read at once that all was known, and concluding that his intention was to hurl her lover into the street before her eyes, struggled, and prayed for mercy. Silently ignoring her entreaties, he dragged her towards the window. A slight scuffling noise was heard. D'Heristal, doubtless in an attempt to get back into the room, hearing what was going on, had dislodged with his weight the old bricks, and the unfortunate man was suspended by one hand over the pavement—fifty feet below.

Varillon must have guessed what had happened, for with renewed persistence he strove to drag his wife to the window to witness the fall that must take place; and she, in despair, caught up a knife from the supper-table, and in insane desperation, drew it across her wrist, as if to try and cut herself free from his relentless grasp.

"And what was the end?" asked Cranstone, as the other paused.

"D'Heristal, when his strength gave way, fell into the street, and was killed instantly. She bled to death, and he had almost crushed her hand in his attempt to drag her to the window. Some of the metacarpal bones were broken, and the rings of her fingers bent, and squeezed into the flesh.

"And at what time did this happen?"

"The servant, who was watching and listening at the door, and through whom the facts transpired, says that, at the instant she drew the knife across her wrist, the clock of Saint Marguerite struck three."

"How long ago did this happen?"

"About five years ago. There was some talk about it, as you may imagine; and Varillon went to live in England. When he returned, about twelve months ago, he brought your pretty countrywoman back with him—having wisely gone to some outlandish place where he was unknown for another wife. How she was induced to marry him I cannot think. Doubtless her parents were poor, and she had just left a boarding-school, and did not know her own mind. However, she is a rich widow now—a better fate than she would have had as his wife. I wonder he allowed her to bring her old nurse with her."

Buvert, having once started, seemed inclined to gossip on forever; but Cranstone, having heard all he wanted to know, managed to escape as soon as he could consistent with politeness.

It was more than a month before Madame Varillon was strong enough to leave for England. Cranstone escorted her to Paris, and turned from watching the departing train with the settled conviction in his mind that he was head over heels in love; that he was a poor man, and she was rich, and that the best thing he could do was to forget all about her as speedily as possible. Easier said than done—three or four years hard work in his profession did not do it. Then came the war with Prussia, the siege of Paris; the outbreak of the Commune, and the second siege by the Versailles troops.

Cranstone saw it all through; and in the hospitals amongst the wounded, or doing his voluntary work under the Prussian guns, he could not banish the remembrance of those soft brown eyes. An unwilling member of the Commune, he still tended their wounded, inwardly hoping for the incoming of the Versailles troops. The day of vengeance came at last, when the streets of Paris became the battle field.

Like a good many more, trusting to the cross of Geneva for protection from both sides, Cranstone sallied out to see how things were going. He had gained a comparatively quiet street, when the scarlet facings of a band of Communists appeared at the head of it coming towards him. Knowing that he would probably be shot out of mere wantonness, he tried to gain entrance into the nearest house until they passed. The assurance that he was a doctor procured him admittance from the porter. An old woman came to the door of the porter's room and looked in; he stood talking to the man about the fighting going on. She gave vent to an exclamation of joy on beholding Cranstone, and caught him by the hand.

It was Madame Varillon's old nurse. Not waiting to answer the doctor's rapid questions, but dragging him frantically by the hand, she led him upstairs. All the doctor could understand amid her incoherence was a reproach directed against himself for never having communicated with her mistress. And then said the garrulous old dame, assimilating herself with her mistress:

"We couldn't live out of Paris where you might be, for we knew you left Souviers; and so we got shut up in this wicked place where they are always killing one another, and have been nearly starved."

By this time they had reached a door of a room on the first floor, and the doctor with a beating heart followed the impetuous old woman, who burst in, crying, "I have got him, I have found him!" And there was the love he had tried to forget. They did not enter into explanations, they were unnecessary, but perhaps the crash of firearms in the street beneath the window frightened her so, that she had to take shelter in the doctor's arms. But that was a noise that she should have been accustomed to. Be that as it may she was there, and in the street a body of Versailles troops had met the Communists and were having it out with them. As she lifted her face to meet her lover's caress she fell on to his breast with a wild gasp of pain. A random ball had found its way through the ill-barricaded window and taken her life. The agonised doctor laid her on the couch. Yes, even as he had seen her in the haunted room with the ghastly blood stain on her white forehead, she lay with the death wound in the same place. The omen was accomplished; he had found his love and lost her. And above the shots and shouts of the combatants, rang out the hour of three. For a few moments he stood motionless and speechless. Then, after one long kiss on the lifeless lips, he turned and sought the street.

The Communists had retreated behind a barricade, hastily thrown up at the end of the street, and their opponents were about to charge it. The doctor stooped over a dead body and took the chassepôt that was in its hand; then, as if struck with another idea, threw it down again, and preferred the sword bayonet.

The Versailles soldiers carried the barricade after a desperate hand to hand struggle, during which they lost half their number. Of the Communists not a man escaped—they fell where they stood.

"My faith!" said the corporal, now in command of the party by the loss of both officers, "But if all the citizens had fought like that one lying there, the Comité Central would never have existed."

His men, looking for their own wounded, and dispatching any insurgent who showed signs of life, had just thrown on one side the dead body of the English doctor.

JERRY BOAKE'S CONFESSION

(1890)

Perhaps one of the most popular fellows on the then newly-opened H— Goldfield, in Far North Queensland, was Jack Walters. Everybody knew him, and everybody liked him, and there was great chaff and much popping of corks 'ere he started down to C— with the avowed intention of getting married. Walters had shares in one or two good mines, and had a tidy sum of money with him when he left the field amidst the congratulations of 'the boys' on his approaching nuptials. Jack was a friend of mine; when he was temporarily crippled by a blasting accident I used to write his love-letters for him.

Three days after he left, Inspector Frost and his black troopers, who all knew Walters, rode into the township. Naturally, the first question asked was, had they met Jack, and how far he'd got on the road?

"Never saw or heard of him," was the unexpected reply, "perhaps he was off the road."

"No, he said he was going down easy and expected to meet you."

"Hum!" said the inspector, "I'm going back to-morrow, and I'll keep a sharp look-out for him."

Fifty miles from H— was a creek with permanent water and a good feed, a favourite camping-place. Frost, who had told the troopers to watch for signs of Jack, had almost forgotten the matter, to which, after all, he did not attach much importance, when a shrill whistle from one of his boys a short distance off the road to the right attracted his attention. The boy had dismounted, and was standing gazing at something on the ground. Frost rode up, and had almost anticipated what it was before he reached the spot. Screened by a few bushes from any chance traveller lay the body of a dead man—Jack Walters. His head was pillowed on his riding-saddle, his blanket was thrown over the lower part of his body, and his pack-saddle and bags were close by, where they had evidently been put overnight. He had been shot through the temple, and in his hand he still held a revolver. To all appearances it was one of those motiveless cases of suicide that now and again puzzle everybody.

A careful examination was made, but nothing seemed to have been disturbed; no money save some loose silver was found. Frost collected all the camp paraphernalia, took careful notes of the position of the body and all the surroundings; then, leaving one trooper to guard the remains, despatched a boy back to H—with the news, and instruction to the police there to come out and take the body—he himself had to proceed on his journey. Casting one more glance around, he noticed a newspaper lying some distance away. Such things were commonly found on old camping grounds, but he walked over and picked it up. It was the *H—- Express*, the journal of the mining township he had left. He looked at it idly for some time, thinking more of the sight he had just witnessed than of the paper in his hand, when he instinctively noticed the date, which suggested a train of thought. Walters had left the field three days before Frost's arrival there. The Inspector remembered that fact well, because there had been some debate as to the spot where they should have passed each other. Three days would make it Monday, and this paper was issued on Tuesday. How had it come into the dead man's camp?

Frost went back and looked at the corpse before the troopers had covered it up with boughs. The revolver taken from the stiffened fingers, he remembered, was but loosely held—it was not in the iron grasp of a dead man's hand, clutched hard at the moment of death. No doubt remained that the case was not one of suicide, but cowardly, cold-blooded murder. Somebody had left the diggings the next morning, had ridden hard and overtaken Walters at the creek, had shared the hospitality of his camp, and had shot him for the sake of the money he had with him. Where was the murderer now?

Frost, who had gold to take down to the port, did not tarry long between the scene of the murder and C—. The second day saw him closeted with the police magistrate, who had just received a telegram from H—, informing him of the arrival of the native police with the news of Frost's discovery. Hardly had Frost told his tale before another telegram arrived—"Jerry Boake left here after Walters. See if he is in C—."

Jerry was a pretty notorious character, and, strange to say, Walters was one of the few men who had befriended him when everybody else had thrown him over.

A very short inquiry elicited the fact that Jerry was in town; also that Jerry was in funds, and had given the barmaid at the 'Rise and Shine' a gold watch and chain. Interviewed, the barmaid produced the gold watch and chain, which were at once recognised as the property of Walters, who had bought them as a present for his fiancée. Jerry was straight-way arrested; and, absurd as the statement may seem, was actually wearing a ring well-known to belong to Walters. He denied his guilt stoutly, stated that Walters had given him the ring and the watch and chain to bring down, and that when he was drunk he gave it to the barmaid. Jerry was remanded to H—, and Frost himself started up in charge of him.

The dusk was setting in when they reached the bank of the creek where the dead body had been found. The party from H—had been there and removed it. Frost pulled up, and looked round. The prisoner, manacled to a trooper, was close to him.

"You're not going to camp here, are you?" stammered Jerry Boake, with pallid lips.

"Why not?" said Frost, sternly, "*you* know nothing about this place, do you?" And without another word he rode straight to the scene of the murder, and got off his horse.

"Turn out," he said briefly.

The troopers dismounted, and began unpacking and unsaddling. Frost undid the handcuff from the trooper's wrist, and refastened it on the prisoner's.

There is only one way in the bush of securing a criminal charged with such a crime as Jerry's, and who would stick at nothing to escape. A light trace-chain is used, and the prisoner tethered securely to a tree. Without a word, Frost, chain in hand, walked to the tree beneath which the body had been found, and beckoned to the troopers to bring the prisoner. Jerry approached; he had summoned up all his hardihood, and called up a look of defiance on his face, but he couldn't control the trembling of his now pallid lips. Frost secured him, and the black trooper brought him his blankets, and sat down a short distance off to watch him.

Darkness closed in, the camp fires blazed up, food and tea were given to the prisoner, and with an air of bravado he pretended to eat; but though the food passed his lips not a bite could he swallow. The tea he drank greedily, and asked for more. The day's journey had been a long one, and the tired men soon dropped off to sleep one after another—but for one man there was no sleep that night. For all that the camp was so quiet, he had an idea that he was being watched, and it gave him a miserable kind of moral support to think that there was someone else awake as well as himself. It would be an awful thing to be the only waking man in that camp.

He had got to the full length of the trace-chain, and must have lost consciousness for a few moments, for, while his heart beat until it nearly choked him, he saw a black shadow under the tree—a dark shadow that was not there before. With an effort he stilled his trembling nerves, and forced himself to gaze at the object. Pah! The moon had risen higher and changed the position of the shadows, that was all. But supposing a man with a bloody smear on his forehead and half-closed dull eyes were really to come and lie down on that spot, while he himself was chained there not able to get away, what an awful thing it would be!

Would morning never come? He thought. Why must he think, think, think, and all about the one thing; his own incredible folly? A few pounds in gold, a few days of drunken 'shouting,' and now—it must be a nightmare, surely—he could not have been led away to do such a madly insane deed. He disliked the man mostly because he owed him many kindnesses, but that was not why he killed him for. No, it was for the few miserable pounds he was carrying.

That horrible black shadow seemed to stop there, although the moon's position had changed. Why did it stop there? Perhaps there was a stain of blood on the ground; he would force himself to go over and see. No, he couldn't do that, he would stop where he was and try to think of other things; but he couldn't. Always the same thought, the same hideous picture—a man asleep with his head on a saddle, and another standing over him with a levelled pistol. And then—well, then, a sight that would never leave him; the moon was young and sickly then, but its light was strong enough to show the dead body of the murdered man, with the bloody smear on his face. Would morning never come? Presently the moon would set, and then the darkness would be horrible. Who knows what hideous thing might not creep on him unawares. The air seemed thick with an awful corpse-like smell; had they buried the body there, where it was found? But this thought was too maddening—he would go frantic if he entertained it. Why did not the bleak shadow shift; the moon was getting low now?

* * * * * * *

Just before daylight Frost was awakened by one of the boys at the door of his tent. "Marmee, that fellow Jerry sing out along of you!" Frost got up and went over to the place. The moon had set, and the night was dark; he told the boys to make the fire.

"My God! Mr Frost," said a piteous voice, "take me away from here, and I'll tell you everything." Frost undid the chain, and led him to the fire. He afterwards said that the look on the wretch's face haunted him for months. Jerry Boake made a full confession—and was hanged a few weeks afterwards.

A HAUNT OF THE JINKARRAS

(1890)

In May, 1889, the dead body of a man was found on one of the tributaries of the Finke River, in the extreme North of South Australia. The body, by all appearances, had been lying there some months and was accidentally discovered by explorers making a flying survey with camels. Amongst the few effects was a Lett's Diary containing the following narration, which although in many places almost illegible and much weather-stained, has been since, with some trouble, deciphered and transcribed by the surveyor in charge of the party, and forwarded to *THE BULLETIN* for publication.

TRANSCRIBED FROM THE DEAD MAN'S DIARY

March 10, 1888.—Started out this morning with Jackson, the only survivor of a party of three who lost their horses on a dry stage when looking for country—he was found and cared for by the blacks, and finally made his way into the line where I picked him up when out with a repairing-party. Since then I got him a job on the station, and in return he has told me about the ruby-field of which we are now in search; and thanks to the late thunder-storms we have as yet met with no obstacles to our progress. I have great faith in him, but he being a man without any education and naturally taciturn, is not very lively company, and I find myself thrown on to the resource of a diary for amusement.

March 17—Seven days since we left Charlotte Waters, and we are now approaching the country familiar to Jackson during his sojourn with the natives two years ago. He is confident that we shall gain the gorge in the Macdonnell Ranges to-morrow, early.

March 18.—Amongst the ranges, plenty of water, and Jackson has recognised several peaks in the near neighbourhood of the gorge, where he saw the rubies.

March 19.—Camped in Ruby Gorge, as I have named this pass, for we have come straight to the place and found the rubies without any hindrance at all. I have about twenty magnificent stones and hundreds of small ones; one of the stones in particular is almost living fire, and must be of great value. Jackson has no idea of the value of the find, except that it may be worth a few pounds, with which he will be quite satisfied. As there is good feed and water, and we have plenty of rations, will camp here for a day or two and spell the horses before returning.

March 20—Been examining some caves in the ranges. One of them seems to penetrate a great distance—will go to-morrow with Jackson and take candles and examine it.

March 25—Had a terrible experience the last four days. Why on earth did I not go back at once with the rubies? Now I may never get back. Jackson and I started to explore this cave early in the morning. We found nothing extraordinary about it for some time. As usual, there were numbers of bats, and here and there were marks of fire on the rocks, as though the natives had camped there at times. After some searching about, Jackson discovered a passage which we followed down a steep incline for a long distance. As we got on we encountered a strong draught of air and had to be very careful of our candles. Suddenly the passage opened out and we found ourselves in a low chamber in which we could not stand upright. I looked hastily around, and saw a dark figure like a large monkey suddenly spring from a rock and disappear with what sounded like a splash. "What on earth was that?" I said to Jackson. "A jinkarra," he replied, in his slow, stolid way. "I heard about them from the blacks; they live under-ground." "What are they?" I asked. "I couldn't make out," he replied; "the blacks talked about jinkarras, and made signs that they were underground, so I suppose that was one."

We went over to the place where I had seen the figure and, as the air was now comparatively still and fresh, our candles burnt well and we could see plainly. The splash was no illusion, for an underground stream of some size ran through the chamber, and on looking closer, in the sand on the floor of the cavern, were tracks like a human foot.

We sat down and had something to eat. The water was beautifully fresh and icily cold, and I tried to obtain from Jackson all he knew about the jinkarras. It was very little beyond what he had already told me. The natives spoke of them as something, animals or men, he could not make out which, living in the ranges underground. They used to frighten the children by crying out "jinkarra!" to them at night.

The stream that flowed through the cavern was very sluggish and apparently not deep, as I could see the white sand at a distance under the rays of the candle; it disappeared under a rocky arch about two feet above its surface. Strange to say when near this arch I could smell a peculiar pungent smell like something burning, and this odour appeared to come through the arch. I drew Jackson's attention to it and proposed wading down the channel of the stream if not too deep, but he suggested going back to camp first and getting more rations, which, being very reasonable, I agreed to.

It took us too long to get back to camp to think of starting that day, but next morning we got away early and were soon beside the subterranean stream. The water was bitterly cold but not very deep, and we had provided ourselves with stout saplings as poles and had our revolvers and some rations strapped on our shoulders. It was an awful wade through the chill water, our heads nearly touching the slimy top of the arch, our candles throwing a faint, flickering gleam on the surface of the stream; fortunately the bottom was splendid—hard, smooth sand—and after wading for about twenty minutes we suddenly emerged into another cavern, but its extent we could not discern at first for our attention was taken up with other matters.

The air was laden with pungent smoke, the place illuminated with a score of smouldering fires, and tenanted by a crowd of the most hideous beings I ever saw. They espied us in an instant, and flew wildly about, jabbering frantically, until we were nearly deafened. Recovering ourselves we waded out of the water, and tried to approach some of these creatures, but they hid away in the darker corners, and we couldn't lay hands on any of them. As well as we could make out in the murky light they were human beings, but savages of the most degraded type, far below the ordinary Australian blackfellow. They had long arms, shaggy heads of hair, small twinkling eyes, and were very low of stature. They kept up a confused jabber, half whistling, half chattering, and were utterly without clothes, paint, or any ornaments. I approached one of their fires, and found it to consist of a kind of peat or turf; some small bones of vermin were lying around, and a rude club or two. While gazing at these things I suddenly heard a piercing shriek, and, looking up, found that Jackson, by a sudden spring, had succeeded in capturing one of these creatures, who was struggling and uttering terrible yells. I went to his assistance, and together we succeeded in holding him still while we examined him by the light of our candles. The others, meanwhile dropped their clamour and watched us curiously.

Never did I see such a repulsive wretch as our prisoner. Apparently he was a young man about two or three and twenty, only five feet high at the outside, lean, with thin legs and long arms. He was trembling all over, and the perspiration dripped from him. He had scarcely any forehead, and a shaggy mass of hair crowned his head, and grew a long way down his spine. His eyes were small, red and bloodshot; I have often experienced the strong odour emitted by the ordinary blackfellow when heated or excited, but never did I smell anything so offensive as the rank smell emanating from this creature. Suddenly Jackson exclaimed: "Look! look! he's got a tail!" I looked and nearly relaxed my grasp of the brute in surprise. There was no doubt about it, this strange being had about three inches of a monkey-like tail.

"Let's catch another," I said to Jackson after the first emotion of surprise had passed. We looked around after putting our candles upright in the sand. "There's one in that corner," muttered Jackson to me, and as soon as I spotted the one he meant we released our prisoner and made a simultaneous rush at the cowering form. We were successful, and when we dragged our captive to the light we found it to be a woman. Our curiosity was soon satisfied—the tail was the badge of the whole tribe, and we let our second captive go.

My first impulse was to go and rinse my hands in the stream, for the contact had been repulsive to me. Jackson did the same, saying as he did so—"Those fellows I lived with were bad enough, but I never smelt anything like these brutes." I pondered what I should do. I had a great desire to take one of these singular beings back with me, and I thought with pride of the reputation I should gain as their discoverer. Then I reflected that I could always find them again, and it would be better to come back with a larger party after safely disposing of the rubies and securing the ground.

"There's no way out of this place," I said to Jackson.

"Think not?" he replied.

"No," I said, "or these things would have cleared out; they must know every nook and cranny."

"Umph!" he said, as though satisfied; "shall we go back now?"

I was on the point of saying yes, and had I done so all would have been well; but, unfortunately, some motive of infernal curiosity prompted me to say—"No! let us have a look round first." Lighting another candle each, so that we had plenty of light, we wandered round the cave, which was of considerable extent, the unclean inhabitants flitting before us with beast-like cries. Presently we had made a half-circuit of the cave and were approaching the stream, for we could hear a rushing sound as though it plunged over a fall. This noise grew louder, and now I noticed that all the natives had disappeared, and it struck me that they had retreated through the passage we had penetrated, which was now unguarded. Suddenly Jackson, who was ahead, exclaimed that there was a large opening. As he spoke he turned to enter it; I called out to him to be careful but my voice was lost in a cry of alarm as he slipped, stumbled, and with a shriek of horror disappeared from my view. So sudden was the shock, and so awful my surroundings, that I sank down utterly unnerved comprehending but one thing: that I was alone in this gruesome cavern inhabited by strange, unnatural creations.

After a while I pulled myself together and began to look around. Holding my candle aloft I crawled on my stomach to where my companion had disappeared. My hand touched a slippery decline; peering cautiously down I saw that the rocks sloped abruptly downwards and were covered with slime as though under water at times. One step on the treacherous surface and a man's doom was sealed—headlong into the unknown abyss below he was bound to go, and this had been the fate of the unhappy Jackson. As I lay trembling on the edge of this fatal chasm listening for the faintest sound from below, it struck me that the noise of the rushing water was both louder and nearer. I lay and listened. There was no doubt about it—the waters were rising. With a thrill of deadly horror it flashed across me that if the stream rose it would prevent my return as I could not thread the subterranean passage under water. Rising hastily I hurried back to the upper end of the cavern following the edge of the water. A glance assured me I was a prisoner, the water was up to the top of the arch, and the stream much broader than when we entered. The rations and candles we had left carelessly on the sand had disappeared, covered by the rising water. I was alone, with nothing but about a candle and a-half between me and darkness and death.

I blew out the candle, threw myself on the sand and thought. I brought all my courage to bear not to let the prospect daunt me. First, the natives had evidently retreated before the water rose too high, their fires were all out and a dead silence reigned. I had the cavern to myself, this was better than their horrid company. Next, the rising was periodical, and evidently was the cause of the slimy, slippery rock which had robbed me of my only companion. I remembered instances in the interior where lagoons rose and fell at certain times without any visible cause. Then came the thought, for how long would the overflow continue. I had fresh air and plenty of water, I could live days; probably the flood only lasted twelve or twenty-four hours. But an awful fear seized on me. Could I maintain my reason in this worse than Egyptian darkness—a darkness so thick, definite and overpowering that I cannot describe it, truly a darkness that could be felt? I had heard of men who could not stand twenty-four hours in a dark cell, but had clamoured to be taken out. Supposing my reason deserted me, and during some delirious interlude the stream fell and rose again.

These thoughts were too agonising. I rose and paced a step or two on the sand. I made a resolution during that short walk. I had matches—fortunately, with a bushman's instinct, I had put a box in my pouch when we started to investigate the cavern. I had a candle and a-half, and I had, thank Heaven! my watch. I would calculate four hours as nearly as possible, and every four hours I would light my candle and enjoy the luxury of a little light. I stuck to this, and by doing so left that devilish pit with reason. It was sixty hours before the stream fell, and what I suffered during that time no tongue could tell, no brain imagine.

That awful darkness was at times peopled by forms that, for hideous horror, no nightmare could surpass. Invisible, but still palpably present, they surrounded and sought to drive me down the chasm wherein my companion had fallen. The loathsome inhabitants of that cavern came back in fancy and gibbered and whistled around me. I could smell them, feel their sickening touch. If I slept I awoke from, perhaps, a pleasant dream to the stern fact that I was alone in darkness in the depth of the earth. When first I found that the water was receding was perhaps the hardest time of all, for my anxiety to leave the chamber tenanted by such phantoms, was overpowering. But I resisted. I held to my will until I knew I could safely venture, and then waded slowly and determinedly up the stream; up the sloping passage, through the outer-cave, and emerged into the light of day—the blessed glorious light, with a wild shout of joy.

I must have fainted; when I came to myself I was still at the mouth of the cave, but now it was night, the bright, starlit, lonely, silent night of the Australian desert. I felt no hunger nor fear of the future; one delicious sense of rest and relief thrilled my whole being. I lay there watching the dearly-loved Austral constellations in simple, peaceful ecstasy. And then I slept, slept till the sun aroused me, and I arose and took my way to our deserted camp. A few crows arose and cawed defiantly at me, and the leather straps bore the marks of a dingo's teeth, otherwise the camp was untouched. I lit a fire, cooked a meal, ate and rested once more. The reaction had set in after the intense strain I had endured, and I felt myself incapable of thinking or purposing anything.

This state lasted for four and twenty hours—then I awoke to the fact that I had to find the horses, and make my way home alone—for, alas, as I bitterly thought, I was now, through my curiosity, alone, and, worst of all, the cause of my companion's death. Had I come away when he proposed, he would be alive, and I should have escaped the awful experience I have endured.

I have written this down while it is fresh in my memory; to-morrow I start to look for the horses. If I reach the telegraph-line safely I will come back and follow up the discovery of this unknown race, the connecting and long-sought-for link; if not, somebody else may find this and follow up the clue. I have plotted out the course from Charlotte Waters here by dead-reckoning.

March 26th:—No sign of the horses. They have evidently made back. I will make up a light pack and follow them. If I do not overtake them I may be able to get on to the line on foot.

END OF THE DIARY

NOTE—The surveyor, who is well-known in South Australia, adds the following postscript:—

The unfortunate man was identified as an operator on the overland line. He had been in the service a long time, and was very much liked. The facts about picking up Jackson when out with a repairing party have also been verified. The dead man had obtained six months' leave of absence, and it was supposed he had gone down to Adelaide. The tradition of the jinkarras is common among the natives of the Macdonnell Range. I have often heard it. No rubies or anything of value were found on the body. I, of course, made an attempt to get out, but was turned back by the terrible drought then raging. As it is now broken, I am off, and by the time this reaches you shall perhaps be on the spot.

THE LAST OF SIX

(1890)

Perhaps no more desolate, depressing scenery can be found anywhere in the world than on the mangrove-flats of Northern Queensland. As you row slowly up some salt-water creek, nothing is visible on either side but low banks of oozy mud, awash at high tide, covered with writhing and distorted trees. Now and then a branch creek breaks the monotony of the scrub, for the shore is here a perfect labyrinth and network of water-courses, whilst the only living denizens visible are armies of hideous crabs, and an occasional evil-looking alligator, which glides noiselessly off the mud into deep water as your boat approaches.

By day it is dismal enough; by night it is worse. The venomous mosquitoes buzz about you in myriads, strange cries resound through the twisted roots of the trees left bare by the receding tide; and, as the night wears on, a white mist, cold and dank, breathes deadly clamminess over all.

It was just sunrise in this delectable region. The rays had even gilded the sombre upper branches of the mangroves with a sparkle of golden colour, although as yet the sullen mist was still rising in white wreaths from the bosom of the sluggish tide. Anchored in mid-stream was a small boat, apparently without occupants, but presently the sail, that in a tumbled heap had been lying on the bottom, was disturbed and a sleepy man emerged from beneath its shelter; as he stood up, another threw the sail back and got up too. They were both towzled, dirty, and looking about as cross-grained as men might be expected to do who had passed the night cramped up in the bottom of a boat, with millions of mosquitoes thirsting for their blood—and getting it.

"No wind!" said the first; "pull again, I suppose, until ten o'clock!" And he stepped forward and commenced to haul up the heavy stone that served as anchor.

"I suppose so," returned the other; "tide against us too, but I think it's just on the turn"—and he settled himself down on the after-thwart and prepared to put out an oar.

"My God! he's coming back!" cried the first and elder man, dropping into the bottom of the boat the stone he had just hauled up. The other sprang up and gazed stupidly at the object indicated, that, carried down by the still-receding tide, passed slowly within an oar's length of the boat.

It was the dead body of a man; the shoulders and the back of the head were alone visible, but the horror of it was unmistake-able—it needed no second glance to tell its character.

"Pull," suddenly cried the younger, dropping on his seat, his voice rising to a shriek; "he's coming aboard!" Released from her anchorage the boat had started to voyage down stream in company with the dead man. A few desperate strokes took them away from the corpse, and then they rested on their oars and gazed at each other with the sweat of fear upon their faces.

"The very alligators won't touch him!" murmured the younger man at last; "let's get out of this. I'm not fit for anything after yesterday."

They pulled a few strokes in silence, then the elder spoke. "Let's get back to camp before we do anything. I'm like you, done up altogether. We'll turn down this creek and then we shan't have to pass him again." And he indicated the direction of the corpse.

The boat was headed down a branch creek, and now went with the tide aided by a few lazy strokes from the men, who silently kept on their course. In about an hour's time the creek widened and the sound of surf was audible; then suddenly they shot out from the gloomy, reeking mangrove swamp into sight of the ocean, and a fresh sea breeze came with a puff in their faces, as if to welcome their return.

"We're close to the camp," said the elder man as they rested on their oars; "we might have got here last night instead of catching fever and ague in that accursed place."

"There's so many of these creeks," returned the other; "we could not have made sure in the dark. However, let's land and go across the spit." Pulling the boat well up the sand and making her fast with a long painter to a straggling mangrove-tree, they stepped ashore; then, having taken the sail out and spread it to dry on the sand they shouldered their oars and ascended the low spit. Before them, within a short half-mile, lay a semicircular bay protected by a sand-bank, on which the long surf rollers were breaking white. Within shelter of the bank lay a small lugger, and on the beach, above high water-mark, were rough sheds, and frame erections indicating that it was a *bêche-de-mer* station.

As the two men approached the camp, a woman came out to meet them; a few aborigines and a Kanaka or two were also visible. The woman who advanced was dark in complexion, with wild black eyes and hair. She was rudely dressed and bare-footed; there was an air of semi-madness about her that was startling, yet fascinating, such awful horror shone in her eyes.

"Well," she said in fairly good English, "you found them?"

"One of them," said the elder man, "and when we've had a feed we'll go and look for the other."

"One of them!" cried the woman; "Which? Which?"

"The one you call Alphonse—the big one."

"Oh!" shrieked the woman, "where is he? Why is he not here?"

"Why! he's in that creek out there, and there he can stop for me; after what you told us he's not fit to be buried."

"Dead!" she returned in an awestruck whisper. "But no! the devil cannot die."

"Devil or not, he's dead; dead enough, and nearly turned our stomachs this morning, for his ugly carcase came drifting right on top of us after we thought he went out to sea yesterday."

"Now, missus," said the other, "suppose you let us get something to eat, for it was nigh this time yesterday when we started."

"You have brought good news," said the woman, "the devil is dead, I will wait on you"—and she hastened to the rude cooking place and soon returned with food and tea.

The meal finished, the two men lit their pipes, the women watching them anxiously.

"You will go again?" she said at last, timidly. One man looked at the other, and then the elder spoke "Well, we'll have another hunt, but I warn you, there's little hope."

"No matter," she said, "but let me go with you."

"I suppose it's not much odds," returned the man. "Come, Jim, the tide's turning now." They shouldered the oars and, followed by the woman, walked back to the boat. The tide was about the same height as when they landed, only now it was flowing. Stepping in they pushed off, and were soon once more amongst the mangroves.

The two trepang-fishers had picked up a leaky boat with a starving crew, a strange crew—two men and a woman— escapees from New Caledonia, whom they brought to the station and fed. The fishers had no intention of handing them over to justice—or, let us say, to the law; the affair was no business of theirs; but if they took them in to Cooktown the capture of their guests would be certain. Then the refugees organised a plan. The two men would take their boat and pull up one of the salt-water creeks to the open country; here they would sink the boat, and make their way, as best they could, through the bush till they happened upon some of the outlying stations. The woman, who spoke good English, could go with the fishermen to Cooktown and take her chance; it was impossible she could stand the hardship of a bush tramp. To this plan the woman vehemently objected, and begged the man she called her husband not to go. Apparently he consented, but during the night the two men slipped away, and in the morning the woman found herself deserted. Then followed a scene of wild lamentation, during which the horrified Englishmen learned some of the ghastly details of the voyage from New Caledonia—horrors that made them shudder and vow that if one of the men ever turned up he should be delivered over to justice. With frantic passion the woman appealed to them to go after the two fugitives and persuade her husband to return; for, she said, the other man had an old and bitter grudge against him, and had only lured him away to his death. Overcome by her entreaties, the two men started and found the body of one man floating in the mangrove creek; of the other they could see nothing, and, returning, were benighted.

Arrived at the spot where the two creeks joined, the boat, with the woman in the stern, was headed up stream with the tide, and they pulled quietly between the dreary groves of trees.

"Have you been up there?" she said suddenly, pointing to an opening on the right.

"No," said one of them, and they turned up the branch.

"There it is!" she exclaimed quickly. "I knew it, I felt it!"

Sure enough there was the Frenchmen's boat just ahead of them, ashore on a small open space, a chance patch of clear ground. They pulled up to her, but the dead body of the second man was visible before they got there. The woman was quite calm, and stood by while her companions examined the corpse. The man had been stabbed in the side and had bled to death; a hideous stain was in the old boat.

"How did Pierre kill him?" she muttered to herself in French. "Ah, I know, he was stabbed from behind, then he turned and knocked the devil overboard. Then he fell and died."

"You will take him back and bury him," she said, in a sad, almost sweet voice. "See, it will be no trouble; just tow the boat;" and she indicated her meaning with a wave of the hand. Then she took her seat in the boat with her dead, the men having thrown the sail over the body, and so they started back.

Arrived at the junction she spoke again. "You will wait, will you not? He will come back, perhaps—I must see myself that the devil is dead."

The men looked at each other, and then, with a few strokes of their oars kept the boat motionless in the tideway.

"He comes!" said the awfully quiet voice of the woman, and with indescribable horror the men saw the now bloated corpse come up the stream once more.

As if influenced by some terrible attraction in the glaring eyes of the woman, the ghastly thing approached the side of the boat where she sat. She rose to her feet, in her hand one of the oars. "Dog! devil!" she cried, dashing it into the face of the corpse. "O you, who ate my child before my eyes. You! who lived on man's flesh to save your life—you who have assassinated my husband! Wolf! what are you now? Dead, dead! And you who ate others shall be eaten by the foul things of this place!" At every epithet she spurned the corpse with the oar until with a hideous, life-like action it slowly turned over and disappeared.

The spell-bound men, who had not understood a word of what she said, for she spoke in French, now started into action, and called to her to sit down. She obeyed; and, hastening to leave the scene the two men, their hearts in their throats, were soon back at the mouth of the creek.

They buried the murdered man, and next morning the lugger hoisted sail for Cooktown having on board the woman, the last survivor of the party of six who had escaped from New Caledonia.

THE SPELL OF
THE MAS-HANTOO
(1890)

Pontiniak, at the mouth of the Kapoeas River, is not a place much visited by Europeans, but one can obtain an exceptional experience there.

Pontianak is the headquarters of the Dutch in Borneo, and the Resident-General has a small joke of his own, which he plays off on the unsuspecting new-chum. As is customary in those torrid settlements, business is generally transacted during the comparatively cool hours immediately succeeding daylight. As you discuss it with the courteous old Resident, he inveigles you into a stroll up and down the verandah, and after a little of this exercise, he informs you that the equatorial line passes right through the centre of his bungalow, and that during the morning walk you have crossed and re-crossed the equator several times.

I have other cause to remember Pontianak. It was my starting-point on an expedition destined to be a very memorable one. I had long contemplated a trip into the interior of Borneo, allured partly by the reports of the half-worked diamond mines, and partly by natural curiosity to see a place so little known. I had accidentally met with a young travelling Englishman, an enthusiastic sportsman, who eagerly jumped at the notion, and the result was that we soon found ourselves at Pontianak, where, after the necessary official permission had been obtained, we made our arrangements for departure.

Travelling there is far more luxurious than in the Australian backblocks. Our destination was the Sintang district, and our highway the river Kapoeas. A large roofed-in native boat, known as a *gobang*, a native crew under a *mandor*, or headman, and a good outfit of stores were obtained, and we started for the land of the Dyaks.

For days our journey was most auspicious. The dense jungle on either hand afforded a good supply of game for my sporting companion, and the native tribes we met were friendly and interesting.

As time went on we found ourselves amongst Dyaks, permission to pass through whose country cost some diplomacy, but patience and a friendly demeanour overcame all objections, and we soon got well into the mountainous districts on the upper reaches of the river. As yet I had not met the object of my search—the abandoned diamond mines, legends of which were often repeated by the coastal Malays. Once or twice I was shown places where gold-mining on a most primitive fashion had undoubtedly been pursued in some long-forgotten age. Circular holes had been sunk in three places in the form of a triangle, and drives had then been made from one to another, but by whom it had been done the Dyaks could not tell. Certainly not by their forefathers. Some told me that it was the work of slaves long ago, when the sultans from India had swept down on the archipelago and enthroned themselves in Java and Sumatra, thence enforcing tribute over Borneo, Celebes, and the smaller islands.

No ruins or inscriptions were to be found indicating that the country had ever been permanently settled by the men of that time. Sometimes I heard mysterious reports of a wild race whose descent was more ancient than that of the Dyaks: they were known as the *Orangpooenan*, or forest men, and were marked with a white spot in the middle of the forehead, an indication, at any rate, of their Hindu origin.

One afternoon about four o'clock the *mandor* came to me and pointed to a rope of twisted rattan stretched across the river—a sign that we were to go no further. Some Dyaks were assembled on the bank, and we went ashore to parley with them.

They were apparently as friendly as usual, and accepted small presents of tobacco, but declined to give us any reason for refusing the required permission to proceed. We visited the village and partook of fruit there, and after dark returned to our boat. Morton was very hurt at our sudden detention, and wished to go on in spite of the natives. I pointed out to him the folly of such a course, and he consented to take things quietly and wait for a day or two. During those two days I made every effort to conciliate our neighbours, and with perfect success excepting in the one direction. We were not to go up the river. I could obtain no reason for this refusal, and concluded that we must perforce return.

My enquiries as to the ancient gold and diamond mines seemed to amuse the old men mightily. One of them told me that I had seen the *Kambing-Mas*. This is a golden sheep which appears to certain doomed men. So infatuated does the victim become at sight of it, that he follows it on through jungles and mountains day after day until he dies of fatigue.

Of legends and traditions I got my fill, but permission to go ahead was not to be had. My old friend who told me of the *Kambing-Mas* asked me if I desired to try for the great diamond which was supposed to be in a lake at the head of a river. This star-like gem, described as of enormous size and unspeakable lustre, can be plainly seen at the bottom, but woe to the rash man who dives down after it! The infuriated spirit-guardians seize and strangle him, and his dead body floats on the surface as a warning to others.

"Perhaps," went on my loquacious host, "you would go to the land of the *Mashantoo*, the spirit-gold?" This district, rich in the precious metal, was cursed by a sultan of old, on account of the death of his son, and although you may go there and fill your pockets with gold-dust and nuggets, they all turn to sand and pebbles when you cross the boundary on your return.

Meanwhile Morton chafed greatly at our delay, and I had to

exercise much tact to pacify him. The third evening I saw him in close talk with the *mandor*; he then left the boat and went to the village, returning about dark with the information that we now had permission to proceed.

It seemed strange to me that I had heard nothing about it, but at the time I had no suspicions. It was a bright moonlight night. Taking the *mandor's* kris, Morton went ashore and severed the rattan rope where it was tied round the butt of a tree. The men took their places and the boat was once more under way.

I dropped off to sleep about ten o'clock. I awoke amidst the crash of boughs and branches, bringing ruin and destruction on us and our craft. Although half-stunned, I managed to struggle from beneath the crushed-in roof, and, as the boat sank, struck out feebly for the shore, which I had no sooner reached than I fainted.

What had happened to us was the result of Morton's rashness. Poor fellow, he paid for it with his life. The villagers had not given him permission to go on, but he had bribed the *mandor* to do so nevertheless. Along the bank of the river the Dyaks had selected certain leaning trees under which we would pass. These had been cut through to breaking point, and temporarily secured from falling outright by twisted rattans. As we passed, these guys were cut, and we were swamped by the falling trees. Morton was killed instantly, but I strangely escaped, and most of the crew were more or less hurt. All this I learned afterwards.

When I came to my senses I was lying by a fire in a small clearing in the jungle, with two or three Dyaks sleeping around. One man was awake, apparently watching. When he saw me looking about he came over to me and brought me a drink. He was very light-coloured, dressed in the ordinary *chawat* or apron with a jacket, called a "*bagu*," on his body. He smiled pleasantly, and, addressing me in the native dialect, said, "Saki (a name they had given me at the village), you were ill advised to seek the Tampat-Mas (gold-mine) here. Why did you not watch the flight of the fish-hawk first?" I asked after Morton, and he told me of his death.

I was well treated, and the fate of Morton, whom they knew to be guilty of the offence, had apparently atoned for our trespass.

On the second day I was much recovered, and Abiasi, the Dyak who had just spoken to me, was sitting by my side showing me how to use the blow-pipe, when a strange old man came from the jungle and advanced in the clearing.

He was tall, white-haired and white-bearded, and on his forehead was a round mark made with a white pigment of some sort. Abiasi rose and said something to him of which I could only catch the word "*Saghie*," another name for the forest men. Presently the old man, who had only a ragged *chawat* on, came over and regarded me earnestly, then he and Abiasi renewed their conversation.

"Saki," said the latter at last, addressing me directly, "if you still wish to see the Tampat-Mas where the Mas-hantoo is, this old saghie will take you there." He then further told me that the old saghie, or *Orangpooenan*, lived in the mountains where there were many old mines, but it was all spirit-gold, that turned into sand and gravel after it was taken away. The saghie thought that the presence of a white man might break the charm. I eagerly agreed to go, and Abiasi gave me many instructions as to my return, lent me a *parang*, or heavy knife, and bade me farewell.

It was evening when we started, and the old man led me through the jungle by a well-beaten path. Although the moon was bright, the shadows were dense where it did not penetrate, and I confess to having felt very nervous as we pushed on in silence, starting at intervals some sleeping bird or a troop of monkeys.

Presently we came to a small opening and halted in front of a low-thatched hut. In answer to his call a young woman, evidently just aroused from sleep, came out; she brought some living embers and made a fire. Like the old man, she was very fair in colour, good-looking, with well-shaped limbs, which, as her only attire was the *chawat*, or apron, were fully displayed.

After eating some rice and fruit, I lay down by the fire and slept for the remainder of the night.

I was not sorry to see a fine large fish cooking on the coals for breakfast, as my returning health brought with it a good appetite. When we had finished the meal the old man and the girl, whom I guessed to be his granddaughter, took a large rush-woven basket between them and started along a narrow path leading through the forest, motioning me to follow.

In about two miles we reached an open space, and before us rose the rugged side of a hill. We followed the base of this round for some time until the face of the hill grew steep and precipitous, and I noticed we were amongst some ancient workings.

At the mouth of what seemed a drive in the cliff the old saghie stopped, and they set down the basket. He then spoke rapidly to the girl, whom he called Suara, and she collected dry wood and built a fire, the old man lighting some tinder with a flint and steel. Suara then broke down the branches of a resinous kind of pine common to the hilly country, and with the assistance of my *parang* dressed them into rude torches. I now understood what these preparations meant, and when we had lit the torches the two picked up the basket and led the way into the tunnel or drive.

As seen by the dim, flaring light, it presented far more finished work than any of the ancient workings I had yet seen. We must have gone at least a hundred yards before the old man stopped, and I then saw that somebody had recently been at work, for there was loose dirt lying about, and some native tools.

The old saghie put down the basket, and motioned to me to come and fill it with the shovel. I did so, and naturally took the opportunity of examining the dirt. I sifted some in my hands, and blew part of the finer dirt away, and am satisfied, even now, that there was a large quantity of coarse gold through it and several specimens, as they are generally called by diggers. Of this I am quite sure, despite what afterwards occurred.

The old saghie was peering over my shoulder while I blew the dust away, and grinned hideously as he saw the gold exposed here and there. I remember wondering at the time what possible ambition could be his for the yellow dross. Perhaps he thought the same of me.

Anyhow, we were both satisfied with our inspection, and I went on filling up the bag until it could hold no more. The old man and the girl picked it up and carried it out of the tunnel. Instead of taking the homeward track as I anticipated, they turned down another one, and in a short time we were beside a small stream which descended from the range. Here there were rude appliances for washing, and I selected, as the most convenient, a shallow baked-clay dish, and commenced washing out a prospect.

Not a speck, not a trace of gold was there. I did not look at my two companions, for it struck me that possibly the dirt at the top of the basket was different from what I had examined in the tunnel. I therefore took another prospect from the very bottom and proceeded to wash it.

It was a strange scene. The narrow path leading down to the small stream, just cutting a thin gap in the dense forest. The shrill chattering and screaming of parrots overhead, and the noises made by the troops of monkeys, which swung from bough to bough, and from one long hanging vine to another. Behind me, as I squatted by the water's edge, the two yellow, semi-nude figures of the old man and the girl, bending over my shoulders in rapt attention.

The dirt was rapidly reduced as I swirled the water round in the dish, and when I tilted it to and fro, there, at either end of the grit and gravel, appeared the yellow sheen of gold. I heard the two behind me heave a sigh of satisfaction as this sight appeared. Surely the spell of the Mashantoo was broken at last?

Suddenly, without a sound of warning, a glistening, flashing object dropped from overhead and struck me and the girl into the water. Blinded and frightened, I staggered to my feet, for the stream was but shallow, and in an instant saw what had happened. A huge boa had dropped from one of the trees above, where it is their custom to hang, watching the paths by which the deer go to water, and snatched its victim from our midst. The old man was crushed against the trunk by three or four folds of the creature, whose tail was still in the branches above, and he was already in the pangs of death.

Suara, who, like myself, had been knocked forward by a blow from a coil of the reptile as it dropped on its prey, was standing near me gazing with horror-stricken eyes on the death-scene. The crunching of the unhappy man's bones was quite audible, but his collapsed body showed that life was over.

The dish had floated on the surface, and was held from going down the stream by a tussock of reeds. Suara picked it up and handed it to me with a look of despair. Instinctively, despite the near presence of the monster, now gloating over its meal. I finished washing the prospect. The spell of the Mas-hantoo held good. Nothing but gravel and sand was in the earthen dish, which I dashed to pieces on a rock.

Together, Suara and I left the spot and made our way to the hut, which we reached that evening and there rested for the night. Next morning she conducted me through jungle paths to within sight of the village where Abiasi lived.

Here she stopped and pointed in another direction, nor would she accompany me a step towards the village; and so, neither able to say farewell to the other in language both could understand, we parted. Abiasi told me afterwards that more of her people lived in the direction in which she had pointed.

Most of our goods had been recovered, and the crew were now nearly all well. A fresh gobang was provided, and I parted from the Dyak villagers with strangely mixed feelings, although it was with some sense of satisfaction that I saw mile after mile increase the distance between me and the mines of the Mas-hantoo.

SPIRIT-LED

(1890)

CHAPTER I

It was the hottest day the Gulf had seen for years. Burning, scorching and blistering heat, beating down directly from the vertical sun, in the open, radiating from the iron roof which provided what was mistakenly called shade. In the whole township there was not a corner to be found where a man could escape the suffocating sense of being in the stoke-hole of a steamer.

The surroundings were not of a nature to be grateful to eyes wearied with the monotony of plain and forest. The few stunted trees that had been spared appeared to be sadly regretting that they had not shared the fate of their comrades, and the barren ironstone ridge on which the township was built gave back all the sun's heat it had previously absorbed with interest.

Two men who had just come in from the country swore that where they crossed the Flinders the alligators came out and begged for a cold drink from their water-bags; and the most confirmed sceptic admitted the existence of a material hell. Naturally there was little or no business doing and, just as naturally, everybody whose inclination pointed that way went "on the spree."

Amongst those who had not adopted this mode of killing old father Time were two men in the verandah of the Royal Hotel. (When Australia becomes republican it is to be presumed that a 'Royal' will cease to be the distinguishing feature of every township.)

The two men in question were seated on canvas chairs in the verandah, both lightly attired in shirt and trousers only, busily engaged in mopping the perspiration from their streaming faces, and swearing at the flies.

"Deuced sight hotter lounging about here than travelling," said Davis, the elder of the two; "I vote we make a start."

"I'm agreeable," replied his companion; "the horses must be starving out in the paddock. We shall have a job to get Delaine away, though; he's bent on seeing his cheque through."

"That won't take long at the rate he's going. He's got every loafer in the town hanging about after him."

"Hullo! what's that?" said the other, as the shrill whistle of a steam launch was heard. "Oh! of course, the steamer arrived at the mouth of the river last night; that's the launch coming up. Shall we go down and see who is on board?"

The two men got up and joined the stragglers who were wending their way across the bare flat to the bank of the river. The passengers were few in number, but they included some strangers to the place; one of whom, a young-looking man with white hair and beard, immediately attracted Davis' attention.

"See that chap, Bennett?" he said.

"Yes, Dick, who is he?"

"Some years ago he was with me roving for a trip; when we started he was as young-looking as you, and his hair as dark. It's a true bill about a man's hair going white in one night. His did."

"What from? Fright?"

"Yes. We buried him alive by mistake."

"The deuce you did!"

"He had a cataleptic fit when he was on watch one night. The other man—we were double-banking the watch at the time—found him as stiff as a poker, and we all thought he was dead, there was no sign of life in him. It was hot weather—as bad as this—and we couldn't keep him, so we dug a grave, and started to bury him at sundown. He came to when we were filling in the grave; yelled blue murder, and frightened the life out of us. His hair that night turned as you see it now, although he vows that it was not the fright of being buried alive that did it."

"What then?"

"Something that happened when he was in the fit, or trance. He has never told anybody anything more than that he was quite conscious all the time, and had a very strange experience."

"Ever ask him anything?"

"No; he didn't like talking about it. Wonder what he's doing up here?"

By this time the river bank was deserted; Davis and Bennett strolled up after the others and when they arrived at the Royal, they found the hero of the yarn there before them.

"Hullo, Maxwell," said Davis, "what's brought you up this way?"

Maxwell started slightly when he saw his quondam sexton; but he met him frankly enough although at first he disregarded the question that had been asked.

In the course of the conversation that followed Maxwell stated that he was on his way out to the Nicholson River, but with what object did not transpire.

"Bennett and I were just talking of making a start to-morrow, or the next day. Our cattle are spelling on some country just this side of the Nicholson. We can't travel until the wet season comes and goes. You had better come with us."

"I shall be very glad," replied the other, and the thing was settled.

Bennett had been looking curiously at this man who had had such a narrow escape of immortality, but beyond the strange whiteness of his hair, which contrasted oddly with the swarthy hue of his sunburnt face, and a nervous look in his eyes, he did not show any trace of his strange experience. On the contrary, he promised, on nearer acquaintance, to be a pleasant travelling companion.

The summer day drew to a close, the red sun sank in the heated haze that hovered immediately above the horizon, and a calm, sultry night, still and oppressive, succeeded the fierce blaze of the day-time. The active and industrious mosquito commenced his rounds and men tossed and moaned and perspired under nets made of coarse cheese-cloth.

The next morning broke hot and sullen as before. Davis had risen early to send a man out to the paddock after the horses, and was in the bar talking to the pyjama-attired landlord.

"You'll have to knock off his grog or there'll be trouble," he said; "he was up all last night wandering about with his belt and revolver on, muttering to himself, and when a fellow does that he's got 'em pretty bad."

"I'll do what I can, but if he doesn't get drink here he will somewhere else," replied the other reluctantly.

"Then I'll see the P.M. and get him to prohibit his being served. It's the only way to get him straight."

At this moment the subject of their remarks entered the bar—a young fellow about five or six and twenty. He was fully dressed, it being evident that he had not gone to bed all night. The whites of his eyes were not blood-shot, but blood-red throughout, and the pupils so dilated that they imparted a look of unnatural horror to his face.

"Hullo, Davis," he shouted; "glad to see a white man at last. That old nigger with the white hair has been after me all night. The old buck who was potted in the head. He comes around every night now with his flour-bag cobra all over blood. Can't get a wink of sleep for him. Have a drink?"

His speech was quite distinct, he was past the stage when strong waters thicken the voice; his walk was steady, and but for the wild eyes, he might have passed for a man who was simply tired out with a night's riding or watching.

The landlord glanced enquiringly at Davis, as if to put the responsibility of serving the liquor on him.

"Too early, Delaine, and too hot already; besides, I'm going to start to-day and mustn't get tight before breakfast," said the latter soothingly.

"O be hanged! Here, give us something," and the young fellow turned towards the bar, and as he did so caught sight of

Maxwell who had just come to the door and was looking in.

The effect of the dark face and snow-white hair on his excited brain was awful to witness. His eyes, blazing before, seemed now simply coals of fire. Davis and the landlord turned to see what the madman was looking at, and that moment was nearly fatal to the newcomer. Muttering: "By—he's taken to following me by daylight as well, has he? But I'll soon stop him;" he drew his revolver and, but that Davis turned his head again and was just in time to knock his hand up, Maxwell would have been past praying for. The landlord ran round the bar, and with some trouble the three men got the pistol from the maniac, who raved, bit, and fought, like a wild beast. The doctor, who slept in the house, was called, and, not particularly sober himself, injected some morphia into the patient's arm, which soon sent him into a stupor.

"By Jove, Davis, you saved my life," said Maxwell; "that blessed lunatic would have potted me sure enough only for you. Whom did he take me for?"

"He's in the horrors, his name is Delaine, and he's out on a station on the tableland. They had some trouble with the blacks up there lately, and, I suppose, it was the first dispersing-match he had ever seen. There was one white-haired old man got a bullet through his head, and he says he felt as though his own father had been shot when he saw it done. He's a clergyman's son; of course he drinks like a fish and is superstitious as well."

"I trust they'll lock him up until I get out of the town; but I'll remember your share of this. Wait until we get away and I will tell you what brought me up here, but don't ask me any questions now. Is your friend Bennett to be trusted?"

"In what way? Wine, women or gold? I don't know about the first two, but the last I can answer for."

"It's a secret. Possibly connected with the last."

"I hope so, I want some bad enough. I think I know where to put you on to a couple of good horses, and then we'll make a start."

CHAPTER II

The stove-like township is three days journey away; four men, Davis, Bennett, Maxwell, and a blackfellow are camped for the night by the side of a small lagoon covered with the broad leaves of the purple water-lily. In the distance the cheery sound of the horse-bells can be heard, and round the fire the travellers are grouped listening to Maxwell who is telling the tale he has never yet told.

"When I fell down on watch that night and became to all appearance a corpse, I never, for one instant, lost either consciousness or memory. My soul, spirit, or whatever you like to call it, parted company with my body, but I retained all former powers of observation. I gazed at myself lying there motionless, waited until my fellow-watcher came around and awakened the sleeping camp with the tidings of my death, then, without any impulse of my own, I left the spot and found myself in a shadowy realm where all was vague and confused. Strange, indistinct shapes flitted constantly before me; I heard voices and sounds like sobbing and weeping.

"Now, before I go on any further, let me tell you that I have never been subject to these fits. I never studied any occult arts, nor troubled myself about what I called 'such rubbish.' Why this experience should have happened to me I cannot tell. I found I was travelling along pretty swiftly, carried on by some unknown motive power, or, rather, drifting on with a current of misty forms in which all seemed confusion.

"Suddenly, to my surprise, I found myself on the earth once more, in a place quite unknown to me.

"I was in Australia—that much I recognised at a glance—but where abouts?

"I was standing on the bank of a river—a northern river, evidently, for I could see the foliage of the drooping ti-trees and Leichhardt trees further down its course. The surrounding country was open, but barren; immediately in front of me was a rugged range through which the river found its way by means of an apparently impenetrable gorge. The black rocks rose abruptly on either side of a deep pool of water, and all progress was barred except by swimming. The ranges on either hand were precipitous, cleft by deep ravines; all the growth to be seen was spinifex, save a few stunted bloodwood trees.

"What struck me most forcibly was that in the centre of the waterhole, at the entrance of the gorge, as it were, there arose two rocks, like pillars, some twelve or fifteen feet in height above the surface of the water.

"Below the gorge the river-bed was sandy, and the usual timber grew on either bank. At first I thought I was alone, but, on looking around, I found that a man was standing a short distance away from me. Apparently he was a European, but so tanned and burnt by the sun as to be almost copper-coloured. He was partially clothed in skins, and held some hunting weapons in his hand. He was gazing absently into the gorge when I first noticed him, but presently turned, and, without evincing any surprise or curiosity, beckoned to me. Immediately, in obedience to some unknown impulse, I found myself threading the gloomy gorge with him, although, apparently, we exercised no motion. It was more as though we stood still and the rocks glided past us and the water beneath us. We soon reached a small open space or pocket; here there was a rude hut, and here we halted.

"My strange companion looked around and without speaking, drew my attention to a huge boulder close to the hut and on which letters and figures were carved. I made out the principal inscription. 'Hendrick Heermans, hier vangecommen, 1670.' There were also an anchor, a ship and a heart, all neatly cut. I turned from these records to the man. He beckoned me again, and I followed him across the small open space and up a ravine. The man pointed to a reef cropping out and crossing the gully. I looked at it and saw that the cap had been broken and that gold was showing freely in the stone. The man waved his hand up the gully as though intimating that there were more reefs there.

"Suddenly, sweeping up the gorge came a gust of ice-cold wind, and with it a dash of mist or spray. Looming out of this I saw for a moment a young girl's face looking earnestly at me. Her lips moved. 'Go back. Go back!' she seemed to whisper.

"When I heard this I felt an irresistible longing to return to my discarded body and in an instant gorge, mountains and all my surroundings disappeared, and I found myself in the twilight space battling despairingly on, for I felt that I had lost my way and should never find it again.

"How was I to reach my forsaken body through such a vague, misty and indeterminate land? Impalpable forms threw themselves in my path. Strange cries and wailings led me astray, and all the while there was a smell like death in my nostrils, and I knew that I must return or die.

"O, the unutterable anguish of that time! Ages seem to pass during which I was fighting with shadows, until at last I saw a sinking sun, an open grave, and men whose faces I knew, commencing to shovel earth on a senseless body.

"Mine!

"I had felt no pain when my soul left, but the re-entrance of it into its tenement was such infinite agony, that it forced from me terrible cries that caused my rescue from suffocation."

Maxwell paused, and the other two were silent.

"You will wonder," he resumed, "what all this has to do with my present journey. I will tell you. You remember Milford, a surveyor up here, at one time he was running the boundary-line between Queensland and South Australia for the Queensland Government. A year ago I met him, and we were talking about the country up this way. In running the line he had to follow the Nicholson up a good way, until finally he was completely blocked. He described to me the place where he had to turn back. It was the waterhole in the gorge with the two rock-like pillars rising out of the water."

Again there was silence for a while, then Davis said musingly.

"It's impossible to pronounce any opinion at present; the coincidence of Milford's report is certainly startling. But why should this sign have been vouchsafed to you? Apparently this being you saw was the ghost of some old Dutch sailor wrecked or marooned here in the days of the early discovery of Australia. Had you any ancestors among those gentry?"

"Not that I am aware of," returned Maxwell, "but if we find the place we shall certainly make some interesting discovery, apart from any gold."

"And the girl's face?" enquired Bennett.

Maxwell did not answer for a minute or two.

"I may as well tell you all," he said then; "I was in Melbourne, after I saw Milford, and I met a girl with that same face, in the street. Strange, too, we could not help looking at each other as though we knew we had met before. That meeting decided me on taking the trip up here. Now, that is really all. Are you ready for the adventure?"

"I should think so," said Davis; "we have fresh horses at the camp, and nothing to do with ourselves for three months or more. Please God, on Christmas Day we'll be on Tom Tiddler's ground picking up gold in chunks."

"One question more," put in Bennett. "Have you ever had any return of these trances or cataleptic fits?"

"Never since, not the slightest sign of one."

CHAPTER III

There was no doubt about the strange proof or coincidence, whichever it should turn out to be. The three men stood on the bank of the Nicholson River gazing at the gorge and the waterhole, from the bosom of which rose the two upright pillars of rock. Two weeks had elapsed since they were camped at the lagoon.

"It is the same place," muttered Maxwell, and, as the overwhelming horror of his fight through shadowland came back to him, he leant on his horse's shoulder and bowed his head down on the mane.

Bennett made a sign to Davis and both men were silent for a while, then Davis spoke—

"Well, old man, as we are not possessed of the supernatural

power you had when you were last here, we'll have to get over that range somehow."

Maxwell lifted his head. "We shall have to tackle the range, but I expect we shall have a job to get the horses over. How about leaving them here in hobbles and going up on foot?"

"Not to be thought of," replied Davis; "why, the niggers' tracks just back there in the bed of the river, are as thick as sheep-tracks. The horses would be speared before we got five miles away. I know these beggars."

"That's true," said Bennett.

Davis eyed the range curiously for some time. "There's a spur there that we can work our way up, I think," he said at last, indicating with his hand the spot he meant. The other two, after a short inspection, agreed with him. It was then nearly noon, so the horses were turned out for a couple of hours' spell, a fire lit and the billy boiled.

"What could have led your Dutch sailor up this way?" said Davis as, the meal over, they were enjoying an after-dinner pipe.

"That is what has puzzled me. I have read up everything I could get hold of on the subject of Dutch discovery and can find no record of any ship visiting the Gulf about that date," replied Maxwell.

"There may have been plenty of ships here, of which neither captain nor crew wanted a record kept. Those were the days of the buccaneers," said Bennett.

"Yes, but with the exception of the ship Dampier was on board of, they did not come out of their way to New Holland," returned Maxwell.

"The Bachelor's Delight and the Cygnet were on the west coast, as you say; why not others who had not the luck to be associated with the immortal Dampier?"

"True; but the Dutch were not noted as buccaneers. However, plenty of ships may have been lost in the Gulf of which all record has disappeared. The question is, what brought the man up into this region?" said Davis.

"I firmly believe we shall find the clue to that secret, when we find the ravine. It seems incredible that a shipwrecked or marooned man should have left the sea-coast, whereon was his only hope of salvation and have made south into an unknown land, through such a range as this."

"Well, boys, we'll make a start for it," said Davis, jumping up; and the party were soon in their saddles.

The range proved pretty stiff climbing, and they were so often baulked, and forced to retrace their steps, that it was sundown before they reached the top.

* * * * * * *

It was a desolate outlook for a camp. A rough tableland of spinifex—evidently extending too far for them to attempt to go on and descend the other side before darkness set in—lay before them.

"Nothing for it but to go on and tie the horses up all night," said Bennett. Fortune, however, favoured them; in about a mile they came on a small patch of grass, sufficient for the horses, and as their water-bags were full, they gladly turned out.

For a time the conversation turned on their expectations for the morrow, but gradually it dropped, as the fire died down. One by one the stars in their courses looked down through the openings of the tree-tops on the wanderers sleeping below, and silence, save for the occasional clink of a hobble, reigned supreme until the first flush of dawn.

"Well, Maxwell," said Davis, as they were discussing breakfast, "hear anything from your old Dutch navigator last night?"

"No, but I had some confused sort of dream again about this place; I thought I heard that voice once more telling me to 'go back'. But that, of course, is only natural."

"I think we are close to the spot," remarked Bennett. "When I was after the horses this morning I could see down into the river, and there appeared to be an open pocket there."

Bennett proved right. In half-an-hour's time they were scrambling down the range, and soon stood in an open space that Maxwell at once identified.

Naturally everybody was slightly excited. Although at first inclined to put the story down to hallucination, the subsequent events had certainly shaken this belief in the minds of the two friends. Maxwell silently pointed to the boulder; there was something carved on it, but it was worn and indistinct. Two centuries of weather had almost obliterated whatever marks had been there.

"They were fresh and distinct when I saw them," said Maxwell, in an awed voice.

By diligent scrutiny they made out the inscription that he had repeated, but had they not known it the task would have been most difficult. The words had not been very deeply marked, and the face of the boulder fronting north-west, the full force of the wet seasons had been experienced by the inscription.

"This is a wonderful thing," said Davis. "There can be no doubt as to the age of that."

"Let's go up the ravine and look for the reef and then get back as soon as possible. I don't like this place. I wish I had not come," returned Maxwell.

They left the packhorses feeding about and rode up the gully, taking with them the pick and shovel they had brought. "It was here, I think," said Maxwell, looking around; "but the place seems altered."

"Very likely the creek would change its course slightly in a couple of hundred years, but not much. That looks like an outcrop there."

"This is the place," said Maxwell, eagerly, "I know it now, but it is a little changed."

The three dismounted, and Davis, taking the pick, struck the cap of the reef with the head of it, knocking off some lumps of stone. As he did so a wild "Holloa!" rang up the gully. All started and looked at each other with faces suddenly white and hearts quickly beating. There was something uncanny in such a cry rising out of the surrounding solitude.

"Blacks?" said Bennett, doubtfully. Davis shook his head.

Once more the loud shout was raised, apparently coming from the direction of the inscribed rock.

"Let's go and see what it is, anyway," said Davis—and they mounted and rode down the gully again, Bennett, who had picked up a bit of the quartz, putting it into his saddle-pouch as they rode along.

Maxwell had not spoken since the cry had been heard, his face was pale and occasionally he muttered to himself, "Go back, go back!" The packhorses were quietly cropping what scanty grass there was; all seemed peaceful and quiet.

"I believe it was a bird after all; there's a kind of toucan makes a devil of a row—have a look round old man," said Davis to Bennett, and they both rode up and down the bank of the river, leaving Maxwell standing near the rock where he had dismounted. Nothing could be seen, and the two returned and proposed going up the gully again.

"You fellows go and come back again, I want to get out of this—I'm upset," said Maxwell, speaking for the first time in a constrained voice.

Davis glanced at his friend. "Right you are, old man, no wonder you don't feel well; we'll just make sure of the reef and come back. If you want us, fire your pistol; we shan't be far off."

The two rode back to their disturbed work and hastily commenced their examination of the stone. There was no doubt about the richness of the find, and the reef could be traced a good distance without much trouble. They had collected a small heap of specimens to take back, when suddenly the loud "Holloa!" once more came pealing up the gully followed instantly by a fainter cry and two revolver-shots.

Hastily mounting, the two galloped back.

The packhorses, as if startled, were walking along their tracks towards home, followed by Maxwell's horse with the bridle trailing; its rider was stretched on the ground; nothing else was visible.

Jumping from their horses they approached the prostrate man. Both started and stared at each other with terror-stricken eyes. Before them lay a skeleton clad in Maxwell's clothes.

"Are we mad?" cried Davis, aghast with horror.

The fierce sun was above them, the bare mountains around, they could hear the horses clattering up the range as if anxious to leave the accursed place, and before them lay a skeleton with the shrunken skin still adhering to it in places, a corpse that had been rotting for years; that had relapsed into the state it would have been had the former trance been death. Blind terror seized them both, and they mounted to follow the horses when an awful voice came from the fleshless lips: "Stay with me, stop! I may come back; I may—"

Bennett could hear no more, he stuck the spurs in his horse and galloped off. Davis would have followed but he was transfixed with terror at what he saw. The awful object was moving, the outcast spirit was striving desperately to reanimate the body that had suddenly fallen into decay. The watcher was chained to the spot. Once it seemed that the horrible thing was really going to rise, but the struggle was unavailing, with a loud moan of keenest agony and despair that thrilled the listener's brain with terror it fell back silent and motionless. Davis remembered nothing more till he found himself urging his horse up the range. The place has never been revisited.

* * * * * * *

In an asylum for the insane in a southern town there is a patient named Bennett, who is always talking of the wonderful reef he has up North. He has a specimen of quartz, very rich, which he never parts with day or night. He is often visited by a man named Davis, who nursed him through a severe attack of fever out on the Nicholson. The doctors think he may yet recover.

THE GHOST'S VICTORY
(1891)

"This is a tough contract," murmured the ghost, as it gazed out of the window of the haunted chamber and looked up and down the almost deserted street. Needless to say it was Christmas Eve, and the clocks had just struck twelve.

It was not at all an awe-inspiring ghost. If one had not known for certain that it was a spectre it might have been taken for a shabby old debt-collector or a hanged bailiff; but it was a genuine goblin, and anybody infringing the trade-mark will be prosecuted.

The house it haunted was an old stone affair, situated on a good-sized allotment in one of the principal streets of Sydney. Most people have passed the place and wondered why it was so dull and murky and desolate, and why a tattered bill always announced that the upper part was "to let." It was owned by an absentee landlord, and there was a law-suit on it, and three mortgages. Around it was a solemn, melancholy waste, tenanted by old jam-tins and goats. The ground-floor was supposed to be occupied as offices, whilst the upper portion was left to solitude—and the ghost.

This was the spectre's grievance. Thirty years before it had cut its throat there, and since entering into the land of spirits it had not had a single opportunity of frightening anybody and achieving a reputation. It had made just one public appearance, and then it fell flat. It was an orthodox apparition, and as such, was strictly obliged to appear only between mid-night and cockcrow; but nobody lived in the house, nobody knew it was haunted, nobody cared whether it was haunted or not. So there it had remained, a poor, forlorn, neglected ghost, living alone in the dark and damp, all forgotten.

"Christmas again," it muttered in spectral grammar, "and I am still unknown. O! if I were only one of those modern young ghosts who go round visiting friends and relations and scaring the wits out of them; but, no! I am old-fashioned and must abide by the rules of the game. Why, I might have heaps of hidden money here to show people for aught the public know." Then it fell to musing over the one chance that had fallen its way.

It had been gazing sadly out of the window as usual at about one o'clock in the morning, when there came the sound of unsteady steps down the street. Presently, a stout old gentleman in evening dress, with his hat on one side and an overcoat on his arm, stopped suddenly in front of the gate and gazed curiously at the building. Would he come in? The ghost's heart beat fast with anxiety.

"Astonishing!" said the old gentleman. "How on earth did I get home so quick? Don't remember the tram—don't remember the train. My house, though, right enough." He opened the crazy gate and lurched in.

"At last, at last!" cried the apparition, restraining itself by a might effort from appearing on the verandah and prematurely flushing its game.

The old gentleman tried to put a latch-key in the door, but as there was no keyhole he failed. Then he kicked, and knocked, and swore. Finally he coiled himself up on the verandah, and after a grunt or two went fast asleep.

Then the exultant spectre passed through the crack underneath the door, and stood contemplating its unconscious victim. But all the old gentleman did was to turn over and say pettishly, as he dragged his coat over his shoulders, "Don't Maria!"

This put the ghost on its mettle. It laid an ice-cold hand on the sleeper, and, in a thrilling whisper, said, "Awake!"

The old gentleman sat up and blinked at the vision of the

dead, and the vision regarded the old gentleman.

"Right, old boy!" said the latter. "I'll wake up in time, never fear. Bring me a stiff brandy-and-soda at it. Good night. Gobless you!" and he laid down again and snored.

This was maddening. A ghost to be mistaken for a waiter and told to bring a brandy-and-soda in the morning! It fled through the top window to the haunted chamber and sat down on the bloodstain and cried.

Time passed, but no other mortal visited the haunted house between midnight and daylight. Other ghosts came. Ghosts who were allowed out at nights; and they used to tell the old deceased inhabitant what joyous times they had; but that only made things worse. Sometimes it thought that a burglar might break in during the small hours and give it a chance; but, then, the occupants of the two alleged offices hadn't enough between them to allure any respectable burglar; and the burglars knew it.

Sorrowfully the poor old apparition mused, and if it could only have repeated the operation of cutting its throat, it would have done so out of sheer desperation and *ennui*.

At that moment the sound of approaching footsteps broke the stillness.

Two men, in earnest conversation, halted opposite the gate, and, by the light of the street lamp, the ghost saw that one of them was the occupant of the offices. He was some sort of agent—general commission—and, as the ghost knew, his principal occupation was hiding behind some old tanks in the back yard when his creditors called, which they did constantly. The old ghost, in its invisible state, used to do a good deal of wandering about in the day-time.

After a few minutes more talk the two men came in, and the agent proceeded to unlock the door.

The ghost nearly shrieked with joy. How should it make the most startling appearance? It decided to await them in the passage and shake its gaunt arms in the shadows.

The agent struck a match, opened the door of his office, and and was about entering, followed by his companion, when by the expiring light of the match, the latter caught a glimpse of the apparition standing at the end of the passage.

"Hallo! Somebody living here?" he said.

"No," said the agent, who had lit another match, and was searching for a candle.

"Thought I saw something at the end of the passage."

"Pooh! Cats, I suppose. This is a regular meeting place of theirs;" and the agent picked up an empty stone ink-bottle and, going to the door, hurled it down the passage, crying, "Shoo! get out!" Then he shut the office-door.

The ink-bottle went clean through the ghost, but the insult hurt it worse. First, to be taken for a waiter, then to be "shoo'ed" at for a cat. It approached the office vowing vengeance, and tramping frantically with the spectres of its old shadow feet on the floor. It was about to pass through the door, and, with a blood-curdling shriek appear before them with its gashed and bleeding throat, but a few words it heard arrested it. The ghost stopped and listened.

"Come, Tom, hurry up and get me those papers I left with you; I must go on board, we start at five sharp," said the younger man to the agent.

Tom sat on the edge of the ricketty deal table, swinging one leg moodily to and fro, but made no attempt to move.

"You know how frightfully hard up we've been?" he said at last.

"Of course I do; has not my sister told me all about it to-day, and, as you know, I gave her all the money I could to keep you going for a bit. I can do no more. Give me the papers."

"Well, then," said the agent, getting up, desperately and defiantly, "I haven't got them."

"Not got them!" repeated the other. "God Almighty, man! what do you mean?"

"Mean what I say."

"What have you done with them?" cried the younger, fiercely.

"The bank has them as security."

The agent's brother-in-law gazed at him in silence. "Do you

know," he said at last, quite quickly, "that you have ruined me?"

"I can redeem them and send them to you overland," muttered the other, with white lips.

"Bah! *you* redeem them; how?" and he glanced round the poverty-stricken room. "Even if you had the money, or could get it, how could you redeem them before Monday? This is Friday, and before you could forward them we should have left Brisbane. You've ruined yourself, and now you've ruined me."

The agent said nothing, and his companion walked impatiently up and down the room.

"How much did you get advanced on them?"

"Five hundred pounds."

"And what became of it?"

"Speculated with it. That was the temptation. I knew of such a safe thing."

"Such a safe thing!" said the other, mockingly.

There was silence for a time. The younger man continued his wild-beast walk, and the agent leant against the table with folded arms and eyes cast down.

Half an hour passed, but the ghost was not impatient; after thirty years of loneliness, this little tragedy was interesting. Besides, it had cut its throat for doing almost the same thing the agent had done. Would the agent cut his throat? In that case he would also become a ghost.

"I dare not go back without those deeds," said the young man at last. "How do you propose to get them back?"

"I think I can borrow the money."

"If that is all I have to rely on, why, they are gone. Well, if it comes to the worst, I must go to the bank and demand their restitution as stolen property. I don't know how the law stands, but I believe they will give them up and—"

"Prosecute me," said the agent.

"I suppose so. I will do my duty, even though it puts you in gaol."

"You will put me in gaol, will you?" snarled the agent, walking up to his companion with an ugly look on his face.

The ghost executed a double shuffle in his joy, and pressed about in the passage. There was going to be a murder, and he would have another ghost to bear him company.

The young man confronted his brother-in-law, and said quietly, "If every other means fails, I must inform the bank, and after that I cannot interfere."

Tom fell back, and said, after a pause, "You had better leave me. I must try and think of some way out of this."

The other seemed in no hurry to stay, and walked to the door merely remarking, "I will see you this afternoon." Then the front door slammed behind him, and the house was left to the agent and the ghost.

Was the agent going to cut his throat? The ghost looked anxiously in; such an opportunity was worth waiting thirty years for.

Was he going to cut his throat? Nothing of the sort. The agent looked quite relieved, as though an unpleasant task had at last been got over. He lit another candle and turned towards the old-fashioned fireplace on one side of the room. The ghost watched him curiously. It was a hearth for burning wood; and the agent prised up one of the side stones, and from a whole underneath took out a large cash-box; put it on the table, and opened it. The spirit rushed through the wall unseen, and looked over his shoulder. The box was full of sovereigns. The agent counted them over with a sigh of relief, replaced the box in its hiding place, and made ready to go.

The apparition had passed through the wall again into the dark passage. It would never do to scare the agent now; he was coming back for that box, and then—the ghost hugged itself in anticipation. The agent closed and locked his door; slammed the front door after him and departed. The ghost stopped behind and chuckled. It was all plain as the proverbial pikestaff, and to be summed up in one word, "bolt." The five hundred pounds had *not* gone in speculation; they were in the cash-box, besides other little pickings. The spectre reckoned it all up on its shadowy fingers; holiday time, crowds travelling about, best chance in the world to get away; he's off, with whatever he can lay his hands on, leaves his wife and children to do the best they can, robs his brother-in-law, and ruins the people who own those deeds; now, how can I circumvent him?

The ghost fell into a brown study. "If I could only materialise myself like some of those new fangled spirits say they can, I might collar that money and tell the young fellow all about it, but I can't. If I appear before him I shall scare him, and then— he might not come back here. I'll best that fellow though if I...."—die for it, the ghost was about to say, but as he had done that already he changed the expression. Just then the daylight lightened the eastern sky, and it vanished, but its face wore a look of satisfaction that was not on it before; evidently the apparition had an idea.

Christmas day passed in the usual manner, so far as the ghost was concerned; that is to say, nobody came near the place, and it either sat on the blood-spot or looked out of the window. Midnight struck, and the ghost was happy. It had six hours of visibility before it, and in a shadowy sort of way it cleared the desk for action.

At half-past twelve the agent made his appearance carrying a small portmanteau.

He struck a match before closing the front door, and dropped it immediately with a yell. Somebody was leaning against the door of his room, a strange, mouldy-looking little man who smelt exactly like a damp umbrella. Resisting the impulse to turn and fly, he waited and listened. There was no sound but the violent thumping of his own heart. He looked round into the street behind him to reassure himself, mustered up his nerve, and struck another match. This time the passage was empty. He wiped the beads of perspiration from his forehead, and laughed with considerable difficulty. Then he unlocked his own door, but he left the front door open. Nobody in his room so far as he could see with a match, so he lit the candle and—it was no fancy. An old man with a ghastly white face and a horrible blood-stain on his white beard and shirt front was sitting loose in the air about three feet above the floor. He might have stood his ground even then, but the thing started to walk through the air towards him, and, smitten with unreasoning panic, he turned and ran through the open door, and the triumphant ghost heard his flying footsteps die away in the distance.

"Now for the other man," muttered the ghost.

One o'clock struck, and in a few minutes the ghost heard someone entering the house. Both doors were still open and the candle still burning, so the newcomer walked straight in. He stopped short inside the room. Seated at the table where he expected to find his relative was a seedy old gentleman who, in spite of the heat, had his coat buttoned right to the neck and his collar turned up. The visitor was silent with astonishment, but the spectre grinned at him in an amiable manner and he faltered at last:

"Who are you, and what are you doing here?"

"So glad you spoke," said the apparition, blandly.

"You see I'm a ghost, and, of course, I can't speak first. Not allowed by the regulations. Now, don't be frightened and run away, because I want to do you a good turn. How do you feel? Quite well?"

"You're a ghost? But I don't believe in them. It's a joke."

"Don't be sceptical, young man. Shall I walk through the table or do any little absurdity of that sort? But, no! you've more sense than that. Listen: Your brother-in-law is a thief, you know, but he is worse than you think. He did not lose the money the bank advanced him. He has it all in a cash box under that stone. Lift it up and see. He was going to bolt. There is his portmanteau."

As in a dream, the live man advanced and did as the dead man directed him. Sure enough he lifted out a weighty cash-box.

"If I were you," said the ghost, "I would go straight to his house with that, and make him open it in front of your sister. His wife, isn't she?"

"Yes."

"Poor woman! Well, good morning, my boy. Wish you luck."

The young man halted at the door. "Is there any little thing I can do, sir, to show my gratitude?"

"There is. Now and again, say at intervals of a few months, persuade someone to come here between midnight and daylight. A sceptic, if possible. I won't give them much of a fright."

"Rely on me. I have half-a-dozen in my mind's eye already;" and he backed rather rapidly out into the street.

"A nice young man," said the ghost. "Now, I wonder if that other fellow is coming back. If he wants to clear out before daylight he'll face anything to get that money."

Sure enough, in about an hour's time, the agent came back. He had been somewhere in quest of Dutch courage, and was pot-valiant. The candle had gone out, but he lit another, and glared about the room.

"Now, where are you?" he cried. "Come out and frighten me again if you can. I've got something here for you." Looking through the wall the ghost saw he was flourishing a revolver.

Cursing himself for a fool for running away before, he put the weapon down and went to the hearth. The cry he gave when he discovered his loss was tremendous. He sprang to his feet, and there, glaring at him across the table, was the old man with the gashed throat. Then three shots were fired in quick succession. Two of them went through the spectre. The third went through the agent.

There are two ghosts in that old house now. One occupies the upper, the one the lower portion—but they are not on speaking terms.

MALCHOOK'S DOOM
A STORY OF THE
NICHOLSON RIVER
(1892)

It was Malchook who told the beginning of this story, and Malchook was supposed to be the biggest liar in the Gulf of Carpentaria, which is equivalent to saying that he was the biggest liar in the world. However, it was on record that he told the truth sometimes—when he was in a blue funk, for instance—and on this occasion his state of funk was a dazzling purple—blue was no name for it.

We were camped on the Nicholson for the wet season. The cattle had been turned out and we had pretty hard work to keep them together, for, after the rain set in and the country got boggy, the niggers commenced playing up and we had to keep going. It was raining cats and dogs that night and we were all huddled together round the fire under a bit of a bark lean-to which we had put up. Malchook was away—his horses were absent that morning and he had been away all day after them. It was about eight o'clock when we heard him coming; he had found his horses and was driving them right up to the camp. Then, instead of hobbling them, he got a bridle and a halter, caught them and tied them up to a tree.

Some of the fellows sang out to him to know what he was doing, but he took no notice, and, after turning out the horse he had been riding, came up to the fire and told Reeve (the boss) that he wanted a word with him. Reeve got up, and the two went over to his tent. Presently Malchook emerged, went over to where his duds were under the tarpaulin that had been rigged up over the rations, and commenced to roll them up. Reeve came back to the fire.

"What's up?" asked Thomas, Reeve's cousin.

"Only that fellow wants to leave to-night straight away, so I gave him his cheque and told him to slide as soon as he liked; he's no great loss anyway."

"What does he want to leave for?"

"Says the camp is 'doomed,' and he is going to put as many miles as possible between himself and us before our fate overtakes us."

There was a general laugh, and just then Malchook came out with his swag and commenced to saddle up in the pouring rain. There was a good moon, nearly full, although of course it was not visible.

The fellows commenced chaffing him, for he was not a favourite; too all-round a liar. He stood it without a word until he was ready to mount then he got on his horse and, turning round, said "Laugh away; this time to-morrow I'll have the laugh of you; this camp is doomed!" He stuck the spurs in his horse and disappeared—swish, swish, swish, through the bog down the bank of the river, and we heard him swearing at his pack-horse as he crossed the sand.

There was much laughter and wonderment at what had sent Malchook "off his chump," but eccentricity was common in those days, from various causes, and presently we all turned in.

I was sleeping under the tarpaulin where the rations were stored, and about two o'clock in the morning I suddenly awoke. It was brilliant moonlight, the wind had changed and the rain ceased, only a little scud was flitting across the sky, giving the moon that strange appearance that everybody must occasionally have noticed—as though she was travelling at express rate through an archipelago of cloudlets. Some impulse made me get out from under the mosquito-net and go to the opening at the end of the tarpaulin and look out.

Everything was very still and quiet; all the horses were camped, for not a bell could be heard, and I stood for some time aimlessly listening and looking at the glistening pools of water lying on the flat between our camp and the bank when suddenly I distinctly heard a human voice in the bed of the river. I waited for a moment to make sure, then I got my Martini and a couple of cartridges and sneaked towards the river. Last full-moon the niggers had nearly clubbed the cook in his mosquito-nets when he was sleeping outside the tent one night; this time, I thought, it would be a case of the bitten bit.

About a hundred yards from the camp I stopped and listened; the voice was much nearer, it was a white man's, it was Malchook's, and he was kicking his knocked-up horse along and dragging the pack-horse after him. I waited behind a tree until he was close up, and then I stepped out. I was only in my shirt, with the carbine in my hand.

"Great God!" he cried, with a kind of choke, "he's here again!"

"What the devil is up with you?" I said; "why didn't you stop away when you went? Got bushed, I suppose, and the horses brought you back?"

He sat on his horse and panted for a few minutes without speaking; then he said: "That infernal old nigger wouldn't let me go. He hunted me back. I've got to share your fate, so let's get it over."

He jabbed his heels in his horse's ribs, but I stopped him. "Don't wake the camp up," I said. "What nigger do you mean?"

"The nigger that Jacky the Span and I roasted in the spinifex. He's headed me back every road I've tried, and I give it up. Let me turn the horses out, and try and get a wink of sleep."

Jacky the Span was an old blackguard of a Mexican who had been knocked on the head about six months before. Everybody said he richly deserved it, and everybody was right.

"When were you up here with Jacky Span?" I asked.

"About two years ago; the time Bratten was killed; but let me turn out the horses and I'll tell you all about it."

We went quietly back to camp, let the tired horses go, and then Malchook laid down on his blankets alongside of me. The tarpaulin was rigged some distance from the other tents, and the boys were done-up and sleeping sound, so nobody awoke. This is what Malchook told me:

Two years before, he and the old Mexican had come up to join Bratten in mustering some horses that had got away from the lower part of the river and were supposed to be knocking about below the first gorge. Like most half-breeds, Jacky the Span (short for Spaniard) was a most inhuman brute towards the natives whenever he got a chance, and Malchook, being a blowhard and a bully, was naturally of the same cowardly disposition—most liars are. One day they spotted an old man and a young gin at the foot of a spinifex ridge that runs in on the Upper Nicholson. I knew the place—real old man spinifex that would go through a leather legging. They rounded the old black up on the top of the ridge, but missed the gin, and Jacky Span said he would make the man find her or he should suffer, and Malchook, in order to keep up his reputation as a flash man and a real old Gulf hand, aided and abetted him.

I suppose the poor devil was too frightened to understand what they really wanted, but, anyhow, all the half-caste devilry, which is the worst devilry in the world, was roused in the Mexican, and Malchook followed suit.

They selected a bank of old man spinifex, and rolled the naked nigger in it for sport. Now, spinifex is beastly poisonous stuff; get your shins well pricked, and it is worse than any amount of mosquito-bites for irritating you and making you itch. Horses will not face it after a day or two in really bad country, and if you run your hand down their shins you will soon see the reason why. Every little prick festers, and their legs are covered with tiny boils and ulcers after a few days in bad spinifex. The niggers always burn it ahead of them before they travel through it. Out in the real Never-Never they have regular tracks that they keep burnt down.

By the time they had rolled this nigger in the spinifex for

some minutes, he must have been in a raging hell of torment; and he knew no more what they wanted with him than he did at the start. Then, according to Malchook, Jacky rolled him into a big bank of dry stuff—they had tied his feet together—and set fire to it. Spinifex is rare stuff to burn, it is full of turpentine, and burns with a fierce heat and a black smoke, so the old nigger was well roasted and when it burnt out they rolled him into another and set that alight. A gust of wind sprung up and started the whole ridge ablaze, and the gin, who had been hidden close by, watching them, sprang out and ran for it, and Jacky Span picked up the old man's club and took after her. He was away about half-an-hour; meantime the old fellow died, groaning awfully, and Malchook began to feel as if he had better have let things alone.

Presently, Jacky Span came back with the club in his hand— big two-handed clubs they use out on the Nicholson—and showed Malchook some blood and hair on it, and laughed like a devil. No need to repeat here all he said.

Now, if Malchook had there and then blown a government road through the brute, there might have been some chance of repentance left for him, but he didn't. He sniggered and let Jacky Span tell him all about it, and camped with him for weeks afterwards. Jacky Span was killed, as I said before, and Malchook assured me, in a sweating blue funk when he spoke, that just at dark he had met his horses coming back, with the old roasted nigger behind driving them. He went on to say that this thing had followed him right up to the river and shrieked at him that he would die in the camp. Then he went on to tell that when he tried to get away from the camp that night the old nigger had met him at every point of the compass, so at last he gave it up and came back.

Now, I knew that there had been an importation of brandy lately into the Gulf country, generally known as the "possum brand," each bottle of which was calculated to make a man see more devils than any six bottles of any other brand. It was very popular, for it would eat holes in a saddle-cloth, so I concluded that Malchook had got hold of some of it, for one of the fellows had returned from Burketown that day. This would account for the ghost of the blackfellow, but the rest of the yarn about Jacky Span I knew to be true, so I told Malchook to clear out and sleep somewhere else—I wouldn't have him under the same tarpaulin with me. He begged and prayed to be allowed to remain, but I told him I would wake the camp and tell everything if he didn't go, so he went, sobbing bitterly. I explained to him that the best thing he could do was to shoot himself; that a man who could follow the lead of a miserable half-caste out of pure flashness was too contemptible to live, but he didn't appreciate my kindness, and slouched away to a bit of a sand-hump about 150 yards from the camp, and I saw him throw his blankets down and then lie down on them. I got into my bunk again and went fast asleep in two minutes.

Reeve woke me up. It was broad daylight. "The niggers were here last night," he said. "Did you hear anything?"

"No," I replied; "but Malchook came back; I saw him."

"Yes. They knocked him on the head—bashed his skull in. He was sleeping out under that tree. I suppose he was ashamed to wake us up."

"Nobody hear anything?" I asked.

"Not a sound. There are the traces of about six niggers coming out of the river towards the camp, and they must have stumbled right on top of Malchook. Poor devil! Polished him off and cleared out. The camp was doomed for him, after all."

I concluded to say nothing, beyond having seen Malchook come back and speaking to him. Sometimes I wonder whether I was not responsible for his death by hunting him away from the camp, but I always console myself with the reflection that he only got what he deserved.

THE RED LAGOON

(1892)

'Where are you going to camp to-night?' asked Mac., the bullocky, as I stopped to have a yarn for a few minutes, on my road down from the tableland.

'I was going to push on to the Red Lagoon; there's good feed there, I hear.'

'Hanged if I'd camp there by myself for any money.'

'Why? Are the blacks bad?'

'No fear, it's the safest place in the North. No nigger will come within ten miles of it.'

'What's up then; devil-devil?'

'So they say, perhaps you'll see if you camp there tonight. I had a mate nearly frightened into the horrors there once. It took nearly a case of whisky to get him straight again. Well, I must be moving. So long!'

Mac. straightened his bullocks up, and I resumed my journey.

It was sundown when I got to the Red Lagoon—so called from a small reddish weed that covered its surface. There was beautiful feed there, and I felt that all the spooks in the world should not prevent me turning out for the night and giving my horses a good show. It was dark before I finished tea, for the twilights are short in tropical Queensland; I had made up a comfortable bed of grass and having fixed up everything snug, lay down for a good smoke. It was a moonless night, and quite calm. Only for the clink of the hobble chains, the tinkle of the bell, and an occasional snort from my horses, there was not a sound to be heard. One has to camp out alone night after night in the bush to thoroughly appreciate the companionship of a horse. As it grew a little chilly I poked up the fire, made myself comfortable under the blankets, and went off into the sleep of the just.

I must have dreamt that I was fighting alligators at the mouth of the Albert River, and that a fearful splashing was going on; at least, that was the impression under which I drowsily came to my senses.

The splashing still continued, however, and came from the lagoon.

'One of the horses has got in and can't get out,' was my first thought, and I jumped up and went in the direction of the sound. All was still when I reached the bank, and by the light of the stars the surface appeared placid and unruffled. Then, for the first time, a superstitious thrill went through me, but I soon shook it off, and, after listening a little longer, I returned to my camp, renewed the fire, and went to see if my horses were all right. The tinkle of the bell in the distance guided me to them; and I found them feeding greedily and contentedly. I remained with them during the time I smoked the heel of a pipe just to get myself into a proper 'daylight' frame of mind, then went back to my blankets.

It was a little while 'ere I went off to sleep, for an owl gave me a start by suddenly commencing to bark right over my head. However, I did drop off and dreamt a very strange dream, I call it a dream, but to me it seemed real enough at the time.

I was awakened, so I thought, once more by the splashing, but this time I had somehow no inclination to inquire into the cause of it. Presently it ceased, and I heard something come stumbling towards my camp. Still I felt neither fear nor any desire to move. The object came into the circle of light and squatted by the fire.

It was an elderly white man, with a remarkably long, grey beard. He was bare-headed, and his shirt and trousers were wet through and clung to him. But that was not all. His head and beard were covered with blood, one eye had been smashed in, and spear-wounds were visible in his cheeks and neck. As to his body, one could not tell, but his shirt was blood-soaked, and the blood dripped from his wrists as he held his hands towards the fire. It was not until I had fully taken in all those details and the hideously gashed face, with its one eye, looked at me across the fire, that terror—unreasoning terror—overmastered me. Then I felt an impulse to yell and jump up, but I was dumb and powerless. The thing arose, and glaring at me with its single eye, suddenly rang a furious peal on a horse-bell.

This broke the charm. I started up; it was broad daylight, the horses had fed back close to camp, and the one with the bell on was just giving himself a vigorous shake.

* * * * * * *

'What's the yarn about the Red Lagoon?' I asked Jack Sullivan, the super of the station, where I camped next night.

'Well,' he said, 'there is a yarn about it, and a very stupid one, too. Why do you ask, you camped there last night. See anything?'

I told him I had been awakened by some mysterious splashing in the lagoon.

'Fish. Lots of big ones there; always jump on dark nights. This is the yarn, some of it, of course, *is* true—it's a matter of history: You know, this country was settled early in the sixties, and afterwards abandoned; all the stations thrown up and the district deserted. This run was one of them, although the old homestead was in a different place. There was a deuce of a lot of 'dispersing,' and cattle-killing going on, and the then manager and some others caught a lot of blacks—all sorts and sexes—at the Red Lagoon, and made short work of the crowd. The blacks, of course, took to the water and were most of them shot in it. Now comes in the embroidery. The lagoon was said to have been quite clear then and has since become covered with the red weed that gives it its name. A natural process I have often witnessed where no one has been killed.

'The super, an elderly man, was afterwards killed by the blacks when camped at the same place. Some of them have since confessed that he took to the water and that they hunted him from side to side until he died. Anyhow, it's true that he was found half in the water, with his head and face frightfully battered, and spear wounds all over. From what I know of them I should say that he was knocked on the head when asleep, and that they then chopped him about and threw his body in the lagoon.'

'Do the blacks ever camp there now?'

'No. But that is not singular. They nearly always shun a place where they have murdered a white man. I know of many instances.'

THE TRACK OF THE DEAD

(1892)

"What's the matter with you; why the deuce can't you sleep?"

"I don't know," returned Alf; "got a touch of insomnia to-night. If I do go to sleep I have the most awful dreams all about men I used to know, men who are dead now."

"Oh, for heaven's sake don't start such talk at this time of night. Sit by the fire and smoke your pipe quietly," I answered, wearily, as I turned my back to the blaze and drew my blanket around me.

"Right you are, old man," he replied, good-naturedly, and I dropped off into unconsciousness.

I awoke with a start. The fire was out, or nearly so, and the camp was silent. Just above the horizon the spectral last quarter of the moon was hanging, throwing ghostly, dim, long shadows around. It was the hour before dawn, the uncanny hour when all the vital forces are at the lowest ebb. Some great general is reported to have said, that the only courage worth a hang was three o'clock in the morning courage. Whether anyone ever did make the remark or not, there is a deal of truth in it.

I roused myself a little and looked around. Alf was sleeping on the other side of the fire, and where he had set his bed down was now in deep shadow, and I could make nothing out. I tried to go to sleep again, but it was useless. Perhaps a smoke might send me off; so, seeing a spark still smouldering, I arose, and blowing the end of a still glowing firestick into a blaze, I lit my pipe, and then, holding the lighted stick up, looked over to where my companion should have been sleeping.

His blankets were tenantless.

May I never experience again such an uncomfortable thrill as went through me when I made this discovery! I put my hand on the blankets where they had been thrown aside. They were cold and the dew had gathered on them; he must have been gone some hours. I listened long and intently, but the night was silent. For a man to wander away from camp in the middle of the night, out in the Never-Never spinifex country, and remain away for hours, is a most uncanny thing. If he had heard the horses making off he would have called me ere leaving; if—but I exhausted all conjectures before daylight dawned. I could do nothing until then.

The light came very slowly, or so it appeared to me. We were camped at the foot of a spinifex rise, on a narrow flat bordering a creek. When the light was strong I could see the horses feeding quietly some short distance away, and picking up my bridle I soon had one caught and saddled, and firing off my rifle two or three times without eliciting an answering shot, I started to look for my missing mate. After some trouble I picked up his track leading straight up the ridge, which, near the crest, was sandy, and the prints of his footsteps were clearly defined. The spinifex was scantier here, and as I gazed intently down I saw something that made me pull up and hastily dismount to scan the tracks closer. Alf, was not alone, somebody was walking ahead of him.

Step by step I followed leading my horse, but I could make nothing of the foremost track, for Alf's almost covered it every time. At last they diverged, and the two ran side by side. It was a bright morning, the sun just glinting under the stunted trees; what little live nature there was in that lonely spot was awake and joyously greeting the day; but I rose up from my examination of that awful foot-mark with the dew of superstitious terror on my forehead. No living man had made that track.

I had to follow on scarce knowing what to think or expect. I tried to persuade myself that the foot-print was that of some attenuated old gin, lean and shrunken as a mummy, but that was against reason. The track was that of the skeleton of a man; and Alf was not following it, but following whatever was making it.

With varying fortune, now finding, now losing the trail I kept on for about two hours; then, halfway down a slight incline, I came upon the object of my search. He was sitting on the ground talking to himself, I thought at first, but when I got closer I saw he was addressing some object on his lap. He was nursing the head and shoulders of the remains of a human being. He lay at full length amidst a patch of rank green grass fertilised by the decayed body, a skeleton with fragments of rotten clothing still clinging to it. Alf had his arm under the skull as one would support a sick man, and was murmuring words of affection. He raised his head as I approached but evinced no surprise.

"This is my brother Jack;" he said. "Fancy his coming to the camp last night to show me where he was. We must take him into the nearest station and bury him, for he can't rest here, it's too lonely."

I could not answer. Alf's mind had evidently given way and I could not reason with him. He carried the body back to our camp and I commenced a ghastly ride to the nearest station over seventy miles away, with a madman and a corpse for companions. The third day after starting we arrived at Ulmalong, then the outside station, and here I learnt the story of Alf's twin brother.

He had been a stockman on the place when it was first settled, and had ridden out on his rounds one day and never returned. There was little doubt that the skeleton we brought in was his, but what led the living twin to its resting place? I held my tongue about the track for they would only think I was as mad as poor Alf.

After we buried the remains Alf relapsed into almost constant silence. He was quite harmless and they found him some light work to do about the place, but he died, prematurely aged, in about a year's time. He was buried with his brother.

BLOOD FOR BLOOD

(1892)

Silence everywhere, the spell of heat on everything. Kites, which had been soaring on strong pinions away back in the dry country, swooping down on the grasshoppers, have had to come in to this lonely waterhole tired out and worried; and now sit dozing on the branches of the motionless coolibah. One who had left it too long has had only sufficient strength to reach the water and flounder in, and stands with bedraggled feathers moping at the edge of the muddy pool. There is no animal nor human life to be seen—just a round clay hole, a few withered polygonum bushes, and some gnarled and warped coolibah trees. Around lies a bare plain with a bewildering heat-mist hovering over it.

The slow, hot hours creep on. The sodden kite standing near the water suddenly topples over and falls dead; at times one of the others flops heavily down from its perch, takes a few sips and flies back again. These are the only sounds, the only living movements that break the stagnant monotony.

There is neither track of man nor beast to be seen, but for all that what was once a man is lying there beneath one of the shadeless trees. It has been lying there for over six months, so there is nothing very repulsive about the poor corpse but its shrivelled likeness to humanity. When it staggered in there alive the hole was dry, and it sank down and died. Since then a quick and angry thunderstorm has passed and partly filled the hole, too late. But no prowling dog has found the body, not even the venturesome crow has been to inspect it; the desert has protected it from white tooth and black beak, and it lies there dry and withered, but the form of a man—and a white man, still.

This is the story of that unburied, unwept, untended corpse. It is a story of thirst, of treachery, of revenge.

Years ago, when stations were valuable and all things pastoral looked bright ahead, three men pushed out beyond the bounds of settlement in search of new country. Two of them were fast friends, although there was a considerable difference in their ages. The third was simply on the footing of ordinary friendship and of about the same age as the elder of the other two. The party was completed by a black boy.

Far beyond the lonely water-hole where the weary kites sit watching the silent dead, they came on to good country—fair, rolling downs and deep permanent holes. At one of these they fixed a camp and inspected the country on all sides with a view of dividing the runs fairly. One day the younger of the two friends and the third man went out together. They took a long excursion northward and finding no water, made, the next day, for a small hole they had passed on their way out. Fatal mistake—the hole was dry, with the body of a misled dingo rotting at the bottom, and with thirsty, tired horses, and nearly empty bags, they were now fifty miles from their camp, the nearest water.

They turned out for a short spell and lay down to catch a few moments of slumber. The young man slept soundly, dreaming of long, cool swims in a river; of watching it sparkling and leaping amongst the rocks; then he awoke suddenly to find himself companionless in the desert. He raised himself on his elbow and looked around. The clear starlight showed him nothing; he was actually alone; his mate and all the horses were gone. He went to where they had hung the water-bags on a tree. They were gone, too. He comprehended it all. His treacherous friend had taken the two freshest horses and the remnant of the water, and started for the camp, trusting that one would get there where two could not. The other two horses had probably followed of their own accord, to die in their tracks.

He had no hope that his companion meant to come back with succour. A man who could do such a deed would never suffer his victim to bear witness against him. He had the choice of two deaths—a lingering one where he was, or a quicker one in a desperate attempt to gain the camp. He chose the latter. He had no expectation that his own old friend would come to his relief, for he guessed he would be deceived by some specious lie.

When the end came, as it soon did, and he fell for the last time, he prayed with his dying breath that the man who had wrought his death might die as he did.

Late that night the survivor, with one remaining horse, reached the camp, and told the anxious occupant how his friend had died of thirst; how he had helped him on to the last, and only left his body when aid was useless and his own life in jeopardy. "I must start at daylight and bring his body in if possible," was the answer at last. Then one lay down to sleep the sleep of exhaustion, the other to watch and mourn.

Over-tired men seldom sleep soundly. Some rambling words from the haunted sleeper roused the watcher's attention. He listened, as the dreamer restlessly babbled out his secret. He understood it all, and for an instant his hand was on his revolver; but no. He would have proof, then—

Next morning, with the black boy, he was on his way before the stars were paling. Proof was easily forthcoming by the tracks. The body of his young friend lay by itself on the plain; no horse-tracks led to it, none from it. He had died by himself, and the story of staying with him to the last was false. What use in following the trail back further? He returned to the camp with vengeance in his heart.

It was easily done. The other suspected nothing. One morning the two rode out together for a last look to the southward before returning. Twenty miles from the camp they stopped at a scanty belt of timber; beyond was nothing but a boundless plain.

"Get up one of the trees," said the avenger, "you may be able to see a little better from that elevation."

The other dismounted and complied. He stood on the highest

limb, no great height, and looked all around; nothing visible but the blue mirage. He looked below. His companion was a hundred yards, or more, away leading his horse. He stopped for an instant and turned in his saddle, and the words smote on the listener's ear hotter than the blazing sun-beams: "As you served that poor murdered boy, so I serve you. If by any miracle you survive and I hear of you again amongst men I will take your life wherever I find you." Then he turned and rode away, deaf to calls and entreaties.

Stumbling over the plain, now cursing in impotent rage, now begging and praying for mercy, the guilty man followed the silent figure leading the horse. Followed it until his sweat-blinded eyes could see no longer, and the poor, abandoned wretch felt the lonely horror of the desert encircle him, for he knew he should never see the face of his fellow man again.

He reached the camp during the night. It was deserted. The threat was carried out to the letter. Aye, more, for a ghost sat there by the dead embers, that he only could see, but it drove him forth into the night, and with desperate, hopeless purpose he made for the haunts of men. Who knows what he suffered before his dying footsteps led him to the dry hole, and he crawled under the nearest shade to pant his life out?

* * * * * * *

Next morning the recruited birds take wing for the drought-smitten plains once more, leaving the body of their comrade to keep company with that of the murderer.

IN THE NIGHT

(1892)

"Steady now, old man; do you feel better? Here! Hold hard! *I'm* not a nigger."

The wounded man had struggled desperately as though still struggling with his foes.

One dead white man, speared through the body; one with his head cut open, whom the speaker was trying to revive, and four dead blacks, lying on their faces with outstretched arms—the posture in which niggers usually die who meet with a violent death. The sun had set, and darkness was rapidly closing in. Presently the wounded man regained his senses somewhat.

"How's Joe?" he asked

"If Joe is your mate, I'm afraid it's all up with him, as it would have been with you if I had not come. Not but what you had done pretty well before I came. I can only account for one," and he motioned towards the dead.

"Yes; I remember. Joe was speared at the start. He was picking wood for the fire. How did you come here?"

"I've been after horses all day, and was on my way home when I heard the row. I got here just as you had this crack on the head; and the niggers cleared. I suppose you fellows were bound for the Cloncurry?"

"Yes. Poor old Joe! Are you quite sure he is dead?"

"Quite sure. Now, what's the best thing to do about you? I suppose you can't rise?"

The other shook his head wearily.

"It's fifteen miles to the station. The boss has got a buggy in there, and we'll bring it out for you if you are game to stop here alone while I go. I'll be back by daylight. There's no fear of the blacks turning up again, I know the run of these fellows."

"I'm game," said the wounded man faintly.

"Right. I'll load your revolver up for you, and be back as soon as I can. Keep your pecker up, you're safe enough here."

With this rough but kindly consolation the stockman departed, and the survivor of the two men who had been suddenly attacked by the natives when camping, was left alone. Not a pleasant position, but nerves are not supposed to be known in the outside country.

There was a first-quarter moon, and the shadows soon got darker and darker beneath its feeble light. The man with the broken head had quite recovered his consciousness but he still felt dizzy and weak. It was an awful time to wait until daylight. Supposing the niggers came back again after all! Then he recalled all the stories he had heard of the blacks mutilating the dead bodies of their enemies. If they came back at all it would be for that. Supposing he was unconscious when they came and they commenced on him! He must watch all night to prevent that. Poor Joe, his mate, he wouldn't like him to be cut up by the darkies.

Surely, he thought, one of the bodies had moved. The moon gave such a sickly half-light now it was sinking that it was impossible to make certain. Yes, it was a dark figure creeping up to Joe's body, not one of the dead ones, for he could still count them—one, two, three, four. A live nigger crawling up to hack Joe about. He took aim and fired. That dropped him, he could see him writhing in the streak of light that broke through a rift in the trees. Go and finish him, to save another shot. On his hands and knees he crawled over, picking up a dropped club on the way. Then the silence of the night was broken by fierce and heavy blows, and he crawled back to his tree and fainted.

The moon had set when he opened his eyes again, but, by the pale light of the stars, he saw, to his horror, another black shadow approaching the dead body of his mate. Another successful shot and, full of rage, he again crept over and used the formidable club. But the savages were not to be deterred; one after another the dark forms came creeping up, to fall beneath revolver and club, until at last the man's senses left him.

The day had broken, but the sun was not yet up, when the stockman and another man drove up in the buggy. They jumped out, and hastened to the apparent sleeper, but he was dead.

"Have the niggers been back and killed him?"

The stockman shook his head. "I can't make it out—look at this club in his hand covered with blood and—"

The two stood up and gazed curiously about. One, two, three, four black bodies and one red heap.

"He wasn't like that when I left him," said the stockman, hastily; "he was speared clean."

The head was pounded out of recognition, the body and limbs smashed by maniacal blows; the corpse of the wretched Joe was beaten out of all semblance of humanity.

"There have been no blacks here since I left."

"What can be the meaning of that club in his hand?" was the reply.

THE GHOSTLY
BULLOCK-BELL
(1893)

"Let's go on to the next water," said Dick impatiently.

"Why, it's seven miles and one of our horses is quite lame. No, this place is good enough for me," I returned.

Dick grumbled; but as there was reason on my side he had to give in, and we were soon unsaddled. Usually a very even-tempered fellow my companion seemed strangely put out about something. I did not take much notice—men often get "cranky" in the bush. He smoked long after our blankets were down, and then I dropped off to sleep and left him staring moodily into the fire.

"I was only a boy!"

I awoke with the words ringing in my ears. The moon had risen, but it was a late moon, and seemed only to make the dark shadows darker, and add to the general loneliness around us.

Dick was standing near the dead fire with his hand stretched out as though keeping something at bay. The sickly light of the dying moon did not reveal his face, but his whole attitude expressed supreme horror.

"What on earth is it?" I asked, getting up with a thumping heart.

He laughed strangely and said, "Listen! Can't you hear them?"

I listened. Some curlews were wailing dismally, and that was all; as I told him, curlews always begin to ring out when the moon rises.

"No, no!" he said, "not that; listen again." I did so. Now, whether it was mere fancy stimulated by my companion's strange manner and my sudden waking, I don't know, but it seemed that I distinctly heard a deep-toned bullock-bell toll slowly and monotonously, as when a belled bullock licks himself.

"Pah!" I said, "it's a lost worker."

"Is it?" he answered with a repetition of his queer laugh. "Go to sleep again, old man, it's nothing to do with you."

The bell, if it was a bell, had ceased, and as I still felt drowsy, I drew my blankets over my shoulders and soon dozed off. When I awoke again it was broad daylight.

Dick was very silent all that day (we were on our way back to the station after delivering some fat cattle at L—).

"Do you believe in warnings?" he asked, when we were camped again that night.

"Presentiments?"

"Yes, that's it. Because I've got one, I shan't see this trip out."

"O, bosh," I naturally replied.

"It was at that last camp I killed my young brother."

I thought Dick had gone mad, for he was one of the best natured of men, but he proceeded, as if he had to tell his story:

"I was only sixteen, and he was a little chap of twelve, but quite different from the rest of us. Very willing and sweet-tempered, but shy, and read every book he could get hold of. Well, at that time dad was doing a bit of carrying, and as he was laid up with rheumatism he sent me on a trip with the team, for I was a dandy bull-puncher even then. He told me to take Ben along and try and make a man of him. You know what cruel brutes boys are. I soon found out that Ben was frightened of going away from the camp in the dark and made up my mind to cure him, and so bullied and chivvied him that the poor little begger became as nervous as a girl.

"Now, there's a yarn hanging to that place where we camped last night—something as to murder done by the blacks in the old times. Ben knew every story there was about the country and could tell them well, too. Of course, he had heard this tale. Now the place was haunted by the ghost of a woman who was always searching for her child who had been killed by the natives.

"I made up my mind to cure Ben once and for all. In the middle of the night I woke him and told him that we wanted to start early, so he must go and bring the bullocks up close to the camp. 'There they are,' I said, 'you can hear the bell.'

"The poor little cove looked at me with great big eyes and shivered, for the bullock just then began to lick himself and his bell tolled out like a clock—one, two, three, up to twelve, and stopped. He begged and prayed me to wait until daylight, but I hunted him off with the bullock-whip and followed him up for a bit to make sure he went.

"It was all quiet for a while, but just about the time he would have reached them I heard that bell again toll out solemnly. Then came such a shriek! I heard it distinctly, though he must have been some way off. I tell you I did feel sorry and ran as hard as I could shouting to him. Half-way I met the bullocks coming up to the camp like mad, but the bell was not amongst them. I had great trouble in finding Ben, for he was on the grass in a dead faint, and the moonlight was not strong. I carried him up to camp and he was an awful sight. His arm was stretched out quite stiff, as if to keep something off, and the poor boy's face was all drawn up with fright and his eyes wide open and staring.

"It was a long time before I brought him round, and when I did he was quite silly, and he never got right again, but died soon afterwards."

Dick was silent and so was I.

"Did you find the bullock-bell?" I asked at last.

"No, and I should like to know who rang that bell—and who rang it last night?" he asked.

"You heard it, too! The yarn about the niggers goes," he went on after another pause, "that they sneaked up to the hut ringing a bullock-bell that they had found so that if the people heard any noise they would fancy it was some stray workers."

* * * * * * *

Dick did not see the end of that trip. We stopped next night at a wayside pub, and he drowned his remorse in rum. Worse still, he fell in maudlin love with a girl there, and Peter, the bush-missionary, turning up—he got married.

She is a perfect devil, and when last I saw Dick he was thin as a rake. Better for him had the presentiment been fulfilled in the orthodox way.

MY ONLY MURDER

(1893)

It was simply a choice between killing a man, and outraging all the finer sensibilities of my nature. Had I not done the deed I should have had to appear in another man's eyes as a cold-blooded, selfish ingrate. I swear to you that it was to spare the feelings of both of us that I took upon myself the terrible responsibility of slaying a fellow-creature.

Do I regret the deed? Not at all.

Twelve years ago, I was just coming to the end of my term of partnership in a North Queensland station, and well pleased I was to get out of it, for pastoral property was falling rapidly. My two partners were not so happy over the matter. The rate at which they were buying me out had, under our agreement, been fixed some time previously, and as prices had since steadily fallen, they had to pay me more than the market value. But, then, had stations gone up, as was anticipated by them when the rate was agreed upon, I should have been forced to accept less than the market value, so it was just the fortune of war.

I had to be up on the station by a fixed date, the wet season had arrived, and there was not a day to spare. If I did not attend on the date specified for delivery, it might form a pretext for the other side to repudiate their bad bargain. The rain came down steadily, and I knew that my work was cut out to reach the place in time. Once across the Banderoar river, I was safe, but when I arrived on the bank it was a swim, and fast rising. There was too much at stake to hesitate; crocodiles or not, I must cross. My horse could swim well, I knew, and so could I. It was growing late, so, without more ado, I undressed, strapped my clothes on the saddle, unbuckled the reins, crossed the stirrup-leathers in front, and started.

As soon as old Hielandman (my horse) was out of his depth and swimming straight, I slipped off and swam alongside him. We were nearly two-thirds of the way across when suddenly Hielandman struck against a submerged snag. The shock and the strong current made me foul him, and ere I could get clear he had clipped me on the head with his fore-foot. I don't remember much about what happened immediately afterwards, only it seemed mighty hard to drown just as I was about to retire with a small competency and get married. Then I felt cold, and oh! so sick, and, after an interval, I found myself ashore with a great singing in my ears, and a taste in my mouth as though I had swallowed all the flood-water in North Queensland.

I had been pulled out by one of a party of men camped on the bank I was making for. He had bravely jumped in without waiting to undress, and after being nearly drowned himself, had dragged me ashore. He was standing by the fire, wringing out his wet clothes, and, with the glow of new-born life within me, I thought he was the most glorious fellow I had ever seen.

'By Jove, old man!' he said to me cheerily, 'if I had waited to take my trousers off you would have been feeding the crocodiles now.'

I did not doubt it, and I told him how deeply grateful I felt, and how I could never thank him sufficiently. To die just then would have been especially bitter, and I said so.

Hielandman had got free of the snag and swum to land safely. Beyond the lump on my head there was no damage done. My new friends were a party of drovers returning from delivering a mob of cattle. I camped with them that night, and next morning, with a light heart, departed for my destination. Needless to say, I had assured Jenkins, my rescuer, of my undying gratitude, and told him that whenever he desired it, my home should be his home, and my purse his purse. He took it all very nicely, told me that he was sure I would have done the same for him, that he wanted nothing; but to oblige me, if ever he did become 'stone-broke' he would remember my kind offer.

Twelve years elapsed. The money I had received for my share of the station had, by judicious investment, turned into a nice little fortune. I was married to a wife exactly suited to me, we had three healthy children, and lived in good style in one of the prettiest suburbs of Sydney. I had often told my wife of the gallant way in which Jenkins, whom I had never since seen, plunged into the flooded river and rescued me, and she as often said that it would crown the happiness of her life to see him and thank him with her own lips.

One day I was accosted in George-street by a bearded and sunburnt bushman dressed in unmistakeable slop clothes, who seized me by the hand and ejaculated; 'But for being told, I should never have known you. You look a different sort of fellow to what you did when I pulled you out of the Banderoar. By Jove, old man, had I waited to take off my trousers you'd have been a gone coon!' It was Jenkins, my preserver.

I was delighted to see him, and insisted on his coming out to stay with me. He agreed willingly, and I was at last able to present to my wife the saviour of her husband. That she was disappointed, I could see; but, being a good little woman, she did not let the guest observe it. Truth to tell, I somehow shared her sentiments. I had, perhaps, rather over done my description, and had made my wife expect to see something akin to one of Ouida's heroes. Jenkins certainly did show to better advantage at his own camp fire than in town, in his newly-creased reach-me-downs; but we forgave all that, and made him royally welcome. At dinner he was rather awkward, and insisted on telling my wife the story of my rescue twice over, always emphasising the fact that, had he stopped to doff his trousers, I should have been drowned.

From that date there commenced an ordeal which I would not willingly—nay, one which I could not—again endure. When Jenkins gained a little confidence he became argumentative and dictatorial. I am a sociable man, and my house was a favourite with my friends; but Jenkins sat upon them all. He asserted his opinions loudly and emphatically, and when unacquainted with the place or topic under discussion, always had some friend of the past to quote who knew all about it. He held views on the labour troubles which were rank heresy to my circle of pastoral friends, but never did he hesitate to loudly assert them. And yet he was a good fellow, evidently looking upon me as a sort of a creation of his own.

'Ah!' he would say, as we stood regarding my pretty house, the sunny, flowering garden, and the children playing on the lawn, 'we should never have seen this if you had gone to the bottom of the Banderoar. If I had stopped to take off—'

I felt this, too, and wrung his hand in response. Perhaps that very evening we had a small dinner-party, and when I saw a demure smile steal over everybody's face, I knew that in the coming silence I should hear Jenkins describing what would have happened had he 'stopped to pull'— Then, I could have slain him. We had not a lady friend to whom he had not confided, in a loud voice, that singular instance of his presence of mind in refraining from undressing. Those male friends whom Jenkins had not insulted, I had quarrelled with on account of their frivolity in always asking me if Jenkins had 'taken his trousers off yet?'

But the worst of it was that the dear fellow really believed that he was affording me the most exquisite happiness in entertaining him. He was convinced that for twelve years I had been pining to pay off my debt, and that now I was enraptured. He was my shadow, and reverenced everything belonging to me. How could I break this charm by declaring that I was tired of him? It would have been worse than heartless.

At last my patient wife began to grow short-tempered and restless. She told me plainly once that Jenkins had not pulled her out of the Banderoar, and that she did not see why she should put up with him any longer. I tried to point out that as she and I were one it really amounted to the same thing, but she replied that it certainly did not. We were not married when it happened, and if I had been drowned she would have married somebody else—perhaps someone not oppressed by having barnacled to him a devoted rescuer who was eternally advertising that he had not taken off his trousers.

I felt that a climax neared—and that something must be done to prevent the breaking up of my once happy home. At times I meditated investing a portion of my capital in a small selection somewhere and getting Jenkins to go and look after it for me, but he expressed himself as being so contented where he was, and so greatly averse to returning to the bush, that I abandoned the idea. Now, too, he began to indulge in sheepish flirtations with the maids, and my wife sternly requested me to 'speak to your friend.' I attempted to do so, but when I saw his mild, affectionate eyes gazing at me, and knew that he was thinking of the time when he struggled beneath the muddy flood waters, without taking off his trousers, I broke down. I could not wound his gentle heart.

It came to me suddenly—the inspiration, the solution of the difficulty. Jenkins must die!

Once resolved, I acted. I knew it was wrong, but I couldn't help it, any more than Deeming could help killing his wives, or Mr. Neill Cream could help poisoning all those poor girls in London. Jenkins was a friendless bushman; I was a man with responsibilities and a family. Their happiness stood first, and it was kinder to Jenkins to kill him at once than to undeceive him.

I shall not enter into details as to the carrying out of my design. Enough to say that it was perfectly successful. I have no intention of teaching the art of murder made easy. Jenkins died peacefully and painlessly. The doctor said that his constitution had been undermined by exposure and hardship. When he was confined to his bed my wife forgave him everything, and nursed him with unremitting care. I have even seen tears in the poor little woman's eyes as she murmured that she was afraid we should lose him. Other people came to see him, and he passed away happy in the firm belief that he left behind him a large circle of sorrowing friends.

I buried him in my own ground in Waverley cemetery, and erected a neat stone with a suitable inscription, stating that he had risked his life in preserving me from death.

All my old friends are back again. Everybody has told me what a manly fellow I was, and how they admired my social pluck in not looking coldly upon an old benefactor who did not happen to be quite up to the Government House standard of dress and manners. My conscience is easy.

AN UNQUIET SPIRIT
(1894)

I.

I hold my father's memory in the greatest respect. I have every reason for doing so.

Although his motives of life and mine were diametrically opposed, this was never made a bone of contention between us. I fell into step and marched dutifully with his views until his death, at a ripe age, left me free to live in a manner more congenial to my disposition.

My father was a squatter—a fine healthy fellow of the old school, that is to say, a man who believed in the work of his own hands, and was never happy when away from the station. He was devoted to cattle and horse-breeding, and, although the chances had many times been presented to him of leasing a huge area, and stocking it with sheep by the aid of a friendly bank, he had always steadily refused. Thanks to this, he died fairly well off.

Many years before his death, I am happy to think, he had succeeded to the height of his ambition. His compact, if small, run was as skillfully divided that it could almost work itself. His cattle were bred to that pitch of perfection that the DAV brand was known throughout Australia. His horses were sought for eagerly as hacks or stock horses. To keep everything up to this standard became the old man's one idea. Method and order were his fetish, and when he died he left me instructions to bury him in his working clothes beside the stockyard. The familiar sound of the trampling hoofs would, he thought, soothe him in the long, last slumber. I am afraid this idea was not a pronounced success.

I was twenty-five when my father died. He had been a widower for twenty years, and soon after I laid him in the grave, in strict accordance with his wishes, I commenced to look out for a manager for Braganall Station. Although I had successfully concealed it during my father's lifetime, I hated bush life as much as he loved it. He died, happy in the thought that his son would be a worthy successor in the management of the station he had created, little dreaming that that son yearned to become a barrister.

I soon found a competent manager named Dodson, took up my abode in Sydney, and began reading for the Bar. I had many advantages; an independent income, a good education, and a first-rate physical training. I worked hard for nearly a year, then, feeling the need of a little relaxation, I ran up to Braganall to spend a few weeks. Everything seemed to be in good working order, although I could not help noticing a falling off in little things from the severe discipline of my father's time, but then I knew he had been a martinet, and laid small stress upon this.

One evening, as the dusk was closing in, Dodson and I sat smoking on the verandah in that meditative silence bushmen enjoy so much. Two of the men, returning to their quarters, passed within earshot.

"Bill," I heard one of them say in the calm stillness of the hour, "did yer put them slip-rails on one side?"

"No, I forgot," replied the other.

"Better go back and do it, or Old Danvers will be around after you!"

Without a word the man turned and went back, and the other walked on.

What on earth did it mean?

"Old Danvers" was my father.

Dodson must have heard the remark as well. The men, evidently, had not noticed us, as we were well within the shadow of the verandah; therefore they had not lowered their voices.

"What does that mean about 'Old Danvers'?" I said.

"I am sure I don't know," replied Dodson.

This I felt was an untruth. "Mr Dodson," I remarked in a severe tone; "I am sure you do know, therefore I expect a plain answer to my question. What did that man mean by saying that my father would be around after him?"

Dodson hesitated, then he blurted out: "The men have some foolish yarn that Mr Danvers, your father, walks."

"Walks!" I repeated. "His ghost appears?"

"Something of the sort. If anything is left neglected the man who did it can't rest—he dreams of your father until he has to get up and go and do what he left undone, even if it's in the middle of the night."

I could not help laughing. "The ghost must be a good overseer," I said; "I suppose your men are always leaving, with this notion going about?"

"Not at all. They are not a bit afraid—they say he always speaks quite kindly to them."

"More in sorrow than in anger," I quoted.

"Precisely so. I saw him once myself. He looked in at my bedroom window; stared at me until I had to get up. Then I found that I had left the garden gate open, and one of the milkers had got in."

I scarcely knew what to think of this communication. Bushmen, as a rule, are not in the least superstitious—they have too much night-work to fancy that the dark hours have uncanny denizens peculiar to themselves. Although I practiced cross-examination on Dodson I could get no more out of him, and, of course, it was useless asking the men. I remained on the station for another fortnight, but heard nothing more about the shade of my departed parent.

II.

Two months after my visit to Braganall, I was sitting in my chambers in Sydney, intent on my work, when, happening to raise my eyes, I saw my father in the room. He was dressed just as he was buried; he advanced to the table, and, without speaking, commenced to put the things on it straight. This was an old habit of his, as I at once recognised. Anything on the table not in its exact place always annoyed him. When everything was neat and square he sank into a chair and smiled kindly at me. Now I felt not the least surprise, strange to say. It seemed the most natural thing in the world for my father to pay me a visit, although I was fully aware that he was buried near the stockyard on Braganall.

"Jimmy," he said, "I don't think you have acted quite fair to me."

"What's the matter, governor?" I asked.

"Why did you not let me know you preferred this sort of thing?" and he indicated the papers on the table. "I thought you meant to look after the place yourself."

"Honestly, I should have told you," I replied, "but I thought you would be more contented if you did not know."

My father shook his head. "I have nothing to say against Dodson," he went on; "he is a very well-meaning young man, but he is going to make a great mistake, and I want you to write and stop him."

I nodded, but kept silence.

My father then went into a detail of station-management with which I need not trouble the reader. I could see (for was I not my father's pupil?) that it was just the kind of mistake that a young and enthusiastic manager like Dodson would fall into. I at once wrote the letter, and enclosed it in an envelope, my father watched complacently. When I had finished he said:

I don't want to annoy you, Jim, but you see it's this way. I'm in Kama at present."

"Kama?"

"Yes, Kama Loka. I am on my way to Devachan, but these little worries rather delay me, for you see Kama is only an astral counterpart of our physical existence, and until I am quite satisfied that I need not bother any more about Braganall my entity will not be properly established in Devachan."

"I understand," I said, but, of course, I didn't.

My father beamed on me with his old kindly look, and left.

He came to see me on little matters, once or twice after that. Several people came in and saw him there, but they only took him for a queer sort of client. Medicine and the law are privileged that way.

Once, however, he put me out a little, and forced me into the meanest action of my life. It was at a garden party, and a swell affair at that, when I suddenly became aware that all eyes were turned my way, and that my father, in his bush dress, was standing by me.

"Jim," he said in an undertone, "I can't help it, I've had no rest for a fortnight. There's the gate-post of the drafting yard been pushed out of place, the gate doesn't hang plumb, and Dodson doesn't get it straightened up."

"I'll send him a telegram about it at once," I answered, hastily.

"You will?" queried the old man. "You know I'll never get to Devachan at this rate."

"I will," I affirmed, and then, for everyone was looking at us, I put my hand in my pocket, then into his hand, as though I was giving alms to a persistent begger, and he went away satisfied.

Now, to pass off the shade of one's father as an intrusive loafer who had to be got rid of at any price, is, I think, the greatest piece of moral cowardice a man can be guilty of. I have never fully recovered my self-respect since.

These constant visits, however, made trouble upon the station. Dodson felt aggrieved that I should be always writing or wiring up about petty little things that might well be left to him, and, moreover, concluded that I must have a spy on the place who supplied me with the information. This led to his resignation, and put me in such a fix that, in desperation, I decided to sell the station.

Our neighbour on Braganall was an old friend of my father's, and a man after his own heart. His two sons, unlike me, were squatters to the backbone; so I wrote to him and put the place under offer. Somewhat to my relief, my father or his astral counterpart, did not object to this. He seemed to think that, failing me, the sons of his old friend would do justice to Braganall. Negotiations were, therefore, soon concluded, and Manxton became the owner of the well-known DAV herd.

I had now some peace from the constant visitations of my father, and about that time I fell deeply in love. Contrary to proverbial wisdom, the course of our true love ran smoothly throughout, and our wedding day was approaching when I received a letter from young Manxton which somewhat unsettled me. We were old friends from boyhood's time, therefore he addressed me without any ceremony. "Look here, old fellow," his letter ran, "when the old man bought this place I don't think he took delivery of any ghosts; at least, they were not mentioned in the agreement. I wish you could induce your ancestral spook to let me manage the station my own way." Young Manxton had a blunt way of putting it, but under the circumstances, I felt I could pardon him.

I saw fresh trouble ahead, but could do nothing but write back and treat his letter as a joke.

III.

It wanted but a week to our wedding day, and Laura and I were deep in confidential conversation one evening when the astral figure of my father appeared. Laura gave a big jump and a little shriek at his sudden appearance, then sat quiet, whilst my father said:

"Jim, you must do something for me. I know you can't properly interfere, but young Manxton is going to sell Silverside and go in for breeding trotters."

At this moment Laura sprang up with a loud cry. "Jim! Jim!"

she half shrieked, "it's your father, I know him from the likeness you showed me. Oh! oh! it's his ghost!"—and she went off
into a faint, and I caught her and put her on the sofa. I looked
reproachfully at the old man and he went out without opening
the door, which was contrary to his usual habit. Then Laura's
mother came in and wanted to know what the matter was and
who the stranger was she met in the hall. I said weakly I did not
know, but would go after him if she would look after Laura, for
I was anxious to get away before she came to.

I passed a restless night, and the next morning the post
brought me a letter of farewell from my sweetheart. She pointed
out clearly that there were but two conclusions to arrive at.
Either my father was not dead and had committed some criminal action which necessitated his disappearance, or it was his
ghost. Now, in either case our marriage was an impossibility—
she could not marry a man whose father had served a term in
gaol; nor could she become the wife of one who had a ghostly
progenitor popping up at convenient and inconvenient times. To
this there was no answer, at least I had none to offer; and it was
not until I had worried my brains for hours that I saw a ray of
hope ahead.

I wrote to Laura and her mother saying that I would offer
them a satisfactory and ample explanation. Then I wrote to
Manxton and asked him to delay the sale of Silverside (one of
the sires of the Braganall stud) until he heard further from me.
Then I sat and waited.

I was not disappointed; my father, looking very penitent,
made his appearance. "I'm awfully sorry, Jim, but I was so upset
when I found out that Manxton was going to sell Silverside that
I came in without thinking."

"It's been my own fault as well," I returned, for I could not
bear to see the old chap so miserable. "However, I think I have
found out a way to put things straight again. In the first place, I
am going to buy Braganall back."

My father shook his head; his business shrewdness was
evidently a portion of the astral counterpart of his physical exis-

tence. "He'll make you pay through the nose when he finds you want it. I know Manxton."

"But I think you can assist me to get it back at my own figure," I returned, and showed him young Manxton's letter.

"Now, can't you make things so ghostly uncomfortable up there that he'll be glad to almost give me the place back?"

My father became perfectly luminous with delight. "Bless you, boy!" he said, and was about to vanish, when I recalled him.

"There's more to be done yet. I have to make it right with Laura. I am going to manage Braganall myself, now that I am about to be married, but, for all that, some little slips may occur which might worry you and delay you on your passage to—where is it?"

"Devachan," said my father.

"Devachan, yes. Do you think you could materialise a letter when you have anything to say? I shall probably keep a room somewhere in Sydney where you could write."

"Certainly I could. Why did I not think of it before?"

"Now, will you be here to-morrow at eleven o'clock, and, before Laura and her mother, give me your word that you will in future confine yourself to letter-writing when anything goes wrong. You see it's this way, Dad. I enjoy seeing you immensely, but the women, you know, are prejudiced."

"I quite understand it," replied the shade, and departed.

I called on Mrs Lyntott, Laura's mother, who is a remarkably strong-minded woman, and laid the whole case before her. She reconciled me to Laura, and they agreed to meet my father at my rooms in the morning.

The inconsistency of womankind! Before that meeting concluded they had taken such a liking to that astral being that they both regretted deeply the compact that had been entered into. "I should have been very glad to see you occasionally, Mr Danvers," said my prospective mother-in-law, and Laura uttered a like wish. However, the thing was done. A ghost must keep its word, once passed; and we parted with mutual feelings of regret.

Before leaving, my father whispered to me: "I gave young Manxton such a night of it last night I expect you'll hear from him to-day."

It is now many years since this happened, and as I have never received a materialised letter, I presume that earthly matters have ceased to trouble the good old gentleman, and my management of Braganall has been satisfactory. His conscious unit has, I hope, passed from Kama Loka to the higher spiritual plane of Devachan.

THE BOUNDARY
RIDER'S STORY
(1895)

THE storm that had been brewing all the afternoon, gathered, towards nightfall, in great black clouds, cleft every now and then by jagged streaks of vivid lightning. Just after dark it burst in a fierce rush of rain and boom and rage of thunder. Blinding as the lightning was, it as only by its assistance that a belated traveller could keep his horse on the bridle-track he was following; for when darkness fell between the flashes, it seemed as though a black pall had been dropped over everything.

With heads bent down, the sodden man and horse plodded on until the rider found himself on a main road into which the track debouched.

"Another mile;" he muttered to himself; "and I'll come to old Mac's." He touched his horse slightly with the spur and glanced nervously round. The travelling now improved, and ere long a dim light proclaimed his approach to some kind of habitation; soon afterwards he pulled up at the verandah of a small bush inn.

"Are you in Mac?" he roared with a voice that outdid the thunder, as he splashed down from his horse into a pool of water, and hastily proceeded to ungirth.

"Who's there?" returned a voice, and the owner of it came out and peered into the darkness.

"Smithson! Lend us a pair of hobbles."

"Jupiter! what are you doing out here such a night as this?" asked Mac as he handed him the hobbles.

"'Cos I'm a fool, that's why," said Smithson as he stooped down and buckled the straps. "Can't go wrong for feed, I suppose?"

"Right up to the back door. Come in and get a change."

Hanging his saddle and bridle on a peg riven into the slab, the late traveller followed his host into the bar. Mac put his head out of the back door and roared to somebody to bring in some tea; then reached down a bottle and placed it, with a glass, before his visitor. Smithson filled out a stiff drink, tossed it off neat, and gave a sigh of satisfaction. Having got a dry shirt and trousers, the traveller proceeded to simultaneously enjoy a good meal and his host's curiosity.

"It's that cursed Chinaman hunted me. The one who cut his throat."

"Did you see him?" asked Mac in an awed voice.

"I did, indeed, with the bandages round his neck just as they found him. I meant to go in to the station and tell the boss he must send out somebody else. When I remembered that you were nearer and came over for a bit of company. Now, don't laugh at a fellow—just you go and stop in my hut for a night or two."

"No fear," returned Mac emphatically.

"Well I thought I didn't care for anything," said the boundary-rider, "but this caps all. You should see—cripes! what's that!" For a long, lugubrious howl sounded outside, followed by the rattling of a chain. Both men forced a very artificial laugh.

"It's Boxer," said Smithson, Suddenly illumined. "I left him tied up, but he's got his chain loose and followed me."

A very wet and woe-begone dog came in at his call. Smithson detached the chain from his collar and they sat down again.

"Boxer didn't fancy being left alone," remarked Mac.

"Seems not. It gave me quite a turn when he howled like that. What do you say?" Taking the hint, Mac arose and the two went into the bar.

"All alone to-night?" asked Smithson.

"Yes, the missus is in town; there's only deaf Ben in the kitchen."

"Well, I hope that d——d Chinaman won't follow the dog."

"Don't get talking like that. How did he come to cut his throat? It was before my time."

"The fellow who had the contract for the paddock-fence lived in the hut with two men, and the Chinaman was cooking for them; he was there for over six months. Chris, the contractor, he paid off the other men; and he and the Chinaman stopped for a week longer to finish up some odd jobs. One morning Chris came in to the station as hard as he could split—the Chow had cut his throat the night before. Chris said he wasn't quite dead, and that he had tied up the wound as well as he could. The super and another man went back with him, but when they arrived the Chinkie was as dead as a door-nail. Now, the strange thing was that the stuff Chris had tied round his throat was quite clean; but when they moved the body, with Chris holding the shoulders, the blood commenced to soak through, and turned them all quite faint. All Chris knew about it was that when he awoke in the morning the Chinaman was lying outside with a sheath-knife in his hand and his throat cut."

"And did you see nothing until to-night?"

"No. Just after dark I heard someone calling, and I went to the door and looked out. I can tell you I just did get a fright, for there by the lightning I saw the Chinaman standing, with bloody rags round his neck, and the knife in his hand."

Mac shuddered and passed the bottle.

"Now," said Smithson, "comes the strange part of it. That shout, or coo-ee, I heard, came from some way off, and that there ghost I saw was not looking at me, but listening for that shout, and smiling like a man who was expecting a friend coming."

"What did you do?"

"I slammed the door to, picked up my saddle and bridle and got out of the back window. I knew my old moke was not far off, but I was that scared I left his hobbles where I took them off. I heard Boxer howling as I rode away."

* * * * * * *

It was a beautiful morning after the storm as Smithson rode in to the head station. So bright and cheerful was it that the boundary-rider felt rather ashamed of the yarn he was going to tell and half-inclined to turn back. However, he went on and had an interview with the superintendent. Naturally, he was laughed at, and this, of course, made him stubborn.

"I'll tell you what I'll do," said Morrison, the super, at last. I'll go back with you this afternoon and stop the night with you, and we'll see if we can't quiet the Chinaman."

Smithson agreed, remarking that perhaps it was only on one particular night he walked, as he had never seen him before.

Morrison turned up an old diary and glanced through it. "Oh, that's nothing," he said, pushing it away.

* * * * * * *

The two men rode up to the lonely hut, Morrison slightly ahead. "There's something queer there," he said, pulling up. Smithson stared eagerly; while Boxer, who was with them, sat down on the road and howled dismally.

Recovering themselves, the two rode on. A man was lying in front of the door stretched out in death. Dismounting, they approached and examined him.

"No, no!" cried Smithson, "don't touch him—we mustn't till the police come."

With an impatient gesture Morrison stooped down and turned the dead face up. In the throat was a rude wound, and in the open eyes a terror more than human.

"It's Christy," said the superintendent in a quiet voice.

"The man who employed the Chinaman?" asked Smithson in an unsteady tone.

"Yes. How, in the name of God, did he come here? Tell me

exactly what you saw and heard."

"I was in the doorway, as I told you," said the boundary-rider excitedly, "standing just there, and by the flash of lightning I saw the Chinaman here"—and he indicated the spot.

"He was standing like this"—and he bent forward like a man watching and listening—looking in the direction the cry came from over there."

"And you saw a knife in his hand?"

"Yes, and he was smiling as though expecting somebody he wanted to see badly."

Morrison put his hand on the other's shoulder and pointed to the knife in the hand of the corpse. "Was it that knife?"

"It looks like it," chattered Smithson.

The superintendent glanced about and shook his head. "No tracks to tell tales," he said.

"No, all the storm was on afterwards."

Morrison mused a bit. "Get a sheet of bark," he said, "or one of those sheets of iron there. We must put him inside, and then I'll give you a letter to take in to the police. You can get back with the sergeant by to-morrow morning, and we'll bury him."

"You're not going to stop here?" said Smithson.

"No," returned Morrison. "I'll get over to Mac's."

They lifted the dead man on to the sheet of iron and carried him into his old dwelling-place, Smithson evidently much averse to the job. Morrison tried to close the staring eyes before they put one of Smithson's blankets over the corpse; but the lids were rigid. "Evidently he didn't like the look of where he's gone to," he muttered. The two set out—one to the little township, the other to Mac's pub.

The night was as calm and fine as though thunder were unknown. Morrison mused deeply over the tragic occurrence, trying to recall all he knew of the past and put a common-sense construction on it, but he failed, and only made himself nervous.

"There's one very strange thing about the affair," he said to Mac, when they were discussing it that evening. "When I paid Chris for the contract—over which he lost, by the way—I gave him separate cheques to pay off his men, including one for the Chinaman of about $30. That cheque was not found, and, moreover, it has never been presented to this day."

"What sort of a fellow was Chris?"

"A good fencer, but a stupid fellow, not fit to take contracts. I often wonder if he took the cheque off the body before he came in."

"Then why didn't he present it?"

"That was his idea, no doubt, at first. But I tell you he could scarcely read or write and I suppose after he heard me tell the sergeant that I would give the bank notice and instruct them to watch for the cheque, he got frightened."

"Before that he imagined that one cheque was the same as another, and that you could not trace a particular one?"

"Yes, just about what he would think."

"Perhaps he killed the Chinaman?"

"Perhaps he did," returned Morrison, after a long and thoughtful pause.

By sunrise Morrison and Mac were at the boundary-rider's hut, and soon afterwards the sergeant and Smithson arrived. The examination did not take long, and they prepared to dig a grave.

"Better not bury him alongside the other," said the sergeant.

"No," replied Morrison. "Let's see, we buried him over against that tree; didn't we, sergeant?"

"Yes, and not very deep either. It was dry weather, the ground was hard, and we came upon a big root."

The obsequies were not prolonged. Sewn up in the blanket, the dead man was soon laid in a damp grave. While the others were filling it up, Morrison, still thinking of Mac's remark, strolled over to the spot where the Chinaman slept, not expecting to see any mark of the place left. He started and turned pale.

"Here! Quick! Come here!" he cried.

The men came hastily, the tools still in their hands. The earth over the old grave had been loosened and disturbed.

"My God! he's got up!" murmured Smithson. "I've heard

they can't rest out of their own country."

"Give me a shovel," cried Morrison; and commenced to carefully scrape the earth away. The sergeant assisted him, and they soon came to the skeleton, for nearly everything but the bones was gone.

"What, do you expect to find?" asked the sergeant.

Morrison was carefully brushing the loose dirt off the thing with a bough.

"Look here!" he said.

Clasped in the fleshless hand was the missing cheque

"It wasn't buried with him, I'll swear," said the sergeant.

"And if it had been, it would have decayed long since," answered Morrison.

"He got up and took it from Chris last night. He was bound to get his cheque back," said Mac.

"Well I'm going to pack up my traps," remarked Smithson.

"I'll send down and have this hut shifted," said Morrison. "Although now he's got what he wanted, I don't suppose, he'll get up again."

"By gum, I won't trust him," said the boundary-rider.

A STRANGE OCCURRENCE ON HUCKEY'S CREEK

(1897)

The heat haze hung like a mist over the plain. Everything seen through it appeared to palpitate and quiver, although not a breath of air was stirring. The three men, sitting under the iron-roofed verandah of the little roadside inn, at which they had halted and turned out their horses for a mid-day spell, were drenched with perspiration and tormented to the verge of insanity by flies. The horses, finding it too hot to keep up even the pretence of eating, had sought what shade they could find, and stood there in pairs, head to tail.

"Blessed if there isn't a loony of some kind coming across the plain," said one of the men suddenly.

The others looked, and could make out an object that was coming along the road that led across the open, but the quivering of the atmosphere prevented them distinguishing the figure properly until within half-a-mile of the place.

"Hanged if I don't believe it's a woman!" said the man who had first spoken, whose name was Tom Devlin.

"It is so," said the other two, after a pause.

Devlin walked to where the water-bags had been hung to cool, and, taking one down, went out into the glaring sunshine to meet the approaching figure.

It *was* a woman. Weary, worn-out, and holding in her hand a dry and empty water-bag. Although only middle-aged, she had that tanned and weather-beaten appearance that all women get, sooner or later, in North Queensland.

With a sigh of gratitude she took the water-bag from Tom's hand and put the bottle-mouth to her lips, bush fashion. There is no more satisfactory drink in the world for a thirsty person than that to be obtained straight from the nozzle of a water-bag.

Tom regarded the woman pityingly. She was dressed in common print and a coarse straw hat, and looked like the wife of a teamster.

"Where have you come from, missus, and what brought you here?"

"We were camped on Huckey's Creek, and my husband died last night. I couldn't find the horses this morning, so I started back here."

"Fifteen miles from here," said Devlin. "We are going to camp there tonight, and will see after it. You come in and rest."

He took her back to the little inn, where she could get something to eat and a room to lie down in. Then they caught their horses and started, promising to look up the strayed animals and attend to everything, according to the directions the woman gave them.

The three men arrived at Huckey's Creek about an hour before sundown. They examined the place thoroughly, but neither dray, horses, nor anything else was visible. The marks of a camp and the tracks bore out the woman's story, but that was all.

"Deuced strange!" said Devlin. "Somebody must have come along and shook the things, but what did they do with the man's body? They wouldn't hawk that about with them."

"Here's the mailman coming," said one of the others, as a man coming towards them with a pack-horse hove in sight.

They awaited his approach, standing dismounted on the bank of the creek. The mailman's thirsty horses plunged their noses deep in the water and drank greedily.

"I say, you fellows," he called out, "you didn't see a woman on foot about anywhere, did you?"

"Yes," replied Tom, "she is back at the shanty."

"Wait till I come up," said the mailman. When his horses had finished he rode the bank to the others.

"Such a queer go," he said. "About five or six miles from here I met a tilted dray with horses, driven by a man who looked down-right awful. He pulled up, and so did I. Then he said, staring straight before him, and not looking at me, 'You didn't meet a woman on foot, mate, did you?'

"I told him no, and asked him where he was going. 'Oh,' he said, just in the same queer way, 'I'm going on until I overtake her.'

"'You'd best turn back,' I said. 'It's twenty-five miles to the next water; and I tell you I'd have been bound to see her.' He shook his head and drove on, and you say the woman's back at the shanty?"

"Yes; it's about the rummiest start I ever come across. The woman turned up at Britten's today, about 1 o'clock, on foot, and said that her husband died during the night; that she could not find the horses, and had come in on foot for help."

"I suppose he wasn't dead, after all, and when the horses came in for water he harnessed up and went ahead, looking for his wife, in a dazed, stupid sort of a way."

"I suppose that is it," said Devlin. "Are you going on to Britten's tonight?" he asked the mailman.

"Yes."

"You might tell the woman that her husband has come-to, and started on with the dray. After we have had a spell, we'll go after him. He can't be far."

"No," replied the mailman, as he prepared to ride off. "He looked like a death's-head when I saw him. So-long."

The men turned their horses out and had a meal and a smoke; by this time they were talking about starting when the noise of an approaching dray attracted their attention.

"He's coming back himself," said Tom.

The dray crossed the creek and made for the old camp, where the driver pulled-up and got out. The full moon and risen, and it was fairly light.

"Don't speak," said Devlin; "let us see what he is going to do."

The figure unharnessed the horses with much groaning, and hobbled them; then it took its blankets out of the dray and spread them underneath and lay down.

"Let's see if we can do anything for him," said Devlin, and they approached.

"Can we help you, mate?" he asked.

There was no answer.

He spoke again. Still silence.

"Strike a match, Bill, "he said; "it's all shadow under the dray." Bill did as desired, and Devlin peered in. He started back.

"Hell!" he cried, "the man *did* die when the woman said. He's been dead forty-eight hours!"

THE UNHOLY EXPERIMENT OF MARTIN SHENWICK, AND WHAT CAME OF IT

(1898)

I knew that Shenwick had been studying the occult for a long time, but being a hardened sceptic, I was not prepared to accept the wonderful progress and results that, he said, had so far rewarded him. All the experiments he essayed for my conversion had turned out failures. Therefore, when he came to me and stated that he had discovered how to resuscitate the dead, provided they were not too long deceased, I frankly told him that I did not believe him.

He was used to my blunt way of speaking, and did not resent it, but proceeded to explain how, after death, the soul hovered about the body for some time, and if you could induce the soul to re-enter the body, the late departed would be given a fresh lease of life.

Several difficulties suggested themselves to me, which Shenwick would not listen to. What, for instance, I said, if a man were blown into fragments by a dynamite explosion, how will you find and unite the pieces? If he were hanged, and his neck dislocated, how would you fix his spine up again? If he had his head chopped off—. Here Shenwick interrupted me to state that he meant only cases of natural death, the decay of the vital forces, not mangling and mutilation. He explained that the emancipation of the spirit for a short period inspired it with fresh vigor, and it came back rejuvenated and strong.

"How are you going to try your experiment?" I asked. "Corpses are not knocking about everywhere."

"I admit that is a stumbling block," he said, "but it may be got over. Would you object to putting a temporary end to your existence in the cause of science?"

I told him in language more forcible than polite that I would put an end, final, not temporary, to his existence first.

He accepted this seriously, and informed me that that would not avail, as I would not be competent to conduct the experiments.

We parted for the time, and I believe he spent most of his time searching for a fresh corpse. I know he applied at the hospital, and was ejected with scorn and derision. He also visited the morgue, but as most of the bodies that came there were "demn'd damp, moist, unpleasant bodies," they were no use to him.

"I've got him," he said, one day, stealing into my room on tiptoe as though he thought that the corpse upon whom he had designs would hear him.

"Got whom?" I asked, "the corpse you have been looking for?"

"No, he's not a corpse yet; I'm not going to make him one. Don't stare like that. He's dying, and I have agreed to keep him in comfort till he dies. He's got a churchyard cough, and drinks colonial beer by the gallon. Will you come and see him this evening?"

I said I would, and went on with my work, as he closed the door, softly and mysteriously, for what reason I know not. I went to Shenwick's that evening. He occupied three residential chambers in a large building, and found that he had given up his bedroom to the subject, who was established in comfort and luxury. As a subject, the man was probably as good as any other, but he was by no means prepossessing, and the language he used to Shenwick was painful to listen to.

"It's unfortunate, you know," said my poor deluded friend, "but since he has been taken care of and doctored, I am afraid he's getting better. Now, he would have been dead by this time if he had been left in the Domain. There was a drenching rain last night that would have finished him off out of hand."

A voice was heard from the next room, demanding beer, adjective beer, in a husky whisper.

"This is my only hope," said Shenwick, as he filled a pint pot from a keg. "The doctor says he is not to have it, but I take the liberty of differing from the doctor."

He took the beer in to his subject, and got cursed for his pains.

"He was quite resigned to death when I picked him up," said Shenwick sadly, when he came back; "but since he has been made comfortable he wants to live."

"Small wonder," I returned, laughing.

"It's no joke; by my agreement for his body I am bound to keep him as long as he lives."

"Well, we must try to upset that, if he does live. I have not seen your agreement; but, speaking as a lawyer, I should say it was not legal."

About three weeks after this Shenwick opened my office door, put his head inside, uttered the mysterious words, "Be prepared for a message this evening," and disappeared. I concluded that the subject had caved in after all, and was on the brink of the grave.

The message duly arrived before I left my office, and after dinner I went to see Shenwick. True enough the subject had departed this life, and his mortal, and very ugly, frame was in the possession of my friend, together with a doctor's certificate. He was now at liberty to conduct his experiments and prove the truth of his theory. He asked me to remain, and witness the result, to which I consented, and as he informed me that the small hours of the morning were most favourable, I took the opportunity of having a sleep on a sofa in the outer room, while Shenwick watched his beloved subject.

Shenwick woke me at about two o'clock. I got up stiff and cross, as a man generally is after sleeping in his clothes on a sofa.

"Hush!" he said, in that mysterious whisper he had affected of late. "I am now sure of success. I tried some passes just now, and I am confident that a spark of animation followed."

I muttered a tired swear word, and followed him into the bedroom. Shenwick lowered the light, and commenced his mesmeric or hypnotic hocus pocus over the dead subject. In the dim light it was a most uncanny exhibition, and the more excited Shenwick grew the more antics he cut with his hands, waving and passing and muttering.

Now what happened is almost incredible, had I not seen it myself; but that grim and ghastly corpse on the bed rose up in a sitting position, gasped and choked once or twice, and then broke out into the vigorous cry of a healthy, lusty infant. For an instant the most cowardly terror assailed me, and I confess that I had it in my mind to cut and run for it, when I noticed Shenwick, after swaying to and from, pitched headlong on the floor in a dead faint. That restored me to my proper senses, and I went and picked him up and tried to restore him.

Meanwhile the hideous thing on the bed still kept blubbering and crying. If you shut your eyes you would swear that here was a baby of forty-lung power in the room.

Shenwick at last recovered. "It was a success," he gasped.

"If you call that row a success, it was," I answered.

He listened intently, and a pained look came into his face. He was evidently greatly puzzled. "Let me go into him by myself," he said at last. I cordially agreed, and he went into the bedroom, and I solaced my nerves with a good strong nip of whiskey. Gradually the crying stopped, and Shenwick came tiptoeing out and told me that the subject had fallen into a nice, quiet sleep.

"It's awkward, very," he said; "but at any rate the experiment succeeded."

"What's awkward?" I asked.

"I left it too long. I told you that the spirit rejuvenated, grow young, after its release from the body. This spirit has grown too young—it's gone back to infancy."

"Then you'll have to rear it as an infant; but you won't find anyone to look after it in its present state."

"I'm afraid not; I'll have to bring it up by hand myself. It's hungry now, poor thing. Isn't there a chemist who keeps open all night?" I directed him to one, and he asked me if I would mind looking after it while he went out and bought a feeding-bottle and some food. "If it cries, try and amuse it," he said, as he left the room; and I heard his footsteps go down the stairs, rousing strange echoes in the great empty building. I called myself all the fools I could think of for having anything to do with Shenwick and his confounded experiments, and settled down to my dreary watch.

Sure enough, the horrid thing woke up, and commenced to cry again. Not being a family man, I had not the remotest idea how infants were to be soothed and beguiled to rest and silence. I had an inane notion that you said, "Goo, goo," or "Cluck, cluck," to them, and snapped your fingers and made faces at them. I tried all these in succession, but the more I goo goo-ed and cluck cluck-ed and made faces, each one more hideous than the last, the more that thing cried and sobbed.

At last, when daylight came, there was a loud knocking at the outer door. I went and opened it, and there stood the caretaker and his wife, the last much excited.

"Where's Mr Shenrock?" she demanded. "What's he doing of with a baby in the room, and ill-treating it, too?"

"There's no baby," I said; "it's a sick man."

"No baby, when I can hear it crying its dear little heart out! You've been smacking and beating of it." She pushed past me and went to the bedroom, saying, "Hush now, my pet; mother will be here directly."

She got as far as the door; then, at the sight of the black-muzzled ruffian sitting up in bed bellowing, she fell down in kicking hysterics. Her husband went to her assistance, but he, too, was struck speechless, with his mouth wide open. In the midst of it, Shenwick came back with a feeding-bottle, patent food, and some milk, having been lucky enough to stick up an early milk-cart. We recovered the woman and Shenwick told her that the patient had just had brain fever, and now imagine himself a baby, and the doctor said he was to be humoured. The woman was only too glad to get away. She had had what she termed a turn, and was not desirous of stopping any longer near this unnatural infant.

It was horribly grotesque to see the man-baby seize hold of the nozzle of the feeding bottle and suck its contents down. When it was satisfied, peace reigned, and the thing slept.

"Shenwick," I said, "you see what comes of interfering with Nature's laws. You will now have to adopt and rear that object in the next room. You were thinking of getting married, I know; but will your wife consent to your bringing home a baby 50 years old! No, she will not—you can consider that settled."

Shenwick groaned, "You needn't rub it in so," he answered.

"Perhaps not, for that little innocent darling asleep in the next room will be a constant reminder."

"Can't you give me some advice on the subject? Although you cannot deny the success of the experiment; yet between ourselves it is of no avail for any purpose. I thought and hoped that the spirit would come back charged with knowledge of the great hereafter. As it has unfortunately turned out, a baby has come back who will grow up with as little knowledge of the past as any other baby does." A long hungry wail came from the other room, emphasizing his statement, and proclaiming that the infant desired further nourishment. Shenwick went and filled the bottle up again.

"There's one chance you have," I said, when he came back. "This aged baby will, most likely, have to go through all the many ills that babies have to endure. I should take care that he died of croup, or scarlet fever, or whooping cough or something or other of that sort."

"What do you mean by 'taking care?'" said Shenwick, looking aghast.

"Nothing at all but what anyone but a fool would understand. I mean, take care of him if he is ill. Now, goodbye, I'm tired." I went home for a bath and breakfast, fully determined to have no more to do with Shenwick, and his dark experiments.

A fortnight afterwards, he came to the office. "I have got rid of him," he said, dropping on to the chair, as though wearied out."

"Buried him?" I asked.

"Oh, no! I called to the doctor who certified his death, and I told him that he had revived, but had come imbecile, imagining that he was an infant. So, after studying the case for some days, he called in another doctor, and he has been removed to an asylum."

"Do you pay for him?"

"Yes, a small sum weekly."

"Well, he will be a pensioner on you all your life, for, according to you, he has another span of years to live. Have you told Miss Colthrope about it?"

"Heavens! no; what would be the good?"

"Best to be open in these matters, however, I won't tell anyone; provided you swear never to have anything to do with this foolery any more."

"That I'll readily do," he said, and he did.

Shenwick married, and years passed, and he had a growing family, when he received a communication from the asylum, stating that the patient had improved so much that they thought he ought to be removed. The fact being that he had grown up into a boy and became more sensible.

Shenwick came to me in despair. "Just fancy, he has the soul of a boy, reared amongst lunatics in an asylum. Of course, he has not been taught anything; what on earth shall I do with him? Will you come out with me and see him? His appearance may suggest something."

I went out with him; ten years had passed since the fatal night of the experiment, and the body containing the boy's soul was that of an old man of sixty-six, looking older on account of the exposure and hardships the body had suffered. It was a regular puzzle. It was evident that he could not take the patient home. And it was pitiful, too. The soul, or spirit, whatever you like to call it, was full of life and vigor, which the palsied, doddering old body could not second. I could think of nothing but a benevolent asylum, and Shenwick agreed to it. The subject never reached it, however. There was a railway accident, and he was badly injured. We went to see him at the hospital. He was unconscious at the time, but death was very near, and he came to his senses just before we left. He recognised Shenwick, and growled out in the husky voice of old, "Hang you, are you never going to fetch that adjective beer?" Then he expired.

Shenwick told me that the last words he uttered at the period of his first death was an order to him, in flowery language, to go and get some beer.

DOOMED

(1899)

Jim Turner sat in the verandah of his modest homestead reading a letter. The mailman had just left the bag, and amongst the miscellaneous contents was a letter from an old friend, one Dick Beveridge, and in the contents was an item of information which made him feel rather uncomfortable.

"You perhaps have not heard that Charley Moore is dead, and how he died. His horse fell on him and crippled him. He lay there for four and twenty hours before he was found, and then he had been only dead for about one hour. The ants were swarming over him. Fancy what he must have suffered! So now that he is gone, you and I are the last of the five."

Five of them. Yes, he remembered it well—five of them, eager, young, and hopeful, who came into the untrodden district just sixteen years ago. They found good country, and each took up a run. Now there was only Beveridge and himself alive, and the other three had all died violent deaths. How distinctly he recalled the occurrence, which had given rise to the looming fate that seemed to be overhanging them.

They were camped one afternoon on the bank of the river; the same river he could now see from the verandah, bordered by luxuriant-foliaged tea-trees, with flocks of white cockatoos screaming and frolicking amongst the bushes, varied by flights of the Blue Mountain parrots crowding and chattering round the white flowers.

"Hullo!" said Moore, "there are some niggers coming."

Across the wide stretch of sand on the opposite bank some wandering blacks from the back country had just put in an appearance. Tired, thirsty, and burdened with their children and their camp furniture, they trooped down the bank to the water, and drank at the grateful pool in the river bed.

"What a start it would give them to drop a bullet in amongst them," said Daveney; "I'm blessed if I don't do it."

"Take care you don't hit one; there are a lot of gins and children amongst them," said Moore.

Daveney took up his carbine and fired. There was a start of dismay amongst the natives, and they bolted up the bank. One stopped behind a black patch prostrate on the sand.

"By heavens, you've hit one, you clumsy fool," said Beveridge, and the whole party went across the sand to the water. Not only one, but two, had been hit. The Martini bullet had gone clean through a gin's body and killed the baby she had been nursing. The gin was still alive. She looked at the white faces still gazing down at her, and commenced to talk. What she said of course none of them could understand, but that it was a wild tirade of vengeance against the murderers of her child and herself they could pretty well understand. Death cut her speech short, and almost at the same time there was a wild yell from the bank above, and a shower of spears fell amongst the run-hunters. Only one man was hit badly, and that was Daveney, the man who fired the fatal shot. The blacks had retreated after throwing their spears, and the whites helped their wounded comrade across to camp. Pursuit was impossible; the evening was well on, and by the time the horses could be got together the blacks would be beyond reach.

Then Turner's memory recalled Daveney's death in raging delirium, when the tropic sun had inflamed his wound, and fever had set in.

"Keep that gin away, can't you? Why do you let her stop there talking, talking, talking? What is she saying? You will all die, die violent deaths. Ha! Ha! Ha! Funny a myall blackgin can talk such good English, but that's what she says, 'You will die violent deaths!' Keep her away, you fellows, can't you? There's no sense in letting her stand talking there!" He died, and was buried in a lovely valley, where never a white man has been near since. Then Strathdon was drowned in the wreck of the Gothenburg, and now Moore had met a horrible fate. Turner got up with a shudder. Who would go next, he or Beveridge? He had no wish to die just then. He had but lately married, and in a few years the station would be clear of all back debt. He took up the letter, and read it through. At the end Beveridge said, "I am coming your way, and will see you in a few days." Turner banished all memories of the past, and went in and ate a hearty dinner and his fair young wife congratulated him on his good appetite.

Beveridge came in due time. Like Turner, he had seemingly banished dull care, and had chosen to ignore the doom that strangely enough seemed hanging over him. Nay, he even declined to talk of it with his host, and resolutely declared it was "all bosh."

It was a sultry, thunderous evening, and Turner and his wife, with their precious first baby, had driven their guest out to a point of interest in the neighborhood, and were returning, when the thunderstorm suddenly burst over their heads. Turner kept his horses going, but the rain overtook them some five miles from the homestead, and pelted them in their faces. Then came a flash, and darkness, as though the electric fluid had struck their eyeballs blind. With the flash came a roar, as though the world was splitting in twain, and then the horses, which had bolted off the road, went headlong into a wire fence, instead of pulling up at the sliprails.

"It's as dark as pitch" said Turner, getting on his legs unhurt. "Where are you all?" There was no answer, and he commenced groping about, and came on the struggling horses. "Whoa! Beveridge, man, where are you? It can't be night, but it's all dark. Didn't you see that cursed old gin standing in the road and startling the horses? Beveridge!"

One of the men fortunately came along and found Turner,

stricken blind, crouching against a tree. One of the horses was dead, with a broken neck; the other was much cut about with the wire. The baby was uninjured, and Mrs. Turner was unconscious; while Beveridge's head had been smashed in by the hoof of one of the struggling horses; he was dead. Mrs. Turner recovered, but her unfortunate husband never did, and to the day when a merciful death took him away from the blind earth, whose beauty he would see no more, he asserted that the last thing he saw was the form of a black gin, with a child in her arms, standing in front of the sliprails and blocking the horses.

THE MOUNT OF MISFORTUNE

(1899)

The hill, or mountain, as it was generally called, stood sheer on the bank of the river, which wheeled sharply around its base. The river was broad and sandy, and in its deeper pools the crocodiles of the Northern Territory disported themselves, and in the sunny hours of the winter days could be seen basking on the sandbanks in sleepy ease and contentment. The mount itself was the termination of a range of some sixty miles long, which started from the locality of a gold field, and all along its course the daring prospector had threaded his way, taking his life in his hand as he did so, for the blacks at that time were still savage and dangerous. On the mount by the river several parties had obtained good results; but, strangely enough, none were able to follow it up. Nearly every party obtained one good prospect, and after that were mocked by the color of gold only.

Worse than all, no party had ever camped at the mount but what death, in some shape, had overtaken one of its members. One had gone to the river to wash his clothes. His mates searched in vain for him when he did not return. The clothes were there, but the crocodiles had got the man. Another had sickened of the malarial fever of the north and died, and been buried there. Another had stuck his pick into his foot, and he, poor fellow, died a dreadful death in the agony of lockjaw. Two had gone there, and only one had come back again, disappeared in a day or two, and the story went round that he had murdered his mate. So the tales ran about the mountain on the bank of the Railly River, and men began to get shy of going there.

"The next lot will get chawed up by the niggers," was the opinion of one old digger. "They haven't had an innings yet, and it's about their turn now."

"Whoever they get, they won't get me. I wouldn't go down there for an ounce a day, unless there was a regular camp," said another.

"What's the matter with the place?" asked a tall young fellow, who was sitting by the fire with the others, a new arrival from Queensland.

They told him the story, and he laughed as all did at first when these yarns were told by old hands.

"Everybody gets a good prospect to start with and then they can never get any more? Hanged if I don't try my luck there."

"We'll find your bones in a black's oven," said the old man who had first spoken.

"Blacks!" returned the other, contemptuously. "You shouldn't talk to an old Palmer man about niggers."

"You may be in nigger country for years, and some fine day, when you're smoking your pipe and reckoning that you're as safe as the Lord Mayor of London, crash will go your skull, and nothing will trouble you any more. I know 'em," said the other.

"So do I," said the young man, "they tackled us like devils when we were on the Roper, when we were coming across, and speared my best horse. I owe them something. But about this mountain, is it a true bill about the prospects?"

"True as gospel; there's men in the camp here who have been there and found it always the same—one good prospect and nothing more."

"It must be traced somehow. I'll have a try, anyhow. By-the-way, a brother of mine came over here about a year ago, and I have never heard of him since. Tall fellow, not unlike me— Sid Thomson was his name—used to be called Lanky Sid!"

"Good Lord!" said the old man. "Thought there was something familiar about the cut of you. Yes, your brother came here, worse luck, but where he is now nobody can say."

"How's that?" said the other, quickly.

"Because he went down to that there mountain, and he never came back again."

"Tell me about it. I came over here from the Palmer, partly in the hope of finding him. Sid and I were always great chums from boys."

"I'll tell you, Thomson, if that's your name," went on Franks, the old digger, "but it's a queer story, mind you, and none too pleasant for you to hear. Your brother Sid, I knew him well. He went down to the Railly River Mountain; would go against all we said, just the same as you, and he hasn't come back yet."

"How long ago was that?"

More than six months. But that's not all. He had a mate with him—a fellow called Radforth. Radforth came back alone. Didn't say much to anyone—and disappeared. Clean gone, nobody knows where."

"Didn't anybody ask about my brother?"

"Of course they did, naturally. But he answered in a way that made 'em think that Sid was still down there, and he had just come up for rations. Leastways, he bought rations, and vamoosed, without a word to anybody. This made some people who didn't like him—for he was an ugly tempered animal—suspect that something was wrong, and a party was made to go down. Well, they went down there, but devil a thing could they find, beyond old tracks and old camps. Some think, maybe, that you brother and Radforth went across the Victoria River, and so on to West Australia, but I don't."

"I'll go down there at once, and alone, too. I'll find this thing out for myself, by God! If my brother has met with foul play, I'll hunt up this Radforth if he's on earth."

"Steady! There's no proof that your brother is dead, nor that Radforth killed him; but the rumour has got about here. Still there may be no truth in it."

"Anyhow, I'm going down to have a look at the place. I

suppose you can tell me how to find it?"

"Simple as possible. You have only to follow the range round, and the mountain is right on the bank of the river. You'll see scores of old tracks. But look out for the niggers! Look here, boy; they'll get the next man."

"I'm going, and I'll find out what's become of my brother," said Thomson; "and I'll start tomorrow."

To a man who had been through the Palmer rush, and finally overland to the Northern Territory, a trip of 60 miles was neither here nor there. Following the range along, he came on the second day to the Mount of Misfortune, round the base of which ran the Railly River. Lonely as was the place, young Thomson did not feel it so, so much was his mind occupied with his brother's fate, but although there were no fresh tracks of blacks about, visible to his experienced eye, he took the precaution of camping some way up the slope of the mountain. There was good food on the flat, and there was no fear of his horses straying far during the night. It was a beautifully clear moonlight night, and Thomson lay for some time smoking and thinking of the quest he was engaged in, when suddenly he heard a sound that caused him to raise himself up on his elbow and listen attentively. There was no mistake. Somebody was working with a pick on some part of the mountain. The night was noiseless, there was not even a wild dog howling, or a breath of wind stirring, and clearly and distinctly came the sounds of the strokes of a pick.

Thomson did not hesitate long. He picked up his Martini carbine, and stole carefully and as silently as possible in the direction of the mysterious sound. It was hard to trace, the echoes amongst the ranges were confusing, but at last he located it, and leaning over the edge of the rocky descent into a steep gully, he saw the worker.

A man was digging down in the bed of the dry creek that ran down the bottom of the gully. Working, and had been working for some long time, as Thomson's digger's eye could see by the long heap of washdirt piled up. Someone had penetrated the mystery of the mountain, and the source of the intermittent patches of gold, and was working it out quietly for himself. Who was the man? "I'll watch till daylight, but I'll find out," thought Thomson.

For hours the solitary worker continued his labor, and the watcher at his post watched him. He congratulated himself on bringing his carbine; a man with the lust of gold in his brain would not hesitate to commit murder to preserve his secret. It was about 1 o'clock in the morning before the digger ceased his toil, put down his tools, and straitened and stretched himself. Then he commenced to follow the gully down, and Thomson strode silently after him. Down, down, following every turn and twist, the two went, for Thomson had now descended into the gully, and kept his man well in sight. Soon the river was in view, and still the stranger kept on until he reached the bank. He never looked back, but descended the path by a well-worn pad, and went out on the sand to the edge of a deep waterhole that extended down the river for a long way. There was an island covered in undergrowth just behind where he had taken up his position, and here Thomson concealed himself, so close that he could hear every word the man uttered. He wondered much that his presence had not been detected before; but the man before him seemed as though he was acting in a trance.

He was sitting at the edge of the water, looking down into its moonlit surface, and talking strangely to himself, as was natural in a "hatter."

"Are you there, Sid? Was it painful when the crocodiles took you? Come up and tell me about it. I've got the lead right enough, and the secret of the mountain. Come up, old man, and don't grin down there. Bah! It wasn't painful—you were killed quick. Come up, man, and see how well I'm getting on."

Thomson could no longer restrain himself. There was no doubt in his mind that this was Radforth, the murderer of his brother in order to gain and keep to himself the secret of the mysterious mountain. He sprang down from the island, and stood beside the talker.

Radforth jumped upright, and looked at him aghast. The

resemblance between the brothers was only a general one, but in the moonlight it sufficed.

"So you've come at last. Come at last," cried Radforth, falling back. "Go, take it; I'll take your place." Turning quickly away, he plunged into the bottomless hole, where the crocodiles that haunted it received him joyfully. He never rose again. Thomson watched for long, but the moonlit surface was unrippled after the commotions of the plunge had subsided.

In the morning he found the camp of the recluse, whom solitude and remorse had evidently driven crazy, and, in a diary, found his worst fears confirmed. His brother and Radforth had discovered what promised to be the true lead of the mountain source of the gold. They had not quarrelled, but the prospects were so rich that the greed of gold grew in Radforth's breast, and he killed his unsuspecting comrade. He took his body to the waterhole, where one could always see the small eyes of a crocodile and a snout floating on the surface. There he left it, but the crocodiles did not touch it. Day after day, night after night, it lay there, and the crocodiles would not touch the dead body, nor hide the murder. Then in desperation he buried it in the sand, and that night the crocodiles dug it up, and in the morning it was floating on the brink of the sand-spit. And there it floated till the flesh dropped from the bone, and the awful thing sank. But the curse was on the man, and every night after his hidden toil in the gully he was constrained to go down to where the bones were lying; and all this he had written down.

In the morning Thomson went down to the edge of the waterhole, and under the clear water opposite where Radforth had been sitting he saw the bones and skull of what he felt sure was his brother's body. He recovered them, and buried them, before he returned to the old camp. He told old Franks and they kept silence, and went back to the mountain on the Railly River.

The first leads of washdirt piled up by the wretched murderer washed out handsomely. The remainder, which they were too disgusted to go all through, contained but specks. The man had been driving himself mad over piling up load after load of

worthless dirt. The mystery of the Mountain of Misfortune is a
mystery still.

THE BLOOD-DEBT
(1899)

Part 1: How the Debt was Incurred

"WELL, I don't see what you have to grumble at, Hunt," said Jenkins to his friend and partner.

"Perhaps not," returned the doctor, looked at from an everyday standpoint; but I've never told you that I ought to have about four hundred thousand pounds to my credit."

"No; you certainly never have. But would you be any happier if you had it? We've a fairly good practice—not astonishing, but rising,—and our patients pay their fees."

"Yes, they pay up, like the good, respectable people they are, and we lead a nice, easy, middle-class existence; but I had a patient once who did not pay up, and never will pay up until I get him in my power some day; and he is one of the richest men in Australia."

"How much does he owe you?"

"One way and another, about four hundred thousand pounds."

"That's a tidy sum. Is this a joke or reality?"

"True as we're sitting here. Lambert Dunaston, whom I suppose you know well enough by name, owes me that figure."

"How did he come to owe you that figure?"

"He bought his life at that price."

"Didn't know you were, or had been a bandit."

"No, it was not that way. I'll tell you how it was. It's a long story, and you'd better know it, and keep it secret to the end, for there's no end to it yet. Dunaston and I went West when the first big "rush" was on. I had no practice then and I thought of setting up out there. By Jove! when we got there it seemed that every hard-up 'medical' in Victoria and New South Wales had been struck with the same idea, and anticipated me. Seeing how things stood, Dunaston persuaded me to invest what little money we had left between us in the purchase of the necessary outfit to join a couple of men, whom he knew, and who were going out prospecting. It was the best thing to do under the circumstances, and I agreed. We clubbed our money and bought camels, and the four of us made a start.

"You've heard of the famous Yellow Spindrift Mine?"

"Who hasn't?"

"That mine was found that trip. The other two men were Winkelson and Martow. Did you ever hear of their names or mine in connection with it?"

"Never. Dunaston is the only one who is known with regard to the Yellow Spindrift."

"Exactly. Winkelson and Martow are dead—murdered, in point of fact. Dunaston, from the sale and what was taken from the mine, cleared eight hundred thousand pounds. Half of that belongs to me. I don't claim any of what he has made since. A majority of the men in the world have two natures. The hidden nature shows out differently in different men. In some, drink brings it to the surface. I suppose you have often noticed how intoxication completely reverses the nature of certain men. Circumstances perform the same thing for others. The man who in town is a mild, pleasant gentleman, becomes a coarse blackguard when out in the "bush" beyond the restraints of civilisation. Dunaston was one of these men. Once we got fairly into the wilderness, he seemed to change into the primal savage which every man is under his veneer. He was viciously cruel, and laid no restraint on his temper until Martow took him in hand and gave him a good thrashing one night. Then he vented his spite on the beasts, particularly the camel he rode—a good camel, too, called Crookshanks, from a malformation of its legs.

"'You'd better go slow, beating that camel,' said Martow to him one evening. 'A camel, like a parrot, never forgets. Some day old "Crookshanks" will get hold of you when you are not expecting it, and then God help you!'

"They were two decent fellows, rest their souls! and if we had not had that devil with us it would not have been so bad, in spite of the wretched desert we were travelling through. As it was, we had a deuce of a hard time of it until luck changed, and we found the 'Spindrift.' What a wonderful find that was! The mine is played out now, but that is since Dunaston sold it. I often dream of it still. What an irresistible influence the sight of gold has upon men! and what a lovely thing it is to find! Clean and heavy. Not like gems that have to be cut before their beauty is apparent. But bright and beautiful from the start—like a pearl that needs no artificial aid."

The doctor paused, and stared hard at the fire. Jenkins did the same.

"It does me good now to think of those days when we had nothing to do but gaze at the gold, and conjecture how deep it would go, and what we were worth each. We were in luck. Nobody had followed our tracks, and we tested the reef, and found it to exceed even our expectations. It was decided that Dunaston and Winkelson should go into Wonderranup, the nearest mining centre, obtain fresh supplies, and apply for the prospectors' claim and reward. There was a 'rock-hole' close at hand that would suffice for the wants of the two of us who remained, and there was a salt marsh about five miles off that would supply water for condensing when that was gone, so they took all the camels with them. It was no good keeping things quiet, for the country swarmed with prospectors, and it was better to announce the find and go straight ahead working it.

"You would have thought it rather lonely for two men by themselves in that gaunt desert country, but, strange to say, Martow and I did not find it so; that gold-reef was the most pleasant and interesting companion men ever had, better than all the books and journals in the world. The choicest wines, the most charming women, the most witty comrades, I tell you, are nothing to a reef full of veins of yellow metal.

"In coming to what is now called the Spindrift township, we had naturally come a very roundabout course, but straight across through the bush it was much shorter, though the track would probably be without water. However, it was not too far to go with camels, unless the country proved very scrubby. Ten days had passed, and we were hourly expecting our two mates back, that being about the time we had calculated on; but they came not. The water in the rock-hole was getting low, and we began to feel anxious; gold would not satisfy hunger or thirst.

"From the top of the ridge, on the side of which was the reef, away to the westward we could see the crest of a granite hill peeping above the black scrub. As most of these bare granite mounds had rock-holes at the base, I proposed that we should go over one day and see if there was not more water there. Martow, however, would not consent to our both leaving the mine, so it was settled that I should go alone, and, as it was a fair moon, I decided to go that night. After our evening meal I started. In rather over an hour I reached the rock-hill, for it was sandy country and heavy walking. I found several rock-holes at the foot of it, but I had gone nearly round it before I came on one much larger than the one where we were camped, and with a good supply of water in it.

While at the back of the hill—that is to say, the side farthest removed from our camp—I thought I heard a faint sound like a distant shot. I listened, but heard nothing more, and concluded it was fancy. Having found the water, I thought I would ascend the mount out of curiosity. From the top there was an extensive view, but by no means a cheerful one—black and gloomy looked the sea of dark scrub around. I had been looking away from our camp. When I turned towards it I saw, to my astonishment, a glow of fire in that direction. It seemed to me to be beyond the ridge where the reef was, and I could not understand it, for there was no grass to burn in that region. Hastily descending, I made back to the camp.

"One way and another, I had been about four hours absent by the time I reached the camp again; and what was my horror to hear cries of pain and sounds of scuffling as I approached. Coming out of the scrub into the open, I saw distinctly, for the moon was directly overhead, and it was bright as noonday. I heard, as I said, groans and cries of anguish, and I saw a camel worrying a man. Instinct told me it was 'Crookshanks' having his revenge on Dunaston. He was literally wiping the ground with him. No wonder the poor wretch shrieked, for of all bites, that of a camel is the most painful, more so than a horse's.

"I was in time to save his life, for 'Crookshanks' was about to make an end of him by dropping on him with his chest and crushing him. I rushed up and blazed my revolver off close before the camel's eyes. I only wanted to frighten him off his victim, for in my heart I rather sympathised with the animal. With shouting and firing another shot, I got Dunaston away, and he was a pitiable sight.

"I was completely bewildered. How did Dunaston come to be there? Where was Martow? However, the only thing to do was to look to the groaning man. I carried him to the camp, put him on the blankets, got a light, and proceeded to examine him. He had had a terrible time of it; no bones were broken, but he was so bruised that I doubted if in that bet climate he would recover. I once had to do my best for a man who was dying from being mauled by a camel. Dunaston not so bad as him, and that was all I could say.

"I had brought a small medicine-chest with me, and I bandaged him up and gave him a quietening draught to take the strain off his nerves; then I made up the fire and looked about the camp, but could find no sign of Martow, living or dead. I had to wait until Dunaston was able to speak. He came to himself when the effects of the soothing draught I had given him had worn off.

"'When did you come back?' I asked.

"'About half an hour ago,' he answered.

"'Where is Martow?'

"'I don't know. I have not seen a soul. I was looking about when that devil attacked me. I'll cut the soul out of him when I am able to get up.'

"'You may never get up,' I said shortly.

"He tried to sit up, but gave a yell of pain, and lay staring at me.

"'What do you mean? Am I fatally hurt?'

"'No, But you are bruised and bitten all over, and only constant attention and care will save you in this climate. For at least two days somebody must be in attendance to change and renew the bandages and keep them moistened with the anti-septic I have put on. Now, satisfy my curiosity. What have you been doing, and why are you alone?'

"'We went into Wonderranup and fixed everything up, and Winkelson will be here in a day or two with the camels. The warden is coming out with him. I was anxious about you fellows, and pushed on before them. Where is Martow?'

"'That's what I must find out. I left him here at dusk, while I went over to a hill three miles away to see if there was any water. I just came back in time to save you from having all the life squeezed out of you.'

"'What do you think can have become of Martow?'

"'I cannot possibly imagine. I am going to have a cruise round.'

"'Don't go far, For Heavens sake, don't go out of hearing.'

"'Don't excite yourself; it's the worst thing you can do. I am not going to leave you just yet.'

"I made him comfortable, and, taking a rifle, went out on what I felt was a hopeless quest." The doctor paused, drank off his whisky, and then resumed.

"Somehow I felt certain Marrow was dead. I went up the ridge to the reef, looked all about where we had been working, fired a shot or two, and waited. No answering shot came. The interior of Western Australia at night is a land without sound; in the dead stillness the slightest noise could be heard; but I heard none. Martow was dead, but who killed him? Dunaston said he came only half an hour before I returned.

"Then I suddenly recalled the sound of a shot that I had fancied I heard when at the granite hill. Dunaston was a liar, and, I began to believe, a murderer as well. I returned to the camp, for there was nothing else to be done till morning.

"I sat down gloomily, scarcely speaking to the wounded man. I began to think that old 'Crookshanks,' the camel, had saved my life. I was safe at present, for the man was helpless. I attended to his bandages during the remaining hours of darkness, and meditated on the position.

"At daybreak I got some food ready, and told Dunaston I was going to make a thorough search for Martow.

"'And leave me here to die,' he cried.

"'You must chance that,' I answered. 'You should have thought of that before you murdered Marrow.'

"For a minute the man was speechless. Then he said in a husky voice—

"'Why on earth should I murder Martow?'

"'Because there would be one less in the reef. You would have done the same by me, but for 'Crookshanks' having a grudge against you.'

"'God! What put such villainous thoughts in your head?'

"'Facts. What has become of Martow? I left him here alive and when I come back I find you here, and he has disappeared. While I was away I thought I heard a shot. When the warden comes with Winkelson there will be a strict search made, if I have not found him before then.'

"A curious expression passed over the man's face. He made an effort to move, and groaned in agony.

"'You said yourself that I should die if not looked after; how can you talk of leaving me?'

"'You *will* die probably; I don't like the look of those bruises at all this morning. I might be able to save you, but duty calls me elsewhere. Martow may be lying wounded in the scrub.'

"'Stay with me, doctor. Oh, for mercy's sake, don't let me die just when I'm going to be rich.'

"'You'll die easy. Mortification will set in, but just before it comes you'll suffer torture.'

"'How can you be such a brute? You're a murderer if you leave me here.'

"'I firmly believe you are one, or I shouldn't talk to you like this. But I must go. I will get you some breakfast, leave everything handy for you, and then spend the day searching for Martow.'

"'Don't go! Don't leave me to die alone like a dog. You can save my life if you stay with me. Martow can take care of himself. Don't leave me, doctor; don't let me die!'

"So the man pleaded in his agony and fear of death.

"I went outside and made up the fire. Looking about, I saw 'Crookshanks,' the camel, who had been caught by his nose-rope in the scrub. I went down to him, and, as he seemed to be in a good temper, I led him up to camp, unsaddled him, gave him a drink, and put him oil some feed. Then I went back and gave Dunaston some breakfast, and had some myself.

"'Doctor,' he pleaded faintly, when I was making ready to start, 'listen! If Martow does not turn up, there will be his share to divide between us two'—

"'Between us three,' I reminded him.

"'Yes. Now, I will give you half my own share, in addition to yours, if you will stay with me and attend to me until I am out of danger.'

"That was my sin and my mistake. I had been gloating over that gold too long, and now I hungered for it. Instead of leaving him at once, to live or die, as Fate thought fit, I lingered.

"'Half my share! Why, man, no doctor in the world ever got such a fee before.'

"I hesitated, then I asked when he expected the others up.

"'Not less than a day or two,' he said.

"'I will stay with you two days on those terms. By then you will either be dead or out of danger.'

"He was not able to hold a pen, but I wrote it down, and he touched the pen while I signed for him. Then I fought with death for forty-eight hours, and I won.

"On the third day Winkelson and the others had not arrived. I told Dunaston that he was safe, and that I would take 'Crookshanks' and go and meet them, and direct them to the other rock-hole, as the one where we were camped was getting very low.

"He agreed, for he could crawl about, and I started, taking, by his directions, the track by which he and Winkelson had gone in. The first day I met no one. The second day I met no one. The third day I came upon a host of tracks making towards the Spindrift on a slightly different line. Much puzzled, I kept on, and met a camel team. We stopped to talk, and they informed me they were pushing out for the new rush, 'Dunaston's Find.' I asked if Winkelson was ahead with the warden. They did not know the name. They were in Wonderranup when Dunaston came in, and they were certain that he came in alone.

"Their words turned me cold, although the day was hot enough. Had there been two murders? I found I was only twenty miles from Wonderranup, so I went on there, and learned the full extent of his villainy. He had come in alone, and the 'Spindrift' was taken up solely in his name. Winkelson must have been treacherously put out of the way on the road down. This was cold-blooded work for you! I joined in with some others going to the new rush, and returned. The place was changed entirely, even in those few days, and was now a busy scene of life. I sought out Dunaston at once; he saw me coming, and managed to get rid of the men he was talking to.

"'Well,' I said hotly, as I came up, 'you had better say your prayers, you d— murdering villain! for I have found out every-thing, and this crowd will think nothing of lynching you when they know what you have done, although it does not often happen in Australia.'

"Dunaston looked at me with provoking coolness. 'If they lynch anybody, or anybody deserves hanging it's you. You left with two mates: you turn up alone with a cock-and-bull story about their having mysteriously disappeared, and I suppose you claim the discovery of this mine.'

"I couldn't speak. The man's astounding audacity and wickedness staggered me.

"'You see the situation, and, I need scarcely say, will accept it—will have to accept it. I know nothing of you, or of the men who went with you. As things go in the constant change and excitement going on now, the disappearance of our friends will not be noticed; but let me draw attention to it, doctor, and you'll find yourself in an awkward position.'

"'Then you mean to deny everything, you diabolical villain! My saving your life from the camel; your bond to me for your life?'

"'Everything,' he calmly replied. 'We were fellow-passengers on board the steamer; since then we have not seen each other. Remember the people who were in Wonderranup when we started are now dispersed all over the goldfields, and were too busy with their own affairs to notice us,'

"The wretch was right. He could easily throw all suspicion on me, and I should have a small chance for life, I simply had my hands tied, and was utterly in his power. He owned the reef; the paper which I held was in my own handwriting; I had not a single proof of any stability to bring forward. Would you believe it? It was not the horror and atrocity of the man's crimes that overwhelmed me at the moment, but the contemplation of what a besotted fool I had been to let this villain get the best of me when I held the game in my own hands.

"'I would to God you were in old 'Crookshanks' clutches again, and I looking on,' I said.

"'You would let him crush me. That is exactly what you ought to have done, doctor, and precisely what I should have done, in your place. However, we can't put the clock hack, and you are a man of sense,—and thoroughly understand the position.'

"I did understand the position, and my blood boils and nearly maddens me, when I think of it. The man is a double-dyed murderer and robber, and I am a struggling physician, but he has the money. Still, I believe that I shall hold trumps one day, and then God help Lambert Dunaston. I'll avenge the deaths of the two men he murdered."

"You found no trace of the lost men?"

"No. I own I did not stay there much longer."

Part 2: How the Debt was Paid

LAMBERT DUNASTON and his bride were passengers on the China steamer *Emperor, en route* for the pleasant and interesting land of Japan. It had been rather a shock to him to find that his old West Australian mate, Dr. Hunt, was taking a holiday by filling the place of the regular ship's doctor that trip, but it was too late to draw back, and as Hunt met him on the standing of a stranger, he concluded that it was simply one of those unfortunate coincidences that happen during a man's life time.

Under shelter of the Great Barrier Reef, along the coast of Northern Queensland, the voyage was through summer seas, and but for the haunting presence of his former friend, Dunaston's honeymoon trip would have been an ideal one. Summer seas, however, are proverbially treacherous, and once past Thursday Island the *Emperor* got into a storm belt, and received some buffeting about.

It was a tempestuous night, and a few passengers had retired early. In the dimly-lighted saloon the doctor groped his way through the bodies of the sleeping Chinese cabin-boys, and went on deck and ascended the bridge. The sea was high, and the wind seemed increasing. The captain was looking at the barometer in the chart-room.

"I'm afraid we'll be caught, doctor," he said, as the other entered.

"How's that; barometer falling?"

"Falling! I should think so. Going to have a typhoon, I'm afraid."

"She's making heavy weather of it now."

"Yes, and I don't want to get into a big blow with her; she's a bad sea boat."

The two men remained silent, holding on during the big rolls the steamer was making. The doctor's thoughts were busy with his schemes against his enemy, and the rhythmical noise of the engines seemed to ring in the chorus, "The time is near." He had no set plan, but he was determined that he would not part with his man again, except on fresh terms.

The whole thing had been quite accidental; he wanted change, and had taken the opportunity offered by the ship's doctor wishing to remain on shore to exchange for the trip. He was as much astonished to see Dunaston on board as Dunaston was to see him, but he was infinitely better pleased. Now seemed the very time to avenge the two murders. Dunaston just married to a beautiful young girl, to whom he appeared passionately attached. Surely the stars in their courses were fighting for him; the man was vulnerable now. Their interviews had been limited, Hunt avoiding the man as much as it was possible to do on board ship, and no one suspected that they had met before.

The captain's foreboding was right. By morning a full-sized typhoon was howling and shrieking behind them, and the Emperor had to turn tail and run right before it. The storm had reached its height about noon, and the steamer was labouring heavily and shipping a good deal of water. Two or three seas had found their way into the saloon, and everything was drenched and miserable. Mrs. Dunaston kept her cabin with her husband.

The wind began to die down after noon, and one or two had struggled to the table, when a sudden jar and the cessation of the engines told of some catastrophe. Hunt climbed on deck, and looked around at the wild tumult of sea, in which the now help-less steamer was tossing and pitching—occasionally heeling far over when a greater wave than usual surged upon her. The worst had happened. The constant racing of the screw in the heavy sea had injured the shaft, and the Emperor had hope-lessly broken down, and was at the mercy of the tremendous seas almost without steering way. A couple of staysails were all the sail that could be made on the apologies for masts, and the coloured crew managed at last to get them spread.

It was a dismal outlook; the rolling of the ship was so violent that even the most practised and active could not keep their feet. The night closed in black and gloomy, and the Emperor was dashed about and banged and lifted seemingly half-way up to the heavens. In the morning she had developed an alarming list, some of the cargo had shifted, and things looked black indeed, for she was now reported to be making water fast. They had been driven out of their course by the typhoon, and not a ship was in sight; but the sea was going down, none too soon. Two boats had been smashed: but the three that remained were large enough to carry all on board comfortably, and they were got out in readiness, for it was now obvious that the steamer would have to be abandoned.

The time had come, and Dunaston was in his cabin putting some matters of importance in his pockets, when the steamer gave a more than usually heavy lurch, throwing him against the bunk, and at the same time his cabin door was slammed and the key turned. He had been locked in to go down with the ship. The boats were on the other side, and in the creaking and groaning of timber that was going on, his cries and shouts were unheard. And if there occurred the least confusion he would not be missed. His wife and the other lady passenger were to go in the first boat in charge of the chief officer. They were in hopes of making Timor in three days. Hunt, of course, had locked him in, out of revenge, and would take care that he would not be missed. The portholes had been screwed tight during the typhoon, and he could not open one in his cabin. He was trapped to die a horrible slow death. If the vessel sank it would not be one quick rush and over; but it would creep in slowly, and he would be hours dying. He beat on the door, and called, and the only sound that answered him was the creaking of the straining timbers.

Hour after hour of agony followed, and then it began to grow dusk, and he felt himself doomed indeed—doomed to die in darkness and loneliness; and he recalled with horror the ghastly rumours that were once spread of men having accidentally been shut up in the water-tight compartments of H.M.S. *Victoria*, and going down with her to die a lingering death at the bottom of the Mediterranean. So passed the long night, in frantic desperation and sullen apathy; several times he thought of suicide, but he had no speedy weapon with which to do the deed. Still the steamer floated and the sea was fast going down, and a dawn he had never expected to see stole in at the port-holes at last.

Dunaston had been sitting on the edge of his bunk, when he started to his feet with a wild shout of hope. He had heard a footstep on the deck overhead. Somebody was on the ship beside himself, or one of the boats had come back, seeing the vessel still floated. No answer came to his hail, but he distinctly heard the footstep pass up and down. After about an hour someone came into the saloon. The motion of the ship was now only a long roll, but the list had become very perceptible. Whoever it was came straight to his cabin, unlocked the door and threw it open.

Hunt stood there, revolver in hand, and ordered him on deck. He was obliged to comply, for the look of the doctor's eyes did not admit of any questioning. On deck he ordered him to sit down, and before he anticipated it, he was shackled to a ringbolt by his ankles. "Now," said Dr. Hunt, "we can talk comfortably." The sky was clear, every trace of the storm had vanished from above, and a fierce equatorial sun was beginning to make its presence felt.

"The steamer's going to float, after all, and we shall have a pleasant little jaunt together. Pity those two fellows, dead in Western Australia, are not here; even old 'Crookshanks' would smile if he saw you."

"I suppose you want money; your share of the reef, in fact. Well, you won't get it," and Dunaston tried to look defiant, but failed.

"I want a full confession. The money can wait, and so can I." Hunt lit a cigar and took a turn or two up and down the deck. The boat now only wallowed with a long sluggish roll; she was very deep, but seemed likely to keep afloat so long as the weather kept fine. Having finished his cigar, Hunt went into the saloon, and came out with some eatables and a bottle of claret, which he proceeded to discuss in sight of his prisoner. "You will be happy to hear that the boats got well away, and Mrs. Dunaston will soon be in safety in Timor. I managed it very neatly, so that we were not missed."

"Are you going to starve me?"

"I'm not going to give you anything to eat or drink until you write down that confession."

"The boats may come back."

"I shinned up the mast this morning as high as I could, and they were not in sight. Besides, you'll never go alive into one of them; I'll take care of that."

"What do you want me to confess?"

"The murders of Winkelson and Martow; then we'll go into the money question."

Dunaston was silent, and Hunt said nothing more. The sun mounted higher and higher; a dead calm reigned, and the blazing heat struck with fierce rays on the man fastened to the ringbolt. Still he held out, but in the afternoon was forced to beg for water. Hunt took no notice of the request. And darkness closed in, and throughout the long hours of the night the derelict was silent, save for a groan of helpless agony and despair wrung at intervals from the prisoner.

It was ten o'clock the next day before he gave in. Hunt brought out paper and pen and ink, then gave his prisoner a little wine and water and some food.

Dunaston wrote. In substance it amounted to what Hunt had guessed. Winkelson had been disposed of on the way down. Dunaston, pushing ahead, had found Martow alone, despatched him treacherously, put his body on the camel, and taking it some distance away, had built a huge fire over it,—the one Hunt had seen from the granite mound. He was going then to wait Hunt's return, when the attack made on him by the camel frustrated his plans, and saved the doctor's life.

This confession he wrote out and signed, and then Hunt fed him again, and the game commenced once more. This time the stake was high, but the cards were all in one hand, and Dunaston had to make a will, giving over a large amount of property, and sign a fat cheque, all in return for value received, the value being half a pint of tepid water, or perhaps a pint, and a little food.

"I shall repudiate all these documents," he said, when the last was signed.

"I suppose you will if you get the chance. I anticipate being picked up soon, and I shall at once give you in charge for the confessed murder of your mate; now that you have given the clue, proofs will soon be forthcoming."

"Don't you intend to release me?"

"Certainly not. But I will keep you alive; we're sure to be fallen across soon."

Another day, and another day, and Dunaston began to feel the effects of the sun.

"I must let him out for a bit to-morrow," thought Hunt, "or he'll go cranky on my hands."

It was another day of unruffled calm, and Hunt had been amusing himself, and maddening his prisoner by dilating on the future stretching before him, and comparing their respective lots when rescued.

"By the way, it will be a pity to separate the money. After you're hanged, perhaps Mrs. Dunaston would not be inconsolable, and I always had a weakness for widows—young widows."

Hunt was looking away at the horizon as he spoke, and did not notice the murderous hand steal up to an iron belaying-pin in the side. It was loose, and Dunaston had noiselessly taken it out, and the next minute launched it with unerring and mad strength at his enemy. Hunt got the blow on the temple, and fell dead on the deck. Dunaston slipped down against the bulwark, and began to laugh sillily and vacantly.

He suddenly realised what he had done, and lost his reason. Hunt had the key of the handcuffs in his pocket, and his body lay beyond reach. The blood from the wound began to trickle towards him along the sloping deck, and the madman greeted it with shouts of terror, and, anon, peals of maniac laughter.

When it reached him he dipped his fingers in it, and wrote meaningless gibberish on the deck.

A boat from a Dutch gunboat boarded the derelict and found the madman still alive, and babbling deliriously, talking to the dead man who lay just beyond his reach, with life and freedom in his pocket. He lingered but a few days.

ON THE ISLAND
OF SHADOWS
(1900-01)

This is the story told by Eugene Tripot, convict from New Caledonia, of what happened to him during the boat voyage when he had succeeded in making his escape.

He died in the hospital at Hong-Kong, insane, having lost his reason through the suffering and privation he went through on that occasion.

He had lucid intervals, during which he repeatedly told this story, and insisted on its truth.

He was rescued from a sandy islet on the outer edge of the Great Barrier Reef, off the coast of Northern Queensland, by a China steamer taking the outside passage. He had been cast away there for some weeks, living on trepang and shell-fish.

Nothing was seen to in any way bear out this story.

* * * * * * *

"Three of us alone between sea and sky—three men with a wolf inside each, wolves that looked at each other out of our eyes. Gronard crouched in the bottom of the boat, gnawing at a piece of wood; Pelrine sat at the stern, with his sheath-knife in his hand, digging savagely at the thwart; I was sitting in the bow.

"The sail flapped idly at every little swing and roll of the boat, just as it had flapped during the last fortnight, never once bellying out.

"Beside us three there was the sun—the sun that hated us so. Hot and eager it rose in the morning—hot and eager to drink our blood. With anger that we should be still alive, it set in the evening. Gronard cursed the sun, Pelrine cursed the sun, and I cursed the sun.

"That was all we did from morning to night. It was all we had to do. It is bad for men to sit silent all day, only speaking to curse the sun, for then the wolf rages and breaks out.

"It broke forth in Pelrine, sitting digging his knife in the thwart, and suddenly he sprang upon Gronard. He would have sprung upon me, just the same, if I had happened to be next to him, for it was the wolf that sprung, not Pelrine, for Pelrine was always a good-hearted man.

"Gronard was taken at a disadvantage, but he was the strongest of us three, and grappled with Pelrine, and in the struggle the boat lurched, and both fell over the side. I saw them go down, down, in the clear water, turning and twisting, and all I thought was, 'They do not feel the sun down there.'

"They never rose, for I saw what looked like long flashes of white light dart at them, and I knew that the sharks that had kept us company so long had them for their sport at last.

"When I raised my head there was a ripple coming fast across the water. If Pelrine's wolf had not broken out just then both he and Gronard would be alive now. I went to the tiller and the sail filled, and the boat moved for the first time for two weeks.

"West was our course—anywhere west, to the great continent that reached for two thousand miles north and south. Merrily blew the wind, and in the evening there were clouds ahead, and a black thunderstorm flashed and muttered in the distance. All through the night there was the pleasant rip and gurgle of water.

"But the wolf gnawed still.

"Morning! and ahead of me I saw white water, but no land. It mattered little whether I died by the wolf or the wave, and I kept straight on. As I got closer to the breakers I saw there was a low, sandy mound visible, with some low bushes growing on it, and to this I steered.

"The northern side looked to be the smoothest, and I endeavoured to make that side; for though there was no sea, the wind having been but light, the sweep and rush of the Pacific rollers was tremendous, and when they broke upon this submerged wall of coral and recoiled broken and shattered, the very air seemed to tremble.

"At the northernmost point of the islet the turmoil seemed less, though the rollers were as big; but the passage was deep enough to let them pass through and expend their fury in a sullen swirl over the flats beyond.

"As I approached I was caught in one of the rollers and swept on with it, with great force and fury. We mounted on the crest of it, and then fell with a rush that made me feel sick. Next moment the boat was dashed on the beach, and I was flung unhurt beside it.

"Then the roller swept back and left us, the broken boat and myself, on the sand.

"It was a miserable little patch of dry land indeed, and when I had rested a little I commenced to examine it, first directing my steps to the low bushes on the highest part. I found it to be a ring of scrub surrounding a depression filled with water. I crashed through the bushes and stooped to drink, scarcely daring to hope that it would be fresh. It was, or at least fairly so, for the spray from the breakers drifted over into it.

"I drank, and the wolf was quiet for a bit, while I lay on the sand and looked around. A line of tossing white ran north and south—the line I had passed through—but to the west was a still sea, broken here and there in patches of shining foam, but mostly still, and of light, transparent green colour. The tide was falling, and by midday there were bare spots of coral showing.

"I went down and searched for shell-fish, or anything left by the tide. I found what was better than all—plenty of the sea-slugs known as trepang. I soon had a quantity collected, and having the means of making a fire, I spent the rest of the day in cooking and eating; and again the wolf crouched for a time.

"That night I slept soundly after the cramped space of the boat, and when the wolf clamoured at daylight I arose. It was a strange thing to be standing there alone on that patch of sand, with the wall of tireless breakers on one side, that looked far above me, as though when they fell they would overwhelm my refuge.

"I fed on trepang, and passed the day idly resting, for now I had tamed the wolf within me. I longed for my companions, but they were in the bellies of the sharks.

"When darkness came I lay down and slept, but awoke in the middle of the night, dreaming that I heard strange sounds, I listened, and at first heard nothing but the boom and crash of the breakers; but presently I heard low voices and the crunching tread of feet on the coral sand. I leapt to my feet, but could see nothing. I called, but got no answer; and still, distinctly, I heard the sound of voices and the tread of feet.

"I hastily traversed the island, but saw nothing, only at times I heard the voices talking, and though I called and called again, none answered me. Then there was silence, and plainly I heard the click and grind of steel meeting steel, the tramp, and quickened breathing of two combatants; and still I saw nothing.

"Suddenly the clashing came quicker and sharper, as though there was a hotly-contested rally, and following it came a fall on the sand, and then a cry in a woman's voice, and a peal of musical laughter. There was low whispering, and the steps died away, heavy and slow, as though they carried a burden, and then there was no sound but the thunder of the tireless billows.

"I scarcely felt frightened—I had been living far too long hand in hand with death. I felt curious, and if terrified at all it was more at the idea that it had been a fancy of my brain—that it was my wits were failing me, for I knew well that loneliness serves some men thus.

"All was quiet for the remainder of the night, and in the morning there were no signs nor tracks of any person but myself.

"Now, although I heard the voices, the tongue that they spoke in was strange to me, but I thought it was Spanish, from the way that I had heard old comrades of mine talk together who were Spaniards.

"Next night the ghosts were there again, and once more the duel, as I took it, was fought on that solitary speck of sand in the great ocean, to the music of the surf.

"That was a strange, unreal life—by day to pace the sandy shore and listen to the waves, and talk to myself, or gather and cook the trepang that supported me; by night to hear the crunch of the sand under unseen feet, and the quick clash of the blades. But stranger still was to come.

"I bethought me, from what information I had gathered, that this reef was the great reef that lay off the coast of Queensland, and that inside, between it and the mainland, ships and steamers were constantly passing up and down.

"My boat was too shattered to admit of my trusting myself in it to the ocean, but could I not patch it up sufficiently to carry me in the still-water channels of the reef? I would only have to keep due west to come out somewhere on the edge of the frequented passage.

"To this end I took to exploring the reef westward as far as I could go during low tide. The second day I came across a submerged object lying on the edge of a deep channel—the wreck of a ship. At low water it was partly uncovered, and the gaunt ribs showed above the surface for some height. It was an ancient hulk, encrusted with marine growth and barnacles. Only the heart of the timber remained; but that was as hard as flint.

"They built stout ships in the days when she left her bones there. She was firmly wedged on the ledge of a reef, and must have been carried to where she lay in some tempest of extraordinary fury. How many years had she been there, and of what nation she was, I had no means of judging just then.

"But day after day I visited her, and in time found that out; I mustered courage to dive down and examine her below the water-mark of low tide. It was not the depth that required courage, but strange things had found their home amidst the waving growth around her. The banded yellow and black sea-snakes of those parts swam in and out, hideous shell-fish with staring eyes and long feelers hid amongst the beams, and, for aught I knew, some loathsome octopus might be lurking in his lair there.

"I pushed on farther and farther by degrees, until I found many casks still preserving their shape and outline, having something within that was of great weight. I burst one open, and inside was tarnished metal so covered with growth and slime that it was impossible to say what it was. After many efforts I broke off a portion of it to examine at my leisure. It was a lump of silver dollars, welded together by marine growth, and discoloured by long submergence.

"I sat aghast at the thought of all those casks there being filled with coin—silver coin—ay, and why not some of them gold? I stood ankle deep in the salt water and looked around. A sea of light and shadow, calm and glassy, of ever-changing colour. Beyond, the restless tossing wall of white froth and foam.

"I had wealth—all I desired of it—in my grasp; and this was my domain.

"Was ever man so situated? When my turn came to die, should I join those ghosts on the isle, who must have been the men who sailed on this treasure-ship. There was blood on these coins, else why were they here, why was that nightly duel fought, what brought this ship so far south of her course?

"I returned to the island and cleaned the coins I held, scrubbed them with sand, and picked them apart with the knife that Pelrine had dropped when he went overboard. They were Spanish dollars, dated 1624 and a few years later.

"In successive journeys I examined some more of the casks, and found that one smaller one was full of gold, and doubtless there were more. It was better they should remain where they were, safer in every way, until I found a way out of my present position. Such a position in every way. With untold riches lying beneath a few feet of salt water of no more value than the leagues of coral north and south of me.

"And if I escaped and gained my fellowmen, of what avail would be my treasure to an escaped convict, who might at any moment be seized and returned to the living death I had fled from. My wealth alone would draw notice to me if I sought to enjoy it. At any rate, I determined to try and escape. I could decide afterwards about the treasure. Perhaps I should be able to purchase my freedom with some of it.

"I determined to wait till the moon was full (it being then half), as it would enable me to make use of the low tide at all hours, and it would also allow me time to patch up my boat, which I commenced to overhaul that day.

"I slept soundly the first part of the night, and awoke as usual at the tread of the ghosts. The moon hung low in the west, and I saw—yes, saw that night the apparitions that haunted that tiny isle.

"The night was clear, save for some angry-looking clouds in the cast, and the setting moon shone with spectral light over the still, shallow waters of the reef. The tide was low, and the passage I had passed through practicable for a well-manned boat with a skilful steersman.

"But was it the ghosts I saw? Half a mile out, or less, lay a ship with lights both in her rigging and streaming through her ports. A boat lay off the edge of the island, and I thought I heard another rowing in from the ship.

"I had no fear, and approached the group gathered on the sand. They were talking seriously, and, though the language was the same as I had always heard, I could now understand every word as though it was my own.

"They took no notice of me as I came near; I spoke to them, but received no answer; I laid my hand on one's arm, and I did not feel him. My sense of touch was dead, my voice was inaudible, my presence invisible. For the time being we had changed places, and the ghosts were the substantial beings and I the impalpable shape.

"There were five of them, all richly dressed in the fashion

of two hundred years ago. One was an elderly man of digni-fied appearance, and the other, who seemed his opponent, was a very handsome young gallant.

"'Before we meet, Don Herrera, and I send your soul to keep company with those of all the traitors since Judas hung himself,' said the elder man in a voice of deep hate, 'I would say some-thing that these gentlemen may remember concerning you.

"'You, a trusted officer of his Majesty, have tampered with the marines of my ship. You tempted them to mutiny, but your vile plot was discovered, and your dupes hung on the yardarm, where you, too, would be hung, King's officer though you be, and noble to boot, but that I reserved you for my own hand.

"'You, who came on my ship as an honoured guest, honoured on account of your standing as my Master's officer, although I knew you for a ruined profligate.

"'You, in your greed for the gold and silver in yon ship, conspired against me, led weak men on to their death, and, above all, sought to dishonour me in a way that only death will wipe out. I would not slay you on my own deck, for death by my hand only would suffice, but I vowed that the first dry land we saw should witness the death of one of us. This spot will serve, and we need not wait for daylight.

"'I call upon you all to hear that this man is a perjured traitor, whom I greatly honour by descending to cross swords with him.'

"The young man answered not, only by an insolent smile, then tossed his hat down, and drew his sword.

"During the time the captain was speaking the other boat arrived at the beach, and two people left and came to us, a priest and a woman. They stopped close to where I was standing, and I saw the most exquisite face illumined by the level moon that I ever saw in my life.

"The priest was dressed in the soutane and broad-brimmed hat of his profession, and looked ill at ease, but his companion flashed a bold glance from her dark eyes at the younger combatant that at once told me the guilty secret, and why the captain had not hung him at the yardarm, but brought him to this patch of sand to kill him himself.

"The fight commenced, warily and cautiously at first, but the two men soon warmed to their work, and then I saw the murderous trick of the young man. He was forcing the old man round, so that he should face the deceitful glare of the setting moon. Bit by bit he accomplished his object; then there was a quick, sharp interchange, and the captain fell, pierced through the body.

"'Bravo!' cried the woman standing by me, and she laughed merrily.

"I shuddered, and the priest darted from her side and knelt beside the dying man. He, too, had heard that devilish laugh, and lifted his head and gazed at his destroyer. He spoke, and his voice was clear and distinct.

"'Behold the judgment of the wicked is close at hand. The gold you plotted for shall never be yours; the beauty you lusted for shall be food for fishes. You shall not linger long behind me.'

"He fell back, as the edge of the ghostly yellow moon kissed the water's edge, its dying rays lighting up the scene of horror, the silent men, the recumbent figure, the dark-robed kneeling priest, holding on high the crucifix; the white sand gleaming out from that great waste of water.

"Suddenly a flash of lightning, accompanied by a peal of thunder, made everyone start. The clouds had banked up in masses to the east, and were covering the face of the heavens. The party hurried off to the boats, taking the captain's body with them, the white breakers were already leaping high, and they quickly pushed off.

"I watched them as they pulled to the passage, and saw the rollers rushing towards them. Then the darkness fell, but out of that darkness rung out cries of despair, and high above all a woman's shriek, the death-shriek of the woman who had laughed at her dying husband. Next instant the tempest burst, and caught the doomed ship. I saw her lights coming closer; saw them, then lost them; then saw them again, and then I knew that she was in the breakers.

"They beat her with successive blows, and hurled her into the passage, a dismasted wreck; hurried her on with the rushing water as the tempest burst in the blackness and fury inconceivable, hiding all things from my view.

"I opened my eyes to a soft, balmy morning, and found myself lying in my usual place on the sand. No sign of the recent storm was visible, my clothes were dry, the sea calm, and the surf lower than usual. Bewildered, I looked around, scarcely believing my eyes. I looked again at the sea, noting how impossible it was for that to have gone down in an hour or two, and as I looked I saw a steamer.

"Instantly the uncontrollable longing to see my fellow-men seized me.

"I made my fire up with a mad haste, piled on it planks torn from my boat, and branches torn hastily from the bushes. A straight column of smoke ascended, and I was seen at once. The steamer stood in, and a boat was lowered. I rushed into the water to meet it. Fear, such as I had never felt in silent, lonely nights, overcame me.

"'Take me from the ghosts!' I cried, as I scrambled in the boat, and fell insensible.

* * * * * * *

"This is a hospital, and they think me mad but the wreck of the Spanish ship is there."

THE HAUNTED STEAMER
(1901)

"Now you fellows speak of it," said the chief engineer of the S.S. *Mainbrace*, as he sat on his bunk, with his legs dangling over the side, addressing two passengers who had already been made free of his state room, "the ship has been haunted ever since Jack Collins went overboard just twelve months ago. Naturally, we don't talk about it, but the passengers find it out sooner or later. We are used to him, and don't mind him."

"He was sitting on the transom in the saloon last night," said the passenger for China, who occupied the camp stool. "I fell asleep on deck and did not wake till everybody had turned in, and when I went below I saw him there. I thought he looked like a stranger but before I could fix him properly he was gone."

"He was on the after hatch a night or two ago," said the pearl-sheller, who was on the settee. "I went up, meaning to speak to him, but when I got close it was the shadow of the wind sail. They play these tricks. There was a schooner up in the Straits troubled the same way."

"How did it happen? There's only the two of us here, and we're not talking men."

"He was our second officer," began the chief, "and a bright young fellow, too, just going up for the master's certificate when he reached Sydney, about a month before last Christmas. He never went up, however. When he got home he found that his wife had cleared out with someone else. Who it was she went with he did not know, and nobody else seemed to know, but she was gone right enough. I think, between ourselves, that not knowing who the man was preyed on him more than anything. If he could have got hold of the pair of them, and could have taken it out of the man and told the hussy a bit of his mind, I don't think he would have felt as bad as he did; but, as it was, he could do nothing, and the idea of going through life not knowing but at any time he might unknowingly meet him, make friends with him, and eat and drink with him—why he told me himself that it was driving him crazy. It was on Christmas Eve that it happened. I suppose the thought of his last Christmas, when he was ashore and just married, was too much for him. Anyhow, he must have gone over the side as soon as he went off watch. He gave the man who relieved him the course, chatted a bit as usual, then went down off the bridge, and nobody saw him again. It might have been an accident for it was a dark night, and there was a heavy sea running."

"I expect he knows now who the other fellow was," said the sheller.

"Did the other fellow know him?" asked the China passenger.

"Possibly not. Queer arrangement, eh? However, they won't meet in this world. Poor Collins made sure of that," said the chief. "Last trip he was often up on the bridge they told me, but this trip he seems to be sticking aft. I have not seen him looking down the skylight into the engine-room, as he used to. Keep it quiet, though: some people are nervous, and don't like this sort of thing."

The curtain hanging in front of the doorway was drawn on one side, and a face looked in. The three men started, but it was not the face of the man who 'walked.'

"You look comfortable," said the owner of the face. "Can I come in?"

"Come in," said the chief, and the sheller shifted a little on the settee to make room for the newcomer.

It was another of the passengers—a man with a fair beard and rather large, light blue eyes. He accepted the accommodation with a nod of thanks, sat down, took out his cigar case, and offered the engineer a cigar—both the other men were smoking already. The subject of conversation changed at once. The engineer gradually glided into the inevitable yarn, and when it was finished the China passenger and the pearl-sheller said goodnight, and left the cabin. A riding light was swinging about midway between the officers' state rooms amidships and the saloon companion-way. As they approached it, another man could be seen coming along the deck, going forward. They should have met just under the swinging lantern, but as they approach the circle of light, the figure faded out of sight.

"Collins," said one with a gasp, and clutched the other's arm.

"Yes," replied the man addressed. "I suppose we shall get used to it in time," and he gave a forced laugh.

They halted at the companion way, and looked back. A bar of light flashed for a moment across the alleyway amidships—it was the third man leaving the engineer's cabin, he could be seen coming along the deck.

"There's Collins again, standing by the skylight of the engine-room," said the pearl-sheller, whose name was Reynolds.

"Looks as they he was waiting for that fellow. Do you know him?" returned the other.

"No; he's been sea-sick, I think; only just shown up since we've been steady."

The third passenger came on. They could see the burning end of his cigar, and when he came in the beam of light he stopped and tossed the stump overboard; then, as he turned, he became conscious of the figure standing at the skylight, apparently watching him. For a moment they stood, the dumb ghost and the unconscious mortal, looking at each other, then the man came on.

"Who's that sulky begger standing by the skylight?" he said, when he reached the others. "Said good-night to him, and he wouldn't answer me."

"His name's Collins; he's a remarkably quiet man," said the China passenger.

"Seems like it," said the other. "Wonder if the bar is still open. Have a nightcap, you chaps?"

"Not for me," said Reynolds.

"Nor me, either," replied Gibson, the China passenger.

"Well, it's a hot night, so I'll get the steward to mix me the namesake of our friend, a 'John Collins.' Wonder if his name is John? I knew a Mrs Collins once," and with a vacant chuckle he descended the few steps that led to the saloon.

"Seems a bit of an ass. What do you think?"

"I think we ought to put the ghost in irons. I shouldn't wonder if this is the man it's looking for. I suppose you didn't do it?"

"Not quite. I've got a very good little wife of my own; but I'd rather have the ghost after me than her if I did such a thing."

"Well, I shall turn in now. I suppose our friend has finished his drink by this time," and they went to their respective berths.

"Steward," said the fair-bearded passenger to the chief steward the next morning, "somebody kept disturbing me last night by looking in my cabin. If it was one of your boys, I wish you'd tell him to stop poking his head in at my door."

The steward made a suitable reply, but watched the other as he ascended to the deck. "Somebody looking in his cabin," he repeated. "Seems to me I have heard tales of that sort before."

It was fine weather, of the hot variety to be expected in the tropics, and was bright and clear, and for once nobody had anything to growl about, and Christmas was approaching. The fair-bearded passenger alone seemed unsettled in mind, now overcheerful, and then despondent; his name was Vincent, and though some got on with him well enough, neither Reynolds nor Gibson liked him.

"Collins is very restless," said the latter one day to his friend. "Kept doing sentry-go on the after deck last night. Vincent was asleep in a chair, and suddenly woke up in a fright, and staggered over to the railing. I collared hold of him, and roused him up, and he said he'd had an awful dream. Dreamt he was in the sea on a dark night, fighting for his life, and watching the lights of the steamer disappearing. I told him he was taking too much whiskey, but he went below and got another nip. Then Collins laughed."

"Here, drop that, old man; ghosts don't laugh, at least the ghosts that I know don't."

"Well, anyway there was a laugh, a very nasty laugh, somewhere about, and I had to visit the steward myself."

The next morning the steamer anchored at Rock Harbour for a few hours.

"How are you, Mr Vincent?" said the Customs officer when he came on board. "Better for your trip?"

"Oh much, thank you; quite right now; naturally upset, you know."

"Know that man?" asked Reynolds when the Customs official had finished his conversation with the other.

"Slightly. He was up here with his wife about six months ago, on his way to England in a B. and A. boat, and a sad thing happened. They were overheard having a rather heated argument in their cabin, and then she rushed on deck, and, it is supposed, jumped overboard. She was never seen again. He was dreadfully cut up, and at Donner's Island changed steamers, and went back again south."

"Where did this happen?"

"About halfway between here and Donner's Island. I must be off. There's the donkey engine starting, and I don't want to be carried on. Good-bye. Remember me to all up north."

About two o'clock the next morning those who slept below were roused by hot words. Mr. Vincent and the chief steward were nearly coming to blows in the saloon.

"I tell you the fellow came right into my cabin, and was bending over me when I woke up. It's an infernal shame that you can't manage your men better, and that passengers should be annoyed like that."

"It's all fancy. My men are much too tired at night, and want to sleep, not go monkeying about looking in people's cabins. None of the other passengers have been annoyed."

Vincent turned to Reynolds, who had been roused by the discussion.

"I was dreaming that confounded dream again, and I woke up in a fright, and there was somebody in my cabin bending over my berth. I assure you there was."

The steward looked at Reynolds over Vincent's shoulder, and made the motion of drinking with his hand, and Reynolds persuaded him to go to bed again. It was blowing hard the next morning, and an unseasonable change had taken place, a reminder of the coming monsoons. The sea was getting up, and it looked as though a stormy Christmas would set in the next day. There had been a small jollification, it being Christmas Eve, and Vincent, who had recovered his spirits, had been exceedingly light-hearted and jovial, and had turned in early rather the worse for wear. It was eleven o'clock, and the chief engineer and the two passengers were taking a walk up and down the short poop when the ship was uncomfortably restless, and they stopped, and sat down for more ease.

"Who is that coming up?" asked Reynolds.

"Somebody in pyjamas, a woman and another man. Why, it's Vincent." And the three men rose.

The steamer gave a heavy roll and a dive just then, and the three figures passed aft on the opposite side of the deck as the ship took a big beam sea on board. Down she went, the screw racing like mad, and the three figures could be seen right aft; but when she straightened up again they were gone. The engineer took about three steps down on to the deck and into the salon, and the other two made their way aft. They looked over at the bubbling wake illuminated by the light from the stern portholes, but if any man's head had been in the water it would not have been seen in that seething turmoil. The alarm was given, and the usual routine gone through, as a matter of form, for there was no earthly hope of ever seeing the man again, and the steamer, after much delay, resumed her passage with the loss of a lifebuoy and a passenger. When the chief hurried into the saloon he went straight to Vincent's cabin, and found it empty, and the steward told him that Mr Vincent had just gone on deck.

"Was he alone, and in his pyjamas?"

"Yes," returned the steward to both questions. The chief went on to the deck again, now crowded and busy, and drew the two men aside.

"There was a man and a woman with Vincent?"

"Yes," they both affirmed; they had seen the three figures distinctly.

"I don't think we'll say anything about them," said the chief. "I wonder whether Vincent saw them, too?"

"Poor devil," said Reynolds. "Dreamt he was in a big sea on a dark night fighting for his life, and watching the lights of the steamer disappearing."

THE GIRL BODY-STEALER
(1901-02)

THE ELDER BACKFORD'S STORY: FEBRUARY 5

Those who persist in saying that I, in any way, consented to the experiment, either lie deliberately, or are entirely ignorant of the circumstances.

Bletchford could bear me out in this if he chose; but he is only anxious to evade all responsibility, although he was the prime mover in the matter.

My younger brother Francis had always been weak and delicate, and possessed a highly imaginative disposition. This did not assist him to regain health and strength: his mind was too vigorous for his body, and was gradually wearing it out.

Many times, when we were boys, have I had to follow him through the house to see that he did not come to harm during his somnambulistic rambles. Gradually he grew out of this habit, but became a confirmed visionary, always attracted by any new speculations on the occult and the unknown.

Fortunately he had too keen a brain to permit of his becoming a prey of the vulgar impostors calling themselves mediums; but where the theory appeared rational and logical he pursued it with avidity.

The separation of the soul from the body during life had a peculiar fascination for him; and he used to fast and experimentalise on himself to see if he could attain the desired object of leaving his body at will.

In vain I remonstrated with him, and pointed out how he was undermining his health, of which he had none too much to spare. He only laughed at me, and told me that because I was robust and found my pleasure in outdoor sports, I was not capable of appreciating such deep and abstruse questions as occupied his time.

It was just then that Bletchford came on a visit to us. At this period I was thirty-six, and my brother thirty. Our parents were dead; we had each a small private fortune, and lived together for the sake of company. Bletchford was an old friend, and I hoped that his coming would rouse my brother, and lead to his interesting himself in less morbid pursuits.

In this, to my great disgust, I was greatly disappointed. Bletchford had caught the craze, and was deeper in the duty of occultism than my brother. Instead of weaning him from his studies he encouraged him to continue in them, and, disgusted and sick at heart, I left them to themselves and sought my own diversions.

About three weeks after Bletchford had been with us he came to me, and, taking my arm confidentially, said "We have completely succeeded, at least in the case of your brother. I am too gross, apparently, to enter into the higher circle."

"Higher humbug," I replied rudely. "What does all this tommyrot mean?"

"It means that your brother can enter at will into the spirit world, leaving his body apparently lifeless."

I forget what I said, though it was something very personal and offensive, but Bletchford took it quietly.

"As yet," he said, "your brother has made no sustained effort, and instead of there being any injury to his health, he looks better and stronger. To-night we are going to prolong the experiment. Will you be present?"

I told him hotly that I would not countenance any such sinful folly. Then I went to my brother, and sought earnestly to dissuade him from dabbling with things better left alone. He only smiled good-naturedly, and told me he was surely old enough to judge for himself. I departed in anger, and left them to continue their experiment by themselves. I declare that I did my best to stop it, and failed.

I saw neither of them again that night, but at breakfast next morning Bletchford turned up, looking very white and haggard. Where's Francis?" I asked.

"He's lying down," he said.

He spoke very little, and I concluded that their precious experiment had failed, and that they both felt ashamed of themselves. Breakfast finished, I rose, intending to go and see my brother, when Bletchford stopped me at the door.

"Are you going up to Francis?" he asked.

"Yes, I am," I answered.

"Don't be alarmed, but he's still unconscious, but it will be right directly. The experiment was only to last three hours, but his soul has not returned yet."

I shook his hand off, and hastened upstairs without a word. My brother lay on his bed fully dressed; his countenance was calm and placid, but there seemed no sign of life about him.

Hastily brushing past Bletchford with a very strong oath, I called our man-servant, and told him to go directly for a doctor. Bletchford tried to speak to me while we awaited the doctor's arrival, but I refused to answer him.

The doctor came and made an exhaustive examination of my poor brother's body.

"He is not dead," he said, when he had concluded. "It is more like a cataleptic trance than anything else. The pulse is extremely weak, but steady. He must be watched continuously, and at the first indication of returning life the vitality must be carefully nursed back with restoratives."

After a few more instructions the doctor departed, and I got everything ready for the return of life. Bletchford wandered about with a hangdog look on his face, but I felt no pity for him.

All at once there was a movement in the inanimate body. A deep sigh escaped the lips, and I hastened to follow out the doctor's injunctions to the letter. With joy I noticed that I was successful. The life seemed to grow while I watched. In a short time he sat up, and looked wonderingly around, then at us in a dazed sort of way.

"Where am I? What's the meaning of this?" Francis said.

Bletchford and I looked at each other, dumb with astonishment. My brother, although so delicate, had a strong manly voice. The voice that asked the above questions was the soft and rather pleasing voice of a young girl.

Then I looked in the eyes, and they were not the eyes of Francis.

"Now, is this some trick?" went on the voice. "Why am I here dressed in man's clothes? It's a very poor joke, and not one gentleman would indulge in."

"Oh, great heavens!" said Bletchford, sinking on a chair, with a look of despair on his face. "There's been a mix up somehow, and the wrong soul has comeback. A girl's soul, too!" and he covered his face with his hands.

"Gracious! What's the matter with him?" said the new Francis. "What does he mean about the wrong soul coming back? Let me think a bit."

We all remained silent. The situation was too tremendous.

"I remember flying headlong out of the buggy," went on the girlish voice after awhile. "Then sparks, and nothing more. What's today?"

"Thursday," I answered, finding my voice at last.

"That was on Tuesday. Where am I?"

"In one of the suburbs of Altonia," said Bletchford, speaking up like a man for the first time. "From what you say you were thrown from a buggy and rendered unconscious?"

"Yes; Jessie Carter bet me a new hat that I couldn't drive the buckboard buggy over a three-feet log."

"Where did this happen?"

"Why, where we live, in the bush at Koorinanga."

"Let me explain," went on Bletchford. "While you have been unconscious, your soul, absent from your body, has entered the body of Francis Backford, then lying in a trance. His soul, therefore, cannot get back to its rightful body, but I think I can put matters straight. If you will permit me to put you into a mesmeric sleep, the soul of Francis Backford will regain its shell, and you will be able to do the same."

"Who am I, after all?"

"At present you are my brother, Francis Backford," I answered. "You have eight hundred a year of your own, and, as my brother was not an extravagant man, I expect there is a balance in the bank. Now I think you will see the reason of submitting to Mr. Bletchford's mesmeric powers, and get rid of a body which must only be an incumbrance to you, and make way for the rightful owner, whom you are keeping out in the cold."

Our strange visitor pondered, and presently raised her—no, I mean his—head, and I saw a wicked gleam in his eyes.

"Now I'm here, I think I'll stop here. I've often wished to be a man; they have much better times than women. Now I have a chance, I'll try what it is like."

"But," stammered Bletchford, "that would be unfair, preposterous, unwomanly"—

"I am not a woman," interrupted Francis; "and I intend to stop."

"But," I said, "your people will bury your real body."

"Let them; I've got this one. Now, a last word. I'm your brother, and you can't deny it, and this is my home. Is this my room?"

"It is," I sighed.

"Then I'll trouble you to go out. I want to overhaul my new wardrobe, and get the hang of these masculine garments."

We left, and I was too downcast even to reproach Bletchford.

MARCH 5

It is just a month since the new Francis arrived, and my hair is rapidly turning grey.

Bletchford has deserted me, and she—no, he—has been going on in a way to blast my brother's character for ever.

Whether it is owing to the new vitality infused in the body of my poor lost brother or not, I cannot say; but it has developed an appearance of health and strength really wonderful.

Every girl in the neighbourhood is in love with him, and I have received countless letters warning me that he would get his bones broken if I didn't stop him from interfering with other men's fiancées; but he only laughs.

His innate knowledge of the sex, I suppose, renders him perfectly irresistible. Didn't Olivia fall hopelessly in love with Viola?

MARCH 9

He informed me to-night that he had joined a 'push.' Says he never imagined that men had such jolly times of it; wouldn't be a girl again for anything. I'll advertise for Bletchford; he left no address. At least he must see me through, for I cannot stand it alone much longer.

MARCH 15

Three communications from different lawyers, stating that unless compensation is forthcoming, writs for actions of breach of promise will be at once issued. Only three! I expected a dozen.

MARCH 16

Had to bail him out of the lockup last night. Thank Heaven! Bletchford has written to say that he will be here to-morrow.

THE STORY OF BLETCHFORD

Backford has told the tale of our unhappy experiment, and has asked me to write the sequel.

But, first, I want to state that I have solemnly renounced all accursed dabblings with things that are wisely hidden from us; and I earnestly entreat all others to do the same, lest they go through the tribulation we have gone through.

Old Backford welcomed me with effusion. Poor fellow, he looks ten years older. The new Francis didn't seem to like my coming at all. I see a gleam of hope. This racketting about has upset his nervous system, and if I get the chance I'll soon have him under control.

Francis has come back. Yesterday a tall, gaunt, powerful man, with a broken nose, came to the door and inquired for Backford. Soon afterwards I heard my name loudly called, and going downstairs found the two standing hand in hand.

"This is Francis—my Francis," said Backford, with tears in his eyes.

I held out my hand in doubt and astonishment.

"Yes, Bletchford," said the man in a deep, hoarse voice, with a villainous accent which I won't reproduce; "I got tired of hanging round waiting for that vixen to let me have my property back, so I collared the first body that came to hand. I'm Boko Ben, a pugilist, at present. 'Knocked out' in a glove-fight at Kooyong City the other night."

We both were delighted, and at once proceeded to discuss our plans.

"Supposing I pick a quarrel with him, and knock him senseless?" said the real Francis, bringing his leg-of-mutton fist down on the table.

"Never do; he wouldn't fight," said his brother. "He'd only scratch and pull your hair."

"Well, we must wait and watch for an opportunity," said the real Francis, alias Boko Ben.

The new Francis did not seem to enjoy the advent of Ben at all; somehow he seemed instinctively frightened of him. So things went on for nearly a week, Francis still continuing to pursue his wild career; whilst poor Ben groaned to witness the way in which his body and reputation were being treated.

I never have seen Miss Sophy Humber in her own proper

person. She might possibly be well-behaved and fascinating; but while she was masquerading in her stolen body there never was such an incarnate spirit of evil, nor one more cordially hated by the three of us.

We'd have poisoned her willingly: but that would only have spoiled everything. During my absence I learned her name from the papers, the incident of her lying at her parents' residence in a cataleptic state having naturally aroused much interest.

We were at dinner one evening, the three of us, when the door opened, and in staggered the new Francis—drunk. This was his first 'Outbreak' in the drink line, and my heart gave a bound as I thought that at last my enemy was delivered into my hand. He held on by the back of a chair, and laughed foolishly, "Givesh glassh wine," he said.

I arose, approached him, and got his eyes under my control. He seemed to get uneasy, and muttered something about "an old ape," and "knocking my blooming head off," but I saw with joy that the fumes of drink were passing away, and I had him in my power.

I made some quick downward passes, throwing all my energy into them, and at my command he relinquished his hold of the chair, and walked steadily over to the sofa and laid himself down.

"Quick," I said to Ben. "Put all your will into it, and be ready to slip into your body directly there's a chance." I very soon had him under my influence, and Boko Ben, an apparently lifeless shell, lay inert in an arm-chair.

I went over to the other, and throwing all the psychic force I possessed into my work, willed the soul of Sophy Humber out of the body of Francis Backford. The eyes were open, and gradually light and life went out of them, and I knew that she was gone.

There was an oppressive silence while Backford and I watched with intense anxiety. Then life kindled again in the eyes, the breath returned, and as Francis sat up in his proper self I dropped fainting and exhausted on a chair.

When I was restored to my senses the brothers were standing by me, and Boko Ben was sitting up in the arm-chair.

"I say," he said, "that was a mean trick to take advantage of a man when he was screwed."

We all three burst out laughing. The girl's voice coming from the frame of the broken nosed bruiser was too funny; the soul of Sophy had taken refuge in Ben's body.

I was about to offer to mesmerise her again, and give her a chance to go back to her own body, which was getting tired of waiting; but Backford whispered to me, "I think four-and-twenty hours in Ben's body would do her good."

I nodded assent, and Backford, turning to the sham pugilist, said, "Here, be off as quick as you can; you've got money in your pocket, and can get a lodging elsewhere."

"What do you mean? I'm not going to be turned out."

"Yes, you are, if you don't go quietly; you've no business here."

"But I won't go. I'm big enough to smash the three of you, and I'll do it."

"No, you won't. You have the size, but only the spirit of a girl inside it. Now go!"

"Send me to sleep, and let me get back to my own body," said Ben, turning to me.

"Not to-night; I'm too tired out," I replied.

Ben rose. He saw there was no help.

"Have a look at yourself in the glass before you go," suggested Backford.

Ben approached the mantelpiece, and looked. He gave one heart-broken wail and went out. The disfigured face and broken nose were too much for the soul of Sophy Humber. For the first time I felt pity.

Next morning about twelve o'clock Ben appeared again, a dilapidated ruin. From what we could learn, he had sought to drown his sorrows in drink, obtained in threepenny "pubs."; had passed the night in the police cell, and had only been just released.

I was about to take pity on him when Backford stopped me again. "Supposing Ben's spirit does not come back for his body," he said; "we don't want the apparent corpse of a pugilist in the house."

I took the hint, and made an appointment with Ben to meet me elsewhere. To make a long story short, I released the soul of Sophy, and as I saw about her wonderful recovery in the paper, I infer that she got back to her body safely. What became of Ben's husk I know not, but as I've heard nothing of a startling discovery, I presume the rightful owner appropriated it again.

The Backfords had to sell their house and leave the district. Sophy had made it altogether too hot for them.

The legal actions were settled, and, altogether, it was a most costly experiment.

M'WHIRTER'S WRAITH

(1901-02)

I had been hard at work all day. The cook had made an effort and cooked a decent dinner. I had finished my smoke, and was just going to take a nip of whisky—a special case that an uncle of mine had sent out from Scotland—when I was conscious of a figure in the room.

I was alone in the house, so far as I knew. I could hear the cook and the two men arguing loudly in the kitchen verandah. The black-boys had permission to go and join a corroboree at the blacks' camp. Who, then, was this stranger?

The figure, first shadowy and vague, grew more distinct, and soon became clearly defined as a tall gaunt man, with a vivid auburn beard and hair, and light-blue eyes. He looked inquiringly at me, and, when I rather plainly requested to know what he was doing in my room, he replied, in a strong Scotch accent,

"I'm M'Whirter!"

"The devil you are," I said. "You're the original M'Whirter, I suppose, who took up this is station and stocked it fifty years ago?"

"I'm the man," he said.

"What brings you here?" I naturally asked. "I thought you died thirty years ago."

"So I did; but, mon, you called me."

Now just before coming in from the verandah I had looked around at the neat and well-kept surroundings of my home, plainly visible under a full moon, and I remember saying aloud,

"If old M'Whirter could see this place now!" and apparently M'Whirter had heard the invitation and accepted it.

I may as well mention that old M'Whirter was a sort of tradition in the place. The legend ran that he was a tall raw-boned Scotchman, who lived on nothing, and made his men do the same, and worked like a cart-horse. The shade before me seemed to about fill the bill, and I began to think that the ghost of M'Whirter actually stood before me.

"Won't you sit down?" I said.

"It's just as weel," replied the shadowy thing.

"Have some whisky?" I asked.

"Mon, it would be guid. I can smell it, but canna taste it. Ye ken I'm but a shadow."

"Is there not something you can do?" I asked. "What the spook people called materialising. I knew a ghost in Sydney that materialised himself into a wig, a mask, and a pair of lazy tongs any time."

"Mon, you're clacking aboot those fechtless bodies called mediums. I'm a genuine ghost. But there may be something in it. A wee drap of whusky would no' be amiss."

"It came to me straight from Dundee." He looked at it longingly. "There's a doctor chiel in Karma that knows a lot," he said. "I'll go ask him," and in an instant he was gone.

I waited patiently, and presently the visitor from Karma returned. At least there he was in the room again, but solid and human; no more shadowy and illusive.

"It is done," he said. "Now, mon, rax us the whusky." He filled out a stiff nip, and a beatific look came over his rugged face. He put his glass down with a sigh of satisfaction.

"Why dinna they keep that brew in Karma?" he remarked; "it would be no so bad then." He sat down, and I handed him a pipe and tobacco, and he commenced to cut up and fill.

"What do you do in Karma?" I asked.

"We just contemplate," he replied, as though somewhat weary.

"Don't you form clubs, get up any whist parties, or cricket, or golf, or anything?"

He looked at me in dumb anger for a time.

"We just contemplate," he repeated; then he reached across for the bottle and helped himself liberally.

"What were you wishing to see M'Whirter for?"

"Well, to see the improvements in the place since he took it up."

"Improvement!" he repeated, and the sneer he threw into it was intense. "Losh, mon, I see no improvement!"

"That's because you don't understand modern things," I replied, hotly.

"Deed, and I don't," he said, calmly. "It's all sinfu' waste and wicked extravagance the way you manage things these times."

"There was not much show of management on this place when I bought it."

"No. There was no' a garden, for one thing," he said, with the utmost contempt. "A guid feed of pigweed was eneuch for a man in those days."

"And you got scurvy and barcoo-rot and every other kind of abomination. And you paid more for curing yourselves than I do for growing a few pumpkins and sweet potatoes."

"Rax me the whusky," said the ghost, and when he had helped himself again he went on: "Noo, the way you use leather on a station is heart-breaking. I would na geeve a bit of green-hide for the leather that was ever made. Oh, but green-hide is good, and bonnie, and mind you, mon, it costs nothing."

"The way you fellows used to live was disgusting," I said.

"Hoot, mon, there's na pleasing you. You maun keep men doon, and no' feed them o'er weel."

"Nonsense, it's just as easy to live well as badly up the bush. You used to eat nothing but weevily flour, just to make out that you were economical."

"And is it economical you are talking? Oh, the sin o't! To talk of throwing away guid flour just because o' a wheen weevils in it! You're awfu' shy with that bottle, mon ! Rax us ma whusky."

That's what it had come to. It was his whisky now, and I

suppose his station and everything. I began to question the sanity of my materialising suggestion. M'Whirter, unaccustomed to liquor for so long, was getting quarrelsome in his cups, and inclined to think that he was on earth again for good.

He finished the whisky and went to sleep with his head on the table, after calling me all sorts of names, amongst which he mentioned that he had his "doots" whether I wasn't a "besom," by which I understood him to mean that I was an old woman.

The morning star was bright when I turned in, but it seemed only five minutes before it was broad daylight and the wall-eyed cook was shaking me.

"There's a man asleep in the next room, and he's been at the whisky, sir. The stink of spirits is something awful there," he said, reproachfully.

At once it flashed across me that the ghost of M'Whirter had not vanished at daylight, and was now on my hands all day. "It's a man came late last night," I said. "I know him. I'll see to him. Bring in breakfast for two, and make some porridge."

"He looks like a man who eats porridge," said the cook, spitefully.

I guessed that there was not a dram left in the bottle. I got rid of him and woke M'Whirter up. He blinked like an owl at first, but gradually came to himself.

"It's awkward," he admitted. "The loon will buke me, and I'll e'en get fined a year or two. They are machty stricht up there; but there, lad, I'll stop with you all day, and gie you a lesson in station management."

I thanked him, and, after freshening up a bit, we sat down to breakfast.

"D'ye no have a 'morning'?" he asked.

"I expect you want one," I said, and opened a fresh bottle. He had a nip, and then sat down to his "parritch," as he called it.

"'Mon!" he said with a shriek, "you are no putting sugar with the parritch? You are but making a pudding of it!"

"Mr. M'Whlrter," I said, "if I like to make a pudding of my porridge, I suppose this is my own station, and I can do it if I like."

"Oh, it's your fash, not mine. But leetle did I think that I'd a sat at my own table and seen a callant eat his parritch with sugar." He put half the salt-cellar on his plate, and groaned.

I groaned too. Fancy having the Scotch host of a pioneer squatter of the old days, with a turn for economy in his disposition, and a disposition to lecture and find fault, on your hands all day. There were six bottles of Dundee whisky left, and I felt all inward conviction amounting to a dead certainty that I would not get rid of him until they were all finished. After he had made a hearty breakfast—I may mention that I had broken my cook in to grill a steak very well, and the M'Whirter growled because his steak was not fried—we walked round the place, and I showed him all the improvements that had been made, and he sneered at every one. The only time he smiled was when we came across a gate that some fellow had pegged with a bit of dry wood—a broken branch, in fact.

"Eh! that looks like old times," he said.

"Does it?" I remarked, for I am rather particular. "It will look like new times directly;" and I went up, gave the man who did it "beans," and sent him down to make a proper peg to put in. We had to go in the store for a tomahawk, and M'Whirter followed us in and leaned against a case and looked round.

"I suppose you keep count of the tobacco by stick, when giving out a pound," he said.

"No; we weigh it now."

"Guid sakes! you lose on every pun' you sell. Twenty sticks to the pun', wet or dry that's fair measure."

"Oh! we don't trouble about those little makes nowadays."

"Little makes ma conscience! Noo there's floor; I suppose you weigh that too?"

"I do."

"A tinnie went to the pun' with me. I've a mighty big thoome, and I always stickit it weel doon in the tinnie when I was measuring. That thoome has stood me in weel"; and he held out the member in question—a great, broad, splay sort of affair.

With lectures like this and some Dundee whisky, I managed to get through the day. In the evening who should come up but a distant neighbour of mine, an elderly Scotchman of the name of M'Phairson. I introduced him to M'Whirter, and mentioned that he was a nephew of the original M'Whirter, which was the only thing I could think of, for it had suddenly occurred to me that M'Phairson must have seen M'Whirter when he was a youngster.

"I remember your uncle weel," said M'Phairson, with the garrulity of age. "You ha'no the bones o'him, and you're no so tall, but you're like—you're like."

This was a good beginning, and I wondered how the ghost liked being told that he wasn't like himself. But that was nothing to what was coming.

"Ah! he was a hard old carle," went on M'Phairson. "Folks about here said the deil got his own when he died. But I always said, and held, that your uncle was too hard a bargain for the deil to touch with his hoof."

I hurried the two inside, talking rapidly and incoherently, while I broached another bottle of whisky. M'Phairson drank his, and asked what ailed me that I was blitherin' at that gate. I couldn't well tell him that he was talking to the ghost of the original M'Whirter, but I had a certain sort of gloomy satisfaction when M'Phairson, under the influence of Dundee, settled down to a real old tirade against the hapless defunct. He left off when he had satisfactorily proved to the supposed nephew that his uncle had been a confirmed cattle and horse stealer and a more than suspected murderer; and by that time the bottle was three parts empty, and the cook poked his head into the door and said that tea was ready, and a singit sheep's-head the dish. I had no sheep, and it seems M'Phairson had brought it over with him in the buggy. As he went into tea the ghost whispered to me, "I forgie him, and I'll go back to Karma content. A singit sheep's head and Dundee whusky is too guid."

Tea passed quietly, and we adjourned for a smoke; then trouble ensued. M'Phairson again got reflecting on the character of M'Whirter's supposed uncle, and I'm afraid he raked up some nasty home truths, which the latter remembered too well. Anyhow it was growing late, and I had nearly dozed in my chair, when I was roused by hot words.

"I will kill you," said M'Phairson, getting up. M'Whirter laughed, and took the biggest nip of whisky I ever saw a man take at one drink. Then he addressed me. "You will come and see this mon kill me?" he asked.

Seeing that he was dead already, I had no objection. "He's going to kill me, ye ken. And I wull gie the M'Phairson the biggest freet ever a M'Phairson got, and they ha'gotten plenty o' freets."

"It's a lee!" shouted M'Phairson.

Peace was now impossible, so we adjourned out in the moonlight to settle matters. Probably, if I had not had to keep pace with a ghost at whisky-drinking, my brain would have been clearer, but as it was I was desperate. The men were fortunately all asleep, and we went round to the side of the house opposite to the kitchen. I was convulsed at the idea of M'Phairson fighting the ghost, but he took it very seriously.

"You will kill me?" said M'Whirter, in whom I noticed a curious change. "Well, begin."

The opponents closed, and then a cry of dismay arose. The M'Phairson's fist had gone right through the now ghostly M'Whirter. He looked at him for one second of palsied horror, and then took to his heels and fled. M'Whirter took after him, calling on him to stop; but M'Phairson, after one turn round the house, rushed into his room and barricaded the door—a very useless sort of proceeding against a ghost. M'Whirter came to me.

"You ha' treated me weel," he said. "You're a wee bit conceited, but ye will grow out o' it. I must move for some reforms in Karma—the taste of that singit sheep's-head and the Dundee whusky will abide by me. Good-bye, laddie, and dinna believe what that cock-sparrow of a M'Phairson tells ye."

Of course, now that he was going, I was quite sorry to part

with him, but we bade each other farewell, and he faded away, and I went to bed.

It took an awful job to get M'Phairson out of his room in the morning. Only that he wanted a drink very bad, he would never have consented to unbarricade his door. But he's very proud of the adventure now, and tells on every available opportunity how he chased "auld Hornie" twenty-five times round the house.

THE LAND OF
THE UNSEEN
(1 9 0 2 - 0 3)

When I first knew George Redman he was an ordinary plea-sure seeking man of the world, with an independent income, which afforded him the means and opportunity to indulge in occasional fads.

Photography was one of them for a time, but of course it was neglected when the novelty had worn off, and something else, "biking" probably, took its place.

For a week or two he dropped out of his usual haunts, and he was often seen in familiar intercourse with an aged man, who was reported to be either an anarchist or a lunatic.

Lunatic or not, he was a man with a striking face and wonderful eyes. The eyes of a visionary or an enthusiast, but certainly not of one deficient of reason.

Gradually Redman withdrew himself more and more from his old friends, and not having seen him for some time, I ventured to call at his rooms one night.

He was at home, and did not seem quite pleased at my coming. However, as we had always been close friends, I did not take any notice of it, and accepted his half-hearted invitation to stay.

His old friend was there, and was introduced to me as Mr. Whitleaf. For a time our conversation turned on subjects to which the old man paid little or no attention, but kept me under a steady fire from his eyes, which made me feel most uncomfortable.

His gaze did not seem so much concentrated on me as on something near me, giving me the uncanny feeling that he was looking at something that I could not see. I was relieved when he changed his gaze, and spoke a few words to Redman in a tongue strange to me.

Whatever he said, Redman seemed greatly relieved, and his manner towards me altered at once, he became quite cordial, and like his old self.

"Did I tell you I am going in for photography again?" he asked.

"No; you know I have not seen much of you lately."

"Well, it is a new phase of photography that I am studying,— or rather, what I hope will prove a new phase."

"Some further advance on the X-rays business?"

"Quite the opposite. The X-rays have developed a wondrous future, but what I hope to arrive at is something far different and far higher."

I noticed that Redman was beginning to get excited, and the old man interposed.

"I will tell your friend," he said, in a clear and singularly fascinating voice, "what is the goal we aim at.

"Listen! I have known for long that the air around us is full of invisible and impalpable beings. Beings I must call them, for want of a better word, but what they are cannot be explained by that word, for they are not—and yet they are.

"They exist—but yet have no existence; they are terrible in their power—and yet they have no power, for they, too, are swayed by an overmastering will. We are their slaves and their masters.

"In this room they are mustering in force, even as we sit here; I cannot see them, but I feel their presence, and know by sure tokens that those that have accompanied you into this room are not inimical to us, therefore I told Redman that we might speak before you.

"Listen again! You may search the universe with the most

powerful telescope that the genius of man has invented; you can track down to the uttermost bounds of infinity almost, the last wandering sun; and the plate of the camera when exposed will give others, and still others, in illimitable spheres beyond those the human eyes can see.

"Why is this? Why should the wonderful power of the camera be able to do what the trained eyes of men cannot? Why can it see through the living flesh and record on its surface the bone it sees beneath?

"Because it has power beyond our feeble strength, because it can search out the stars hidden in immeasurable distance, and make them visible to us. And it, too, when we have found the right method to use it, will seize these unseen forms that surround us and reveal them in actual shape.

"They are around us now in countless numbers, but we move through them unknowingly and unwittingly; and yet they, too, are fraught with all the powers of good and evil that sway the human heart.

"That is the work we are engaged in now, and if we succeed, we bridge, at one step, the gulf between the known and the unknown, the seen and the unseen, that has existed since matter was formed from chaos."

In his excitement the old man had arisen from his chair, and with burning eyes and eager hands emphasised his speech, as though he actually saw the formless beings he spoke of hovering in the seemingly empty air.

"It is true, Cameron," said Redman, after a pause.

"I have been studying the matter closely, and am now assured of the existence of these invisible companions crowding the space that surrounds us. Why am I assured? Because we have attained a partial success. Dimly and indistinctly; constant experiments with the camera have given us some results.

"I will show you them tomorrow. Why should it not be? The bones of the body are no longer hidden from view. The stars shining in the immensity of space, so distant that a telescope fails to find them, reveal themselves on the plate.

"So will these invisible beings in time, and I tell you I dread the day of our triumph."

"Why so?"

"Why so? The Gorgon's head that turned the rash onlooker into stone will be as nothing to what the man is doomed to witness who first solves the dread secret.

"Do not suppose these forms will be human; they will be the embodiment of the good and evil passions of those that have passed before; what awful shape they will take I cannot guess—something so fearful that the first glance may blast the eyesight of the man who looks. But, on the other hand, they may be beneficent and blessed."

"But surely you are not reviving the old jugglery of ghost photographs?"

"Pshaw! We are searchers for the hidden secret, honest and straightforward, not shuffling charlatans, gulling a foolish public. But come to-morrow and see what we have done. Don't talk of this outside."

I rose and took my leave, for it was nearly midnight, and as I walked the almost deserted streets I seemed to be haunted and followed by a ghostly company of phantoms. Horrible, because I could not guess their shape; awful on account of their impalpability.

They thronged around me, and shed their unholy influences on my sleepless pillow for the remainder of the night. I had taken the first rash step into the forbidden, and was suffering the penalty.

The next morning I went to Redman, according to my promise. He took me to his gallery, which had been enlarged and improved since I saw it last, and in it we found old Whitleaf working amongst some chemicals.

"I promised to show you how far we had got," said Redman, opening a locked drawer. "Look at this."

It was a large photograph of the interior of an empty room that he had put into my hand, but at first I could see no more than that. He smiled slightly at my openly-shown disappointment, and, taking it from me, placed it on a frame, and bade me look through a splendid magnifying glass fixed above.

Then I saw.

I saw, and I did not see. The room stood out in bold perspective. It was empty, and it was not empty.

Shadows obscured the light from the windows where no shadows should have been. There were eyes, of that I am certain; such eyes—eyes that could kill with a glance if one only saw them plainly and clearly.

The room was full of beings without shape, without form, but stamping their invisible presence by a way that was felt and not seen.

As I looked, entranced, I prayed that I should not see them, for the mere thought of the possibility brought cold terror to my heart and the limpness of death to my limbs.

"Look not on what is forbidden," was the mandate I seemed to hear, as by an effort I turned away, shuddering, and caught my friend's arm.

"Oh, they are here!" I gasped, "the awful ones. Seek no further. Man must not see their shape."

"They are there," repeated the deep voice of Whitleaf. "Ay, and they are here."

I covered my eyes with my hands and tried to forget, while every nerve and fibre shrank with dumb terror.

"Look again," said Redman.

I could not refuse, though my whole being revolted at the ordeal. I looked.

He had changed the photograph, and now I gazed on the sea, calm, motionless, and lifeless. And as I looked there gradually grew on me a monstrous horror.

It was not in sea or sky, but it was there. A momentary resemblance of evil—evil made palpable, such evil as man could not conceive, could not execute.

The maniac homicide would have recoiled, shuddering, from the mere suggestion of it, and died, shrieking with terror at its presence.

And the awful thing was still not there in form and substance, only in its dreadful influence.

I withdrew my eyes and sat down on a chair.

"Can such things be about us?" I asked.

"Do you not know that they are?"

"But why seek to make them visible when the vision would bring madness?"

"There may be more beyond—there is more beyond," said Redman. "Look at this." He changed the picture.

I hesitated.

"Nay, it will restore your courage."

Once more I gazed through the glass. It was a bedroom, and on the bed lay a corpse composed for burial.

Slowly there stole over me a wonderful feeling of peace, of everlasting happiness.

I strained my gaze to find out what caused it; it seemed to me that if I once succeeded in seeing that benign presence I should sorrow no more, but joy eternal would be mine. All my former fear and horror vanished.

"They are gods in good and evil," I said as I looked up. "Will you ever rest till you see them?" I went on, forgetting all I had said before.

"Never!" said both men together.

I became now as infatuated with their prospects of success as my friends were, though I could do little to help them, and circumstances called me away for six months.

When I returned I hastened to see Redman, having learned from his letters that a discovery was shortly expected. I found Redman and Whitleaf waiting together, and learned that I had just arrived in time to witness the success or failure of a trial they were then making.

The plate was even then exposed in the gallery. Both men, I could see, were in a condition of strongly suppressed excitement, and when at last the time expired Whitleaf proceeded to the gallery alone, under some pre-arranged agreement.

Redman paced up and down, repeatedly looking at his watch.

"He must have seen by this time," he said at last, and as he spoke a cry thrilled through the house and pierced our ears—a cry for help, a cry of terror and horror, indescribable overpowering horror, so great that you felt your heart stand still, paralysed and aghast.

We rushed to the gallery.

Whitleaf lay on the floor, with stony eyes and bloodstained mouth. He was dead—dead, with wide-open eyes that spoke still in silent testimony of the death he had died—killed by the shock of seeing what man should never see.

With a shuddering hand Redman closed the eyes that had seen more than mortality is allowed. There was black blood on his lips and white beard, and seemingly it had welled from his mouth.

The plate had fallen from his failing grasp, and lay on the floor, broken, pulverised, and ground to powder—by whom?

Redman said little; he seemed stunned and bewildered at the terrible power that had shown itself.

There was a medical examination into the cause of Whitleaf's death, and the doctor certified it was caused by sudden stoppage of the heart's action.

I had a chance to go away again, and gladly accepted it. I was cured for a time of any desire to pry into such fearful mysteries as Redman's pursuit seemed to lead to.

As for him, blank disappointment had fallen on him. I know what his thoughts were: what use was it to make absolute this fresh discovery of science when the success of the experiment meant the death of the investigator?

And yet I could see he had an irresistible longing to look on the sight that had blasted Whitleaf's eyes for ever. I urged him to seek travel and change.

I did not see him again for more than six months, and then his mood had greatly altered for the better.

The gloomy effect of the catastrophe of Whitleaf's death had disappeared in a great measure, if not entirely; and, above all, he had fallen in love with a young girl who, both in mind and body, seemed in every way fitted for him, and worthy of the utmost affection.

Yet this fair young girl, who was devoted to my friend, was the means of plunging him back into the blackness of madness.

One day I met him with his fiancée and her mother, going to lunch at his rooms, and he invited me to accompany them. During the meal his prospective mother-in-law asked him if he continued his photographic pursuits.

He answered "No," and the old lady, prompted by the devil, proposed that he should take a likeness of her daughter, and to my surprise Redman consented.

The gallery had been locked up since the fatal day of Whitleaf's death, and Redman led the way there, and unlocked it. Dust lay thick everywhere, and the place was close and unpleasant, and I, for one, felt the evil impression of it.

Redman placed Miss Torrance in position, got his apparatus ready, and took her likeness in two or three different attitudes, then leaving the plates in the dark room to develop at another time, we left the room, I, glad indeed to get away from the place.

Next morning I went to call upon Redman, and to my surprise and grief found him sitting on a lounge, haggard, wild-eyed, desperate, and half-mad. He looked like a man after a long drinking bout, on the eve of delirium.

"Good Heavens, Redman! what's the matter?" I asked.

He turned his awful eyes on to me, and spoke—"I have seen them, and live."

With the words came back to me the old thrill of cold horror, and I looked at him without answering.

He spoke again with an effort—"I developed those portraits I took of Miss Torrance, and there was one," here his voice dropped, "that must have been on one of the plates that Whitleaf and I prepared. *They* were there!"

He stopped, and leaned back with the beads of perspiration standing on his forehead.

Presently he arose, and asked me to come with him to the gallery, "Not to see that," he added; "it is utterly destroyed."

We entered the gallery, and he brought me the negatives. I held them up to the light, and looked at them. They were all happily caught, one in particular in which she was seated leaning back with a smile on her face. So might a young mother have smiled at a child at her knee.

He selected that one.

"It was almost in the same position as this," he said; "and when I looked on it but for an instant, I saw the horror there. Seated in her lap it seemed to be—that awful thing of loathsome evil! And she smiling down on it. It was but an instant I saw it, and then it was snatched from my hand, and ground into powder there. He pointed to a place where some fragments lay.

"Snatched from your hand?" I repeated in amaze.

"Yes; I know no more. When I came to myself I was on the floor of this place, with the moon shining through the glass overhead. Fancy, in one moment all my happiness cast to the winds.

"Can I marry that girl knowing that she sat there smiling and innocent, and in her lap a being of hell, a vile monster that could slay humanity with its basilisk glance if it were permitted?

"Oh! the raging torment I passed that night in—for that one glance has cut me off from my fellows for ever. Would that I had died like my poor friend!"

"What was it like?"

"Like? How describe what human language is not capable of describing? How describe what is so far removed from humanity, so utterly beyond and apart from it that no words of mine can make you apprehend it? One thing only I saw, that there were eyes in the monster-eyes that were darts of death.

"Ask me nothing more. This marriage once broken off, I shall leave this."

The marriage was broken off. Redman's strange, sudden, and unaccountable change of manner led to not unjust suspicions of insanity, and Miss Torrance never knew the frightful secret.

He, poor fellow, wandered through the world a haunted man.

I met him a year afterwards. He was worn down with grief,

and I doubt not his brain was disordered.

Morbidly his imagination dwelt continuously on the unseen horrors by which mankind are surrounded, and unconsciously walking amongst.

He shuddered at the mention of photography, and kept himself almost entirely shut up.

At last a change took place. It seemed as though he had mustered up a despairing courage to meet and fight his unseen foes.

He resumed his photography, and avowed to me his intention of following his discovery to the bitter end—giving his life to it.

There was a large public gathering shortly coming on, and he told me that he would try his next experiments there. He asked me to call on him the day after the function had taken place.

It was in the morning that I went, and found the servants relieved to see me.

Redman was locked in his photographic gallery, and about half an hour before they had heard a loud fall in there, but no cry; and since then all their knockings and callings had received no attention.

Suspecting the worst, I hurried to the gallery door, and at once forced it open. Redman was, as I expected to find him, dead on the ground.

He had been writing at the table, when a heavy iron rod, one of the supports of the glass skylights, had fallen, with no apparent cause, on his head, killing him instantly.

The photograph was in minute splinters and powder on the floor; but the writing on the table was addressed to me, and I immediately took possession of it. It ran as follows:—

"I took the photograph on the prepared plate, and developed it this morning. So strung were my nerves from the constant contemplation of this subject that I contemplated the negative without more than a momentary spasm of terror.

"Would you believe it, that the large crowd was scarce to be seen; blotted out and hidden by the unseen creatures, now made visible. I had not more than time to take in the details, when it was again snatched from my hand and crushed to atoms. This I anticipated.

"I had noticed the plate well in that brief glance I caught, and saw what I had seen before, that the eyes I told you of were directed against me from all quarters, and I gather from that that these beings are only secure in their invisibility, and fear their discovery.

"Are they the source of all evil, restrained and limited in their action by the occasional Presence among them of a Supreme Power, omnipotent and beneficent? It may be so, and they shrink from being observed.

"Would it end in their leaving for another planet world if they should become visible like men?

"I have seen them and live; and lest anything should happen to me, I will leave you, Rupert Cameron, directions to prepare the plate, so that my secret will not be lost.

"In the first place, you...."

* * * * * * *

Here the bar had descended, and a splash of blood on the white paper was all that was left.

The terrible and fatal secret had not descended to me.

WHAT THE RATS BROUGHT

(1904-05)

It was during the prolonged drought of 1919, just about Christmas time, that the steamer *Niagara* fell in with an apparently abandoned barquentine about fifty miles from Sydney.

It was calm, fine weather; so, failing to get any response to their hail, the chief officer boarded her.

He returned with the report that she was perfectly seaworthy and in good order, but no one could be found on the ship, living or dead.

The captain went on board, and, being so close to port, he was thinking of putting some hands on her to bring her into Port Jackson, when a perusal of the barquentine's log-book in the captain's cabin made him hesitate.

From the entries it appeared that the crew had sickened and died of some kind of malignant fever, the only survivors being three men—a passenger, one sailor and the cook.

The last entry, which was nearly three weeks old, stated that these three had provisioned a boat and intended leaving the vessel in order to make for Australia, as the only chance of saving their lives, as they felt sure that the vessel was infested with plague.

The value of the barquentine and cargo being considerable, and the weather settled, the captain determined to take her into port.

He put three volunteers on board to steer her, took her in tow, and brought her into Port Jackson, and anchored off the Quarantine Ground.

On reporting the matter to the medical officer, he was ordered to remain at anchor until it was decided what course to take.

The season was very hot and unhealthy, and when the story spread it occasioned a slight scare amongst the citizens.

Both vessels were quarantined, and the barquentine thoroughly examined.

When it was found from the log that the deserted craft had sailed from an Indian port where the plague that had so long devastated Southern Asia was then raging furiously, the consternation grew into a panic.

It was determined to take the vessel to sea and burn her, for nothing less would pacify the public.

The claim of the owners and the salvage claim for compensation were rated, and the *Niagara* towed the derelict out to sea, set fire to her, and then returned to undergo a term of quarantine.

Nothing further occurred, and in due course the *Niagara* was released, and the people forgot the fright they had entertained.

The drought reigned unbroken, and the heat continued to range higher than ever.

Then, when the winter had passed, and the dry spring betokened the coming of another summer of drought and heat, a mortal sickness made its appearance in some of the low-lying suburbs of Sydney.

When it had grown to an alarming extent, grim stories got to be bruited about, and a tale that one of the sailors of the *Niagara* had told was repeated.

He was on watch the night before the vessel was to be destroyed, the two ships lying anchored pretty close together.

It was about two o'clock when his attention was drawn to a peculiar noise on board the ship.

He listened intently, and recognised the squealing of rats, and a low pattering noise as though all the rats on the ship were gathering together.

And so they were.

By the light of the moon his quick eyes detected something moving on the cable

The rats were leaving the ship.

Down the cable they went in what seemed to be an endless procession, into the water, and straight ashore they swam.

They passed under the bow of the *Niagara*, and the sailor declared it seemed nearly half an hour before the last straggler swam past.

He lost sight of them in the shadow of the shore, but he heard the curious subdued murmur they made for some time.

The sailor little thought, as he watched this strange exodus from the doomed ship, that he had witnessed an invasion of Australia portending greater disaster than the entrance of a hostile fleet through the Heads.

The horror of the tale was augmented by the fact that the suburbs afflicted were now haunted by numberless rats.

People began to fly from the neighbourhood, and soon some of the most populous districts were empty and deserted.

This spread the evil, and before long was universal in the city, and the authorities and their medical advisers at their wits' end to cope with and check the scourge.

The following account is from the diary of one who passed unscathed through the affliction. Strange to say, none of the crew of the *Niagara* were attacked, nor was the boat, with the three survivors ever heard of.

* * * * * * *

The weather is still unchanged.

It seems as though a cloud would never appear in the sky again.

Day after day the thermometer rises during the afternoon to 115 degrees in the shade, with unvarying regularity.

No wind comes, save puffs of hot air, which penetrate everywhere.

The Harbour is lifeless, and the water seems stagnant and rotting.

And now, dead bodies are floating in what were once the clear sparkling waters of Port Jackson.

Most of these are the corpses of unfortunates, stricken with plague-madness, who, in their delirium, plunge into the water, which has a fatal fascination for them.

They float untouched, for it is reported, and I believe with truth, that the very sharks have deserted these tainted shores.

The sanitary cordon once drawn around the city has long since been abandoned, for the plague now rages throughout the whole continent.

The very birds of the air seem to carry the infection far and wide.

All steamers have stopped running, for they dare not leave port, in case of being disabled at set by their crews sickening and dying.

All the ports of the world are closed against Australian vessels.

Ghastly stories are told of ships floating around our coasts, drifting hither and thither, manned only by the dead.

Our sole communication with the outer world is by cable, and that even is uncertain, for some of the land operators have been found dead at the instruments.

* * * * * * *

The dead are now beginning to lie about the streets, for the fatigue-parties are over-worked, and the cremation furnaces are not yet available.

Yesterday I was in George Street, and saw three bodies lying in the Post Office colonnade. Dogs were sniffing at them; and the horrible rats that now infest every place ran boldly about.

There is no traffic but the death-carts, and the silence of the once noisy street is awful.

The only places open for business are the bars; for many hold that alcohol is a safeguard against the plague, and drink to excess, only to die of heat-apoplexy.

People who meet look curiously at each other, to see if either bear the plague blotch on their face.

Religious mania is common.

The Salvation Army parade the streets praying and singing.

The other day I saw, when kneeling in a circle, that two of them never rose again. They remained kneeling, smitten to death by the plague.

The "captain" raised a cry of "Hallelujah! More souls for Jesus!" and then the whole crew, in their gaudy equipments, went marching down the echoing street, the big drum banging its loudest.

As the noise of their hysterical concert faded round a corner, a death-cart rumbled up, and the two victims were unceremoniously pitched into it, one of the men remarking, "They're fresh 'uns this time, better luck!"

Such was the requiem passed on departed spirits by those whose occupation had long since made them callous to suffering and death.

All the medical profession stuck nobly to their posts, though death was busy amongst their ranks; and volunteers amongst the nurses, male and female, were never wanting as places had to be filled.

But what could medical science do against a disease that recognised no conventional rules, and raged in the open country as it did in the crowded towns?

Experts from Europe and America came over and sacrificed their lives, and still no check could be found.

All agreed that the only chance was in an atmospheric disturbance that would break up the drought and dispel the stagnant atmosphere that brooded like a funeral pall over the continent.

But the meteorologists could give no hope.

All they could say was that a cycle of rainless years had set in, and that at some former time Australia had passed through the same experience.

A strange comet, too, of unprecedented size, had made its appearance in the Southern Hemisphere, and astronomers were at a loss to account for the visitor.

So the fiery portent flamed in the midnight sky, further adding to the terrors of the superstitious.

It was during one night, walking late through the stricken city, I met with the following adventure.

My work at the hospitals had been hard, but I felt no fatigue. The despair brooding over everyone had shadowed me with its influence.

Think what it was to be shut up in a pest-city without a chance of escape, either by sea or by land!

I wandered through the streets, Campbell's lines running in my head, "And ships were drifting with the dead to shores where all was dumb."

Suddenly a door opened, and a young woman staggered out, and reeling, almost fell against me.

I supported her, and she seemed to somewhat recover from the frightful horror that had apparently seized her.

She stared at me, then said, "Oh! I can stand it no longer. The rats came first, and now hideous things have come through the window, and are watching his breath go out. Are you a doctor?"

"I am not a doctor," I answered; "but I'm one of those who attend to the dying. It is all we can do."

"Will you come with me? My husband is dying, and I dare not go back alone, and I dare not leave him to die alone. He has raved of fearful things."

The street lamps were unlighted, but by the glare of the threatening comet that lit up the heavens I could see her face, and the mortal terror in it.

I was just reassuring her when someone approaching stopped close to us.

"Ha, ha!" laughed the stranger, who was frenzied with drink; "another soul going to be damned. Let me see him. I'll cheer him on his way," and he waved a bottle of whiskey.

I turned to remonstrate with the fellow, when I saw a change come over his face that transformed it from frenzy of intoxication into comparative sobriety.

"Your name, woman; your husband's name?" he gasped.

As if compelled to answer, she replied,

"Sandover, Herbert Sandover?"

"Can I come too?" said the man, addressing me in an altered tone. "I know Herbert, knew him of old; but his wife doesn't remember me."

"Keep quiet, and don't disturb the dying," I said; and giving my arm to the woman, went into the house.

We ascended the stairs and entered a bedroom; the rats scampered, squeaking, before us.

On the bed lay a man, plague-stricken, and raving in delirium. No wonder.

On the rail at the head of the bed and on the rail at the foot sat two huge bats.

Not the harmless Australian variety that lives in the twilight limestone caves; nor the fruit-eating flying-fox; but a larger kind still, the hideous flesh-feeding vampire of New Guinea and Borneo.

For since Australia became a pest-house the flying carnivora of the Archipelago had invaded the continent.

There sat these demon-like creatures, with their vulpine heads and huge leathery wings, with which they were slowly fanning the air.

And the dying man lay and raved at them.

Disturbed by our entrance, the obscene things flapped slowly out of the open window, and the sick man turned to us with a hideous laugh, which was echoed by the strange man who had joined us.

"Herbert Sandover," he said, "you know me, Bill Kempton, the man you robbed and ruined. I'm just in time to see you die. I came to Australia after you to twist your thievish neck, but the Plague has done it. Grin, man, grin—it's pleasant to meet an old friend."

I tried to stop him, but vainly; and from the look on the dying man's face I could see that it was a case of recognition in reality.

The woman had sunk upon her knees and held her head in her hands.

Kempton still continued his mad taunting. Taking a tumbler from the table he poured some whiskey into it, and drank it.

"This the stuff to keep the plague away," he shouted; "but you, Sandover, never drank. Oh no! too clever for that. Spoil your nerve for cheating. But I'll live, you cur, and see you tumbled into the death-cart."

So he raved at the dying man, and one of the great vampires came back and perched on the window-sill.

Raising himself in bed by a last effort, Sandover fixed his eyes on the thing, and screamed that it should not come for him before his time.

As if incensed by his gestures, the vampire suddenly sprang fiercely at him, uttering a snarl of rage.

Fixing in talons in him and burying its teeth in his neck, it commenced worrying the poor wretch and buffeting him with its wings.

Calling to Kempton, I rushed forward to try and beat it off, but its mate suddenly appeared. Quite powerless to aid, I picked up the woman, who had fainted, and carried her out of the room.

Kempton, now quite mad, continued fighting the vampires, but at last, torn and bleeding, he followed us into the street.

I was endeavouring to restore the woman, and he only stopped to assure me that the devils were eating Sandover, and then reeled off.

When the woman came to her senses I left her by her own request, to wait till the Death-Cart came round.

I called there the next morning, but never saw her again.

Amidst such sights and scenes as these the summer passed on, burning and relentless.

The cattle and sheep were dying in hundreds and thousands, and it looked as though Australia would soon be a lifeless waste, and ever to remain so.

* * * * * * *

One morning it was pasted up that news had come from Eucla that the barometer there gave notice of an atmospheric disturbance approaching from the south-west.

That was all, and no more could be elicited.

The line-men at the next station started to ascertain the cause of the silence; and after a few days they wired to say that they had found the men on the station all dead.

But the self-registering instruments had continued their work, and the, storm was daily expected from Cape Leuwin.

The days preceding our deliverance from the pest were some of the worst experienced; as though the approaching storm drove before it all the foul-brooding vapours that had so long oppressed us, and they had assembled to make a last stand on the East coast.

One morning I felt a change, a cool change in the air.

Going into the street, I saw, to my surprise, many people there, gathered together in groups, and gazing upwards at a strange sight.

The vampires were leaving the city.

Ceaseless columns of them were flying eastward, and men watched them with relieved faces, as though a dream of maddening horror was passing away.

Then came a sound such as must have been heard in the quaint old city of legendary lore when the pied piper sounded his magic flute.

The pest rats were flying.

Forth they came unheeding the people who stood about; and Eastward they commenced their march.

All that day it continued, and some reported that they plunged into the sea and disappeared.

At any rate, they vanished utterly, and with them other loathsome vermin that had been fattening on the dead and the living dead.

Everyone seemed to see new life ahead.

Men spoke cheerily to each other of adopting means of clearing and cleansing the city, but that work was taken out of their hands.

That night the cyclonic storm that had raged across the continent burst upon us. All the long-dormant forces of the air seemed to have met in conflict.

For three clays its fury was appalling. The violent rain and constant thunder and lightning added to the tumult.

No one stirred out during those three days of tempest and destruction.

Nature in her own mighty way had set to work to purge the country of the plague.

It was while this storm was at its fiercest that the Post Office tower and the Town Hall tower were shattered and hurled in ruins to the ground. No one, so far as I know, witnessed the catastrophe.

The morning of the fourth day broke calm, clear and beautiful.

At midnight the tempest had lulled; and when daylight came, the sun rose in a sky lightly flecked with roseate morning clouds.

Accompanied by a friend, I started out to see the ruined city, and those who were left alive in it.

The streets still ran with flood-water, but the higher levels had pretty well drained off; and once they were gained, our progress was easy.

Martin Place was choked with the ruins of the tower, and many other buildings that had succumbed; while not a single verandah was left standing, in any street. We went to the Harbour.

The tide was receding, carrying with it the turbid waters that rushed into it from all points, carrying with it, too, wreckage and human bodies.

A strong current was setting seaward through the heads, and bore out to the Pacific all the decaying remnants of the past visitation.

The deserted ships in the Harbour had been torn from their

moorings and either sunk or blown ashore.

Wreck and desolation were visible everywhere, but the air was pure, cool, and grateful; and our hearts rose in spite of the difficulties that lay before us, for the looming horror of the plague had been lifted.

* * * * * * *

Of what followed, your histories tell you.

How the overwhelming disaster knit the states together in a closer federation than legislators ever had forged.

How from that hour sprung forth a new, purged, and purified Australian race.

All this is the record of the Australian nation; mine are but some reminiscences of a time of horror unparalleled, which no man anticipated would have visited the Southern Continent.

THE KADITCHA: A TALE OF THE NORTHERN TERRITORY

(1907)

I.

The heat was something to be forever remembered, although the surroundings had barely as much to do with it as the all-dominant and overpowering sun—sand-ridges uniform in direction, red and fiery in hue, and but scantily veiled with the hostile and venomous spinifex and a few stunted and thinly-foliaged trees.

A small cavalcade, consisting of three white men, one black-fellow, and five 'ships of the desert,' were painfully toiling across the killing regularity of the sand ridges. When they reached the crest of one, the party halted, and temporarily sought refuge, after dismounting, in the most ample apology for shade that could be found; while the camels relieved their wounded feelings by grunting and snarling at each other and the state of things in general.

The men who dismounted to rest their sun-dazzled eyes resembled the general run of sojourners in the unoccupied parts of central Australia. The youngest was a man of over thirty-five, who looked as though, when divested of his uncared-for beard, and when the deep tan had faded from his face, he would resume easily the tall hat and frock coat of civilisation.

"Well, Barrett," he said to an elder man with more of the confirmed bushman about him, who had drawn a note-book from his pouch, and was consulting some figures on it. "How do we stand now?"

"Close to it, I think, and if there were any landmarks about, I could tell our position to a certainty, but this confounded desert is as flat as a billiard-table when you take the level of the crown of the ridges. But that ridge which we are about to tackle looks a shade higher than the others, and we must be about near the place."

"Let us hope this salt lake will turn up trumps, for our camels are done up negotiating these sand waves."

"The lake is always dry," said Barrett, "it is only a courtesy title, but the niggers say that the little soak close to it at this end never fails them. Hope they're right."

The third man, who had not yet spoken, and seemed a little inferior in station to the other two, here broke in. "We'd better be making a start, Mr Glendower; old Sir Hack-a-rib is getting to look uncommonly ugly, and beginning to blow bladders, as if he meant to play up if he doesn't get water soon."

"Right, Joe!"

Wearily the men remounted, and again emerged into the full force of the blistering heat, now augmented by the rising of a hot wind. Barrett led the line, and they descended the slope of the ridge and commenced to ascend the one opposite. By the time they had reached the top the hot wind was terrible, and it was as much as the camels could do to struggle to the crest. Once there, Barrett waved his hand, exclaiming, "There's the lake."

The so-called lake was but a distant sheen of white, glistening salt, an elongated arm of which wound and twisted almost to the foot of the ridge that they had just painfully surmounted. A lake! To call by such a name was worse sheer blasphemy. A lake should be something that suggested the deep and cool repose of sleeping water, dark shadows wavering and shimmering under o'erhanging, green leaves, that trailed and dipped and kissed the surface when the wind—not a hot wind—rustled and played with them. This lake threw back the glaring heat that smote its burnished front with more painful refraction than did the red sand-dunes; but it was the lake they were bound for, and Barrett led the caravan towards the nearest end of it.

The heat that radiated from the bare surface of encrusted salt struck them with unrelenting wrath and fierceness as they rode on, and they were just upon the edge of a shallow hollow that merged its dry channel into the lake, when Barratt stopped suddenly, and gave an exclamation of astonishment.

A few paces in front of him, on the bare, hot sand, lay the corpse of a blackfellow.

They dismounted, and gathered round. The native had seemingly died of thirst; he was making for the soak, and, finding it dry, had laid down to die. He had been dead not many hours, but already the oven-like blast of the hot wind had commenced its shrivelling work. "This looks bad for us," said Barrett, "when even the natives of the land come to grief."

"He's stuck to his waddy to the bitter end," said Glenlyon, pointing to a formidable club the dead hand still grasped; "but what is he carrying his dancing-pumps for; what are they for?" he asked, turning to Barrett.

Joe stooped and took from the back of the corpse a pair of slippers, apparently, that had hung round his neck, with some native string. He handed them to Barratt with a look of intelligence. "Kaditcha," he said.

"And what the mischief do you mean by Kaditcha?" asked Glenlyon.

Joe, who did not seem a man of many words, said briefly— "Why murder shoes; but he'll tell you."

Thus appealed to, Barrett took up the task of explaining the problem.

"Certainly they were his dancing-pumps, which he carried to hide the fall of his fairy footsteps when he stole upon his sleeping enemy to hit him on the head with that big club he was so burdened with. He'll never do it again, and it looks as though we shall share the same fate!"

"Are the treacherous things common?"

"No; not very; they are principally used by the blacks of the M'Donnell Ranges, not far to the eastward of here. The blacks of the spinifex desert, away to the nor'-west, wear shoes, too; but theirs are harmless ones made of plaited spinifex to shield the soles of the feet from the burning sand."

"What are these made of then?"

"I'll tell you by and by, if we live; but we must see about what is the best thing to do in this fix. There's no water to be got in this soak. See." He pointed with the last word to the dried-up remains of innumerable birds that lay about, and amongst them the corpse of a dingo, with the wild dog snarl still curling its lip.

"Well, we have plenty of water still left for ourselves; but the camels will never manage to get back to the last water; it's nearly a hundred and fifty miles away. Joe, there's the soak down there; have a look, and see if there is any chance to clean it out."

Joe unstrapped the shovel from where it was carried handy on one of the packs, and strolled off on his errand. Presently his tread was heard returning. "Blacks been following it down already, and found it as dry as a bone," was his laconic comment.

There was a somewhat moody silence for a time; then Barratt, who had been intently watching the camels, and particularly Senachherib, who was busily browsing on something, and looking uncommonly bland and smiling, suddenly said: "Blessed if there isn't a chance of our pulling through after all."

"Sirhaggarib find 'em Parakheelia," said the blackboy, at the same time.

"What's all this?" asked Glenlyon.

"Parakheelia growing about here," said Barrett. "It's a plant that as good as a drink to camels, and old Senachherib spotted it already. Bully for the evil-tempered old cuss."

"Let's camp here, then," said Glenlyon. "Let them get a bellyfull if it does them any good."

"Does them any good, dear fellow? It's saved their lives, and ours too. It's a wonderful plant, although it looks so insignificant. We'll camp here all night, a bit away from that dead nigger, though."

"I'll take the shoes of murder first. I'll take them down to Melbourne as a curiosity."

"Oh, they have some there; that's where I first heard about them."

After selecting a suitable spot, they packed and formed a camp, and over a pipe Barrett told all he knew about the Kaditcha.

"The accepted notion is that they used for the purpose of secret murder. D'ye see how cunningly they are made without heel or toe; alike at both ends, so that there is no track left to show the direction the wearer has gone; and, as for being noiseless, no list slippers are anywhere near them. The uppers are woven of human hair, and the soles of dry grass caked with gum and human blood, with a dressing of emu feathers. What the dead owner was doing with them so far from the range I don't know."

That night the camels had a satisfactory feed, and, in a day or two, the party got safely back to the little outside camp from which that had started on their interrupted prospecting trip.

II.

It was Cup Day in Melbourne, a brilliant Cup it had been, too; the wealth had been all that could be desired, and the ring had been hit hard, for the favourite had won.

In the crowded street, one of Melbourne's leading thoroughfares, two men met each other with a glad note of pleased surprise.

"Why, Barrett, I'm as glad to see you as I was when the favourite flew past the post first. Never expected you would tear yourself away from that lovely country."

"Oh, I've sold out very well, and am going to have a bit of a spell; think I deserve it."

"By Jove, you do," returned Glenlyon, "we must have a yarn

about old times, and that devil of a trip we had together. When will you come out and have dinner, my wife knows you well by repute, and will be delighted to know you personally. Gad, she looks upon you as a second Livingstone."

As Barratt laughingly protested at this estimate, another man sauntered up and accosted Glenlyon, who greeted him in return cordially. A few words only had been interchanged, when the newcomer turned to Barrett, remarking he had had the pleasure of meeting him once. To this Barrett returned a cold acknowledgement. But Glenlyon noticed nothing strange in his manner and rattled on—"So glad you fellows are old friends, now look here, you and Carlisle, come out and have dinner on Thursday. Settling-day, I've won a pot of money to-day, and you must come and have a feed, and stay the night to signalise the event. Consider it settled—good-bye till then, Carlisle, I must have a bit of a chat with Barrett."

"Where on earth did you pick up that fellow Carlisle?" asked Barrett, when they were done.

"Carlisle? Oh, he's a first-rate fellow, only he's rather out of luck just now. Must have lost more than he knows how to pay over the races to-day. That's why I asked him out; besides, I don't want to seem cold to him, for he was a one-time pretender to my wife's hand. She can't bear the sight of him. But I feel sorry for the poor devil, especially now that he's been hit so hard."

"Well," said dogged Barrett. "I confess I wouldn't trust the man as far as I could sling him. There were some worse than shady stories about him up north, where I knew him. I'm not a married man, but I'll bet your wife's instinct is right, and I'd not go against it."

But Glenlyon's cheery nature rejected the idea, and he changed the subject, with a parting toast to the memory of Senachherib.

* * * * * * *

On the appointed afternoon, Barrett found himself at Glenlyon's pretty villa. He had been asked early, in order to make the acquaintance of his friend's wife, and was soon enjoying the chat with his hostess. The liking was mutual, and Barrett found himself telling her all the details of their northern journey.

"Oh, those horrible murder shoes! My husband has them still, but I must insist on his getting rid of them. Do you know, Mr Barrett, it may be gross superstition on my part, but I believe that there is an uncanny influence about those shoes. If a man wore them I feel convinced he would be irresistibly impelled to murder somebody, if he was inclined that way. I shall never be happy till they are out of the place."

"I know many people about the part where they are used," replied Barrett, "who have just the same feelings about them. Why that man, Joe Keeting, who was with us when we got them, and as decent a fellow as ever lived, has since been murdered by a native wearing similar slippers."

"Oh, how awful! Walter shall not keep them another hour. I wouldn't sleep another night in the house with the fatal things."

During dinner, the conversation tended towards the outside experience of Glenlyon and his friend in Central Australia, and Barrett took the opportunity of telling his host about Joe Keeting's death.

Glenlyon was greatly moved by the news, especially when he learned of the details of the murder. "Now, Walter," said his wife, "I have often mentioned my aversion to those murder-shoes you preserve so carefully, I insist on your making a bonfire of them."

Glenlyon rose abruptly, and said, "I will fetch them at once, and we will burn them after dinner; they would always be associated with poor Keeting's murder."

"Pardon me, Mrs Glenlyon," said Carlisle. "Will you allow me to take over the seemingly fatal responsibility of their custody? I have a small collection of native curios, and they would be a great addition to it."

When Glenlyon returned with the Kaditcha, his wife said—
"Mr Carlisle has put in a plea for them, and he can have them, as long as he takes them away with him, and I never see them again."

Carlisle took the shoes from his host, and said—"Your unfortunate friend must have aroused the revengeful feelings of the blacks by some probably unintentional wrong. I believe these shoes are used when tribal injuries are avenged."

"No," exclaimed Barrett, somewhat hotly. "Keeting never did an ill-turn to the blacks—on the contrary, for a man in his position he was exceptionally kind and humane to all he came in contact with. As we learnt afterwards, he was the victim of a mistake. The blackfellow who stalked and killed him unawares mistook him for a man known up there as Jim Dawson, who was noted for his inhumanity, and to tell the truth would have deserved whatever he got."

Carlisle glanced at the speaker with a look of deadly hatred, but restrained himself. Glenlyon looked uncomfortable, and his wife, whose eyes had been intently fixed upon Carlisle, rose to leave, saying, "The conversation is getting too horrible for me; perhaps after a cigar you will find a less gruesome subject."

She gave an unobserved motion to Barrett, who sprang and opened the door for her. As she went out she said to him in an undertone, "Are Carlisle and Dawson the same man?" Barrett nodded, closed the door, and resumed his seat.

There was an awkward silence for a while, then Carlisle spoke—

"I presume you meant me when you made that remark just now, Mr Barratt. I thought both you and Glenlyon were acquainted with the reasons that I have for resuming my own name, as well as those for using the name of Dawson for a brief time, but I was unaware that I had earned such calumny while so doing."

"I must apologise to you and Mrs Glenlyon," said Barrett to his host, "But the feeling of friendship I had for Keeting must be my excuse—men feel strongly in the outside country. If you have been slandered, Mr Carlisle, I am glad to hear that the stories of your cruelty to the blacks are false; they are certainly widely reported in the north."

"Let it pass at that," said Glenlyon. "I am sure Barrett meant no intentional offence. Those Kaditchas seem indeed to breed trouble."

The incident was dropped, and the men finished their cigars in outward amity.

* * * * * * *

An unseasonably cool night has succeeded a hot day, but Barrett tossed and tumbled, unable to sleep. This was an unusual mood to afflict him. As a rule he was a sound and healthy sleeper, and, at last, he rose to seek the bushman's solace of a pipe of tobacco. But his long-tried friend had been left in the room where they had been sitting, and he had nothing in the bedroom. He thought for a moment, and decided that, as everybody in the house was sleeping soundly this cool night, he would chance making a noise, and go and seek it. The more he thought of it, the more desirable did it seem, until, at last, he had fully persuaded himself that he could not exist without a pipe.

A distant clock struck two as he opened his door, and passed into the dark passage. "I wish I had the Kaditchas on," he thought, as he lingered for a moment, and reflected that even bare feet made very audible tread in the utter stillness. Suddenly, he experienced a strange thrill, as if some unseen figure had passed him, and, with a start, he stepped out, and turned towards the head of the stairway. There was a window on the next landing, and again he shuddered, for, surely, a dim and noiseless shadow had flitted between him and the light. He recovered his nerve in an instant, and, inclined to smile at his folly, he moved to the head of the staircase, and commenced carefully to descend. Again in the hall the queer feeling attacked him that a hostile figure was moving without sound ahead of him, but the hall was exceptionally dark, and he could see nothing. Moving cautiously along, fearful that he would suddenly wake every echo by stumbling against something, he thought himself of the exact position of the smoking-room. Yes, right at the end of the right-hand side, and opposite was the room which Glenlyon used as his office. Then he paused in a start of amazement. The unmistakable sound of a key cautiously inserted into a keyhole caught his ear. His courage returned with the sudden beat of his heart. This was no shadowy being from another world, but a flesh and blood burglar, who had no terrors for him. A streak of pale light was visible for an instant, and was then obscured, the silent visitor had entered the office and closed the door. Many thoughts crowded into Barrett's mind. Glenlyon had told him that he had a considerable sum of money in the house that night, and had left it in the desk in his office. His late winnings and some other money were there.

Carlisle, the man who was on the brink of ruin, was after it.

Evidently he must be desperate, for, as Barrett thought the matter hastily over, he comprehended how, equipped with the silent shoes of murder, he must have had the audacity to enter Glenlyon's bedroom, and take the keys from the toilet-table without disturbing either of the sleepers. There was no longer any necessity for caution; the more noise the better. In two or three quick steps, Barrett had reached the door and thrown it open. There was a large window in the room and a street light opposite, so the surroundings of the room could easily be seen. Carlisle was standing at the open desk, paralysed at the interruption.

"Bowled out," said Barrett, and advanced upon him.

"It's you, is it?" returned the other, recognising the hated voice. "Look here, Barrett, I'm desperate; there's more than ruin hanging on this. I'm in a corner, and I'll fight. Stand off, for I'm armed."

Not answering a word, Barrett closed with him immediately. Both men were well matched, and clothed only in their pyjama suits. But to Barrett there was a weird unreality about the struggle, for his adversary's feet made no noise, whilst his own stampings were noisy enough and resounded through the silent house. It was almost like wrestling with a ghost, but a most substantial one. Carlisle was armed with a sheath knife, while Barrett was, of course, just as he had jumped out of bed. Barrett had fast hold of the man's wrists, and, although he had received one or two slight scratches, he felt that he could hold him until assistance came, in spite of his frenzied efforts to get away.

They were locked together when the door opened, and Glenlyon and his wife appeared with a light. Both were in their night-dresses and had evidently been aroused by the alarming sound of the fight. The conflict stopped, and Barrett, releasing his grasp, allowed the baffled thief to draw back. Then there was a minute's silence, broken by the loud panting of the combatants.

"Good God, Carlisle!" said Glenlyon, when he had taken the scene in.

"Yes. I was going to take your money; but this man stopped me, and now there's nothing left for me but revenge, and I mean to have it, too." What with shame and rage the man was mad for the time being.

"I don't like talking to a man with a knife in his hand," returned Glenlyon. "Hand it over, that's better."

Mrs Glenlyon slipped hastily out of the room. When she returned, having donned a dressing-gown, the heated feelings had somewhat cooled down.

"I shall not prosecute you," her husband was saying. "The disgrace and ruin that, according to your own showing, are awaiting you, will be bad enough, and punishment enough in all conscience. Clear out as soon as it is daylight, and don't let us set eyes on you again."

"And don't forget to take the murder shoes with you," added Mrs Glenlyon.

Carlisle disappeared, and the one or two frightened servants who had been huddled outside the door were hunted back to bed. After bandaging the one or two slight knife cuts that Barrett had received in the fray, the rest retired to their rooms to resume their interrupted slumbers, Glenlyon first bestowing the cash in a safer place.

* * * * * *

Six months had passed away, and Glenlyon and his wife were seated at their breakfast, Glenlyon, man-like, taking his with his newspaper. Suddenly he uttered an exclamation, "Good heavens, Connie, it is impossible!" His wife sprang up and went to look over his shoulder; together they read the announcement;- "News just to hand by the mailman is to the effect that a treacherous murder has been committed in Arconwatta. The victim is a well-known and popular mine-owner of the name of William Barrett, owner of the battery just erected at the Sennachherib mining claim, from which there has been lately such wonderful returns. The unfortunate victim was evidently murdered in his sleep, and a horrible detail is the fact that the murderer had evidently adopted native tactics and muffled his approach with the silent shoes or kaditchas of the blacks, a discarded pair being found at the murdered man's door. Two thousand ounces of gold were taken.

"Later—A clue to the murder has, it is thought, been discovered, as the kaditchas have been recognised as having been seen in the possession of a man who is well known. There is only one policeman on the place, but about a dozen smart bush-men have volunteered, and are now on the tracks of the suspected man, whose capture is only considered a matter of time."

"Capture him I hope they will," said Mrs Glenlyon, "and hang him with those horrible shoes around his neck."

But the judgement that fell on the wretched man was less merciful than that of hanging. The avengers of blood found him dead, with the gold still beside him. He had died of thirst, for when he found the hole he was making for was dry he dared not turn back, but to the last struggled on, hugging the stolen gold.

BIBLIOGRAPHY

MY STORY (*The Queenslander*, in two parts, 6 and 20 February 1875)

THE LADY ERMETTA; OR, THE SLEEPING SECRET (*The Queenslander*, 25 December 1875)

THE MEDIUM (*The Queenslander*, 12 February 1876)

THE DEAD HAND (*The Bulletin*, 16 April 1881)

JERRY BOAKE'S CONFESSION (*The Bulletin*, 8 March 1890)

A HAUNT OF THE JINKARRAS (*The Bulletin*, 5 April 1890)

THE LAST OF SIX (*The Bulletin*, 19 April 1890)

THE SPELL OF THE MAS-HANTOO (*The Bulletin*, Christmas Edition, 20 December 1890)

SPIRIT-LED (*The Bulletin*, Christmas Edition, 20 December 1890)

THE GHOST'S VICTORY (*The Bulletin*, Christmas Edition, 19 December 1891)

MALCHOOK'S DOOM: A STORY OF THE NICHOLSON RIVER (*The Bulletin*, 23 January 1892)

THE RED LAGOON (*The Bulletin*, 23 April, 1892)

THE TRACK OF THE DEAD (*The Bulletin*, 23 April, 1892)

BLOOD FOR BLOOD (*The Bulletin*, Christmas Edition, 17 December 1892)

IN THE NIGHT (*The Bulletin*, Christmas Edition, 17 December 1892)

THE GHOSTLY BULLOCK-BELL (*The Bulletin*, 26 August

ABOUT THE EDITOR

JAMES DOIG works at the National Archives of Australia in Canberra. He has edited several volumes of colonial Australian supernatural fiction, including *Australian Ghost Stories* (Wordsworth Editions, 2010). He has also edited single-author collections by H. B. Marriott Watson and J. S. Leatherbarrow, and has published articles on obscure authors of horror and the supernatural, including R. R. Ryan, Keith Fleming, and H. T. W. Bousfield. He has a Ph.D. in medieval history from Swansea University in Wales.

Lightning Source UK Ltd.
Milton Keynes UK
UKHW011447220719
346610UK00002B/719/P